'40,0㴑㴑   㴑
which lay before him
in a heap of gold
and banknotes.'

Fyodor Dostoevsky
The Gambler
and
A Nasty Business

Translated by
Ronald Meyer

PENGUIN BOOKS

PENGUIN BOOKS

UK | USA | Canada | Ireland | Australia
India | New Zealand | South Africa

Penguin Books is part of the Penguin Random House group of companies
whose addresses can be found at global.penguinrandomhouse.com.

This translation first published in Penguin Classics 2010
Published as a Pocket Penguin 2016

001

Translation and Notes copyright © Ronald Meyer, 2010

Set in 10.36/12.8 pt Haarlemmer MT Pro
Typeset by Jouve (UK), Milton Keynes
Printed in Great Britain by Clays Ltd, St Ives plc

A CIP catalogue record for this book is available from the British Library

ISBN: 978-0-241-25958-0

www.greenpenguin.co.uk

Penguin Random House is committed to a
sustainable future for our business, our readers
and our planet. This book is made from Forest
Stewardship Council® certified paper.

Fyodor Dostoevsky

Born 1821, Moscow, Russia
Died 1881, Moscow, Russia

'A Nasty Business' was first published in 1862. *The Gambler* was first published in 1866 as a means to pay off the author's roulette debts.

Contents

The Gambler	1
A Nasty Business	177
Notes	243
Appendices	
I Names in Russian	256
II Table of Ranks	257
III A Note about Money in 'The Gambler'	258

The Gambler

A Novel (From the Notes of a Young Man)

Chapter 1

I've finally returned from my fortnight absence. Our party has already been in Roulettenburg[1] for three days. I thought that they would be waiting for me God only knows how eagerly; however, I was mistaken. The general had a confident air about him, spoke to me condescendingly and sent me to see his sister. It was clear that they had borrowed money from somewhere. I even thought that the general was a bit ashamed to look at me. Marya Filippovna was extremely busy and hardly spoke to me; however, she took the money, counted it and listened to my whole report. Mezentsov, the little Frenchman and some Englishman were expected for dinner: as usual, as soon as there's money, there's a Moscow-style dinner party. Upon seeing me, Polina Alexandrovna asked me why I had been away so long, and without waiting for my reply, walked off somewhere. It goes without saying, she did this on purpose. However, we need to have a talk. A lot of things have built up.

I've been given a small room on the fourth floor of the hotel. They know here that I belong to *the General's suite*, which one can see has managed, somehow, to make an impression. Everybody here thinks that the general is a very wealthy Russian grandee. Even before dinner he found time, along with other commissions, to give me two thousand-franc notes to be changed. I changed them in the hotel bureau. Now they'll think we're millionaires, for a whole week at the very least. I wanted to take Misha and

Nadya out for a walk, but on the stairs I was summoned to the general; he had thought it fit to enquire where I was taking them. This man absolutely cannot look me straight in the eyes; he would like to, but every time I answer him with such an intent – that is, disrespectful – look that he becomes embarrassed, as it were. In a highly bombastic speech, in which he piled up phrase upon phrase until finally he became thoroughly muddled, I was given to understand that I should walk with the children somewhere in the park, as far away as possible from the casino. In the end, he became thoroughly angry and added sharply:

'Otherwise, you might take them to the casino, to the roulette tables. You must excuse me,' he added, 'but I know that you are still rather frivolous and are capable, perhaps, of gambling. In any event, although I am not your mentor and do not wish to take on such a role, at the very least I have the right to desire that you, so to speak, do not compromise me . . .'

'But I don't even have any money,' I answered calmly, 'you need to have some money in order to lose it.'

'You'll have some immediately,' the General answered, flushing a bit, he rooted around in his bureau, consulted his accounts book, and it turned out that he owed me approximately 120 roubles.

'How shall we go about figuring the amount?' he began, 'it has to be converted to thalers.[2] Here, take a hundred thalers, a round sum – the rest, of course, won't go missing.'

I took the money in silence.

'Please, don't you be offended by my words, you're so quick to take offence . . . If I made an observation, it was only, so to speak, to warn you, and I do, of course, have a certain right to do so . . .'

As the children and I were returning home before dinner, I met a whole cavalcade. Our party had gone to have a look at some ruins. Two splendid carriages, magnificent horses! Mlle Blanche in one carriage with Marya Filippovna and Polina; the little Frenchman, the Englishman and our general were on horseback. The passers-by stopped and stared; they made an impression, but it does not bode well for the general. I figure that with the 4,000 francs that I brought, plus whatever they evidently had managed to borrow, that they now had seven or eight thousand francs; that's much too little for Mlle Blanche.

Mlle Blanche is also staying in our hotel, together with her mother; and our little Frenchman is somewhere here as well. The footmen call him 'Monsieur le Comte', and Mlle Blanche's mother is called 'Madame la Comtesse'; who knows, perhaps they really are *comte et comtesse*.[3]

I just knew that Monsieur le Comte would ignore me when we gathered for dinner. The general, of course, would not even think of introducing us or even recommending me to him; and Monsieur le Comte has spent time in Russia and knows the insignificance of this thing called *outchitel*.[4] He, however, knows me only too well. But I confess that I made my appearance at dinner uninvited; it seems the general forgot to make any arrangement; otherwise, he would certainly have sent me to dine at the *table d'hôte*.[5] I came of my own accord, so the general looked at me with displeasure. Kind-hearted Marya Filippovna at once found me a seat; but it was my meeting with Mr Astley that came to my aid and willy-nilly I found myself a part of their party.

I first met this strange Englishman in Prussia, in a railway car, in which we were seated opposite each other, when I was travelling to meet our party; then I ran into him as I was entering France, and finally in Switzerland; two times in the course of this fortnight, and now I suddenly meet him here in Roulettenburg. Never in my life have I encountered a person who is shyer than he; he's shy to the point of seeming stupid, and he realizes this himself, because he's not at all stupid. He is very nice and gentle, however. I managed to get him to talk at our first meeting in Prussia. He said that he had spent the summer at North Cape and that he very much wanted to go to the fair in Nizhny Novgorod.[6] I don't know how he became acquainted with the general, but he seems to be boundlessly in love with Polina. When she entered, he flushed crimson. He was very glad that I sat next to him at the table and seems to consider me his bosom friend.

At the table the little Frenchman set a peculiar tone; he was offhand and pompous with everybody. But in Moscow, I recall, he would talk a lot of twaddle. He'd go on an awful lot about finance and Russian politics. The general would sometimes venture to contradict him, but modestly, only as much as was possible without doing real injury to his own self-importance.

I was in a strange mood; it goes without saying that even before the dinner was half over I had managed to ask myself my usual and unchanging question: Why was I hanging around with this general, and why hadn't I left them long, long ago? From time to time I would steal a glance at Polina Alexandrovna; she didn't notice me at all. It ended with me getting angry and making up my mind to be rude.

It all began with me suddenly, for no apparent reason, butting into their conversation loudly and without asking their leave. Most of all I wanted to pick a quarrel with the little Frenchman. I turned to the general and suddenly made the observation, rather loudly and distinctly, and I think, interrupting him as well, that it was almost utterly impossible for Russians to dine in hotels at *table d'hôte* this summer. The general directed a look of astonishment at me.

'If you are a self-respecting man,' I continued, 'then

you'll certainly be inviting abuse and must endure the most extraordinary insults. In Paris and on the Rhine, even in Switzerland, there are so many wretched little Poles, and their little French sympathizers, at these *tables d'hôte* that it's impossible to get a word in if you're a mere Russian.'

I said this in French.[7] The general looked at me in bewilderment, not knowing whether he should get angry or merely be astonished that I had so forgotten myself.

'So somebody somewhere gave you a good lesson,' said the little Frenchman, carelessly and scornfully.

'In Paris I first fell out with a certain Pole,' I replied, 'then with a certain French officer, who was defending the Pole. Then later a group of Frenchmen came over to my side, when I told them that I wanted to spit in the monseigneur's coffee.'

'Spit?' the general asked with pompous bewilderment, and even looked around. The little Frenchman examined me mistrustfully.

'Just so, sir,' I replied. 'Since I was convinced for two whole days that it might be necessary to make a short trip to Rome in connection with our business, I went to the office of the Embassy of the Holy Father in Paris in order to get a visa for my passport. There I was met by a little abbé, a dried-up man of about fifty with a frosty expression on his face, who after hearing me out respectfully but extremely coldly, asked me to wait. Although I was in a hurry, I of course sat down to wait, took out my *Opinion nationale*[8] and began to read the most terrible diatribe about Russia. Meanwhile, I heard somebody pass through the adjacent room to see the monseigneur; I saw my abbé bow to him. I repeated my previous request to him; he even more coldly asked me again to wait. A bit later somebody else came in, also a stranger on business – some Austrian – he was given a hearing and immediately escorted upstairs. Then I became very annoyed; I got up, walked over to the abbé and told him in no uncertain terms that since the monseigneur was receiving, then he could deal with me as well. Suddenly the abbé drew away from me in extraordinary surprise. He found it simply incomprehensible that a lowly Russian could presume to put himself on the same level as the monseigneur's guests. As if delighted that he might have the opportunity to insult me, he looked me up and down and shouted in the most impudent tone: "Surely you cannot suppose that the monseigneur will put aside his coffee on your account?" Then I, too, began to shout, but even more loudly: "You should know that I would spit in your monseigneur's coffee! If you don't finish with my passport this very minute, I'll go see him myself."

'"What! When he has the cardinal with him!" the little abbé shouted, and moving away from me in horror, he rushed to the door and spread out his arms as if he were on the cross, assuming the attitude that he would rather die than let me pass.

'Then I answered him that I was a heretic and barbarian, "*que je suis hérétique et barbare*", and that I cared nothing for all these archbishops, cardinals, monseigneurs and so forth and so on. In a word, I assumed the attitude that I would not back down. The abbé looked at me with boundless malice, then snatched my passport and took it upstairs. A minute later the visa was ready. Here, gentlemen, would you like to see it?' I took out the passport and showed the Roman visa.

'You, however,' the general began . . .

'What saved you is that you declared yourself to be a barbarian and a heretic,' observed the little Frenchman, grinning. '*Cela n'était pas si bête*.'[9]

'But must I really follow the example of our Russians? They sit here – not daring to utter a word and are likely ready to deny that they are Russian. At least in my hotel in Paris they began to treat me more attentively when I had told everybody about my fight with the abbé. The fat Polish *pan*,[10] the person most hostile to me at the *table d'hôte*, retired into the background. The Frenchmen even bore with me, when I told them that two years ago I had seen a man whom a French *chasseur*[11] had shot in 1812 simply because he wanted to unload his rifle. This man was then a ten-year-old child and his family had not managed to get out of Moscow.'

'That cannot be,' the little Frenchman flew into a rage, 'a French soldier would not shoot a child!'

'Nevertheless, that's what happened,' I answered. 'A respectable retired captain told me, and I myself saw the scar on his cheek from the bullet.'

The Frenchman began talking a lot and speaking quickly. The general started to back him up, but I suggested that he read, for example, at least excerpts from the *Notes* of General Perovsky, who had been taken prisoner by the French in 1812. Finally, Marya Filippovna began talking about something else in order to cut the conversation short. The general was very unhappy with me, because the Frenchman and I had almost begun shouting at each other. But Mr Astley seemed to enjoy my argument with the Frenchman; as he was getting up from the table, he invited me to drink a glass of wine with him. In the evening, I duly succeeded in talking with Polina Alexandrovna for a quarter of an hour. Our conversation took place while we were out for a stroll. Everybody had gone to the park by the casino. Polina sat down on a bench across from the fountain, and let Nadenka[12] go play with some children not far away. I also let Misha go play by the fountain, and we were finally alone.

We began, of course, with business first of all. Polina simply became angry when all I had to give her was

700 gulden. She was certain that I would bring her back from Paris at least 2,000 gulden, if not more, after pawning her diamonds.

'I must have money, no matter what,' she said, 'I must get it; otherwise, I'm simply lost.'

I began to question her about what had happened in my absence.

'Nothing except that we received two pieces of news from Petersburg: first, that Grandmother was very poorly, and two days later that apparently she had died. This news was from Timofey Petrovich,' Polina added, 'and he's a very reliable man. We're waiting for final confirmation.'

'And so, everybody here is in a state of anticipation?' I asked.

'Of course: everybody and everything; for six whole months they've been hoping for nothing else.'

'And do you hope, too?' I asked.

'You see, I'm not related to her in any way, I'm only the general's stepdaughter. But I do know for a fact that she will remember me in her will.'

'I imagine that you'll get a great deal,' I said earnestly.

'Yes, she loved me; but why do *you* imagine this?'

'Tell me,' I answered with a question, 'our marquis, it seems, is also privy to all the family secrets?'

'But why does that interest you?' Polina asked, looking at me sternly and coldly.

'It would be surprising if it didn't; if I'm not mistaken, the general has already managed to borrow some money from him.'

'You have guessed quite correctly.'

'Well, would he have given him money if he didn't know about Granny? Did you notice that at dinner on three occasions when speaking of Grandmother he called her Granny: "*la baboulinka*".[13] Such close and such friendly relations!'

'Yes, you're right. As soon as he finds out that I'm going

to get something from the will as well, he'll start courting me at once. Is that what you wanted to know?'

'What do you mean start courting? I thought that he'd been courting you for a long time now.'

'You know very well that he hasn't!' Polina said crossly. 'Where did you meet that Englishman?' she added after a minute's silence.

'I just knew that you would ask about him now.'

I told her about my previous meetings with Mr Astley on my travels.

'He's shy and amorous and of course he's fallen in love with you already, hasn't he?'

'Yes, he's fallen in love with me,' Polina replied.

'And of course, he's ten times richer than the Frenchman. Why, is it certain that the Frenchman has anything? That's not subject to any doubt?'

'No, it's not. He has some sort of château. The general spoke about it to me yesterday as a matter of fact. Well, is that enough for you?'

'In your place I would certainly marry the Englishman.'

'Why?' Polina asked.

'The Frenchman is handsomer, but he's viler; while the Englishman, apart from the fact that he's honest, is also ten times richer,' I snapped.

'Yes, but on the other hand, the Frenchman is a marquis and cleverer,' she replied very coolly.

'Is that so?' I went on in the same manner.

'Absolutely.'

Polina took a terrible dislike to my questions, and I saw that she wanted to make me angry by the tone and the absurdity of her reply; and I told her so straight away.

'Well now, it really amuses me to see you get so upset. You ought to be made to pay, if for no other reason than that I allow you to ask such questions and make such conjectures.'

'I really do consider myself entitled to ask you all sorts of questions,' I replied calmly, 'precisely because I am prepared to pay for them any way you wish, and I don't set any store whatsoever by my life now.'

Polina burst into laughter.

'Last time, on the Schlangenberg,[14] you told me that you were prepared, as soon as I gave the word, to throw yourself down head first, and it's a thousand feet there, I believe. One day I will say that word if only to see how you'll pay up, and you can be certain that I will stand firm. You're hateful to me – precisely because I've allowed you so many liberties, and you're even more hateful, because I need you so much. But as long as I need you – I must take care of you.'

She started to get up. She had spoken with irritation. Of late she always ended a conversation with me with malice and irritation, with genuine malice.

'Allow me to ask you, what exactly is Mlle Blanche?' I asked, not wishing to let her go without an explanation.

'You know yourself what Mlle Blanche is. Nothing more has been added. Mlle Blanche will probably become the general's wife – if, of course, the rumour about Grandmother's death is confirmed, because Mlle Blanche and her mother and her second cousin the marquis – they all know only too well that we are ruined.'

'And is the general truly in love?'

'That's not the point now. Listen and remember: take these 700 florins and go and play, and win me as much as you can at roulette; I need money now, no matter what.'

Having said this, she called Nadenka and set off for the casino, where she joined the rest of our party. I, on the other hand, turned left at the first path I came upon, deep in thought and marvelling. It was as if I had been hit on the head with her order to go and play roulette. It was a strange thing: I had more than enough to ponder, and yet

THE GAMBLER

I became completely absorbed in analysing my feelings for Polina. Indeed, it was easier for me during the fortnight of my absence than now, on the day of my return, although during my journey I had yearned for her like a madman, rushed about like one possessed, and even saw her before me constantly in my dreams. Once (this was in Switzerland), having fallen asleep in the train, it seems that I began to speak aloud to Polina, which amused all the passengers sitting with me. And once again I now asked myself the question: Do I love her? And once again I was unable to answer it; that is, to put it more precisely, I answered myself for the hundredth time that I hated her. Yes, she was hateful to me. There were moments (to wit, at the end of every one of our conversations) when I would have given half my life to strangle her! I swear, if it were possible to slowly sink a sharp knife into her breast, then I believe that I would have snatched it up with delight. And yet, I swear by all that is holy, that if she had indeed said to me on the Schlangenberg, on that fashionable peak: 'Throw yourself down', then I would have thrown myself at once, and even with delight. I knew that. One way or another, this must be settled. She understands all this surprisingly well, and the thought that I recognize altogether unmistakably and certainly the extent of her complete inaccessibility to me, and the complete impossibility of fulfilling my fantasies – this thought, I am certain, affords her extraordinary pleasure; otherwise, would she, she who is so careful and clever, be on such intimate and frank terms with me? It seems to me that until now she has regarded me like that empress of antiquity who would undress in front of her slave, since she did not consider him a man. Yes, she has not considered me a man several times . . .

However, I had a commission from her – to win at roulette, no matter what. I had no time to ponder why or how soon I must win or what new designs had come into being in that perpetually calculating head. Moreover, during this fortnight a multitude of new facts about which I still had no idea had evidently come into play as well. All this must be gone into, gotten to the bottom of – and as soon as possible. But there was no time now – I needed to set out for the roulette tables.

Chapter 2

I confess that I found this unpleasant; although I had decided that I would play, I had not at all counted on beginning by playing for other people. This had even thrown me off some, and I went to the gaming rooms feeling greatly annoyed. From the first glance I disliked everything. I can't stand the bootlicking one sees in the feuilletons[1] the world over and particularly in our Russian newspapers, in which almost every spring our journalists write about two things: first, the extraordinary magnificence and splendour of the gaming rooms in the roulette towns on the Rhine, and second, the piles of gold supposedly heaped on those tables. It's not as though they're paid to do this; they do it out of disinterested obsequiousness. There's absolutely no magnificence to be found in these rubbishy rooms, and not only are there no piles of gold on the tables, there's hardly any ever to be seen. Of course, every once in a while during the course of the season some character turns up, either an Englishman or an Asian of some sort – or a Turk, as happened this summer – and he either loses or wins a great deal; but the rest play for small stakes, and on average there's very little money on the table. Once I had entered the gaming room (for the first time in my life), I could not make up my mind to play for some time. Moreover, it was crowded. But even if I had been alone, even then I think that I would have sooner walked away than started playing. I confess that my heart was pounding and I had not pulled myself together; I knew for certain and had decided long ago that I would not leave Roulettenburg as I had arrived; something radical and final would take place in my destiny without fail. That is how it must be, and that is how it will be. It may seem ridiculous that I should expect so much from roulette, but I find even more ridiculous the routine opinion, accepted by all, that it is silly and absurd to expect anything at all from gambling. And why is gambling worse than any other means of acquiring money, trade, for instance? It's true that only one out of a hundred wins. But – what does that have to do with me?

In any case, I had planned it so that I would first have a good look around and not begin anything serious this evening. If something did happen this evening, then it would be by chance and of no consequence – that's what I had decided. Moreover, I needed to learn the game itself; because notwithstanding the thousands of descriptions of roulette that I had always read with such eagerness, I understood absolutely nothing of how it worked until I saw it for myself.

In the first place, it all seemed so filthy – somehow morally sordid and dirty. I'm not at all referring to those greedy and anxious faces, which cluster round the gaming tables by the dozens, the hundreds even. I definitely see nothing filthy in the desire to win as quickly as possible and as much as possible; I have always found very silly the view of a certain well-fed and well-to-do moralist, who to somebody's excuse that 'they were playing for small stakes', replied, 'So much the worse, because the greed is so petty.' As if petty greed and massive greed weren't the same thing. It's a matter of proportion. What is petty for a Rothschild[2] is wealth for me, and as far as gains and winnings are concerned, people everywhere, and not only at roulette, are always doing somebody out of something or winning something. Whether gains or winnings are vile is another question. But I will not solve that here. Since I myself was utterly possessed by the desire to win, all this greed and all this greedy filth, if you will, were somehow suitable and familiar to me as I entered the room. It is a most pleasant state of affairs when people don't stand on ceremony, but act in the open and unbuttoned. And what's the point of deceiving oneself? A most futile and imprudent pursuit! At first glance, what was particularly unsightly about this roulette riff-raff was the respect for the pursuit, the seriousness, and even the deference with which they crowded round the tables. That's why there's a sharp distinction here between the kind of game that is called *mauvais genre*[3] and the kind that is appropriate for a respectable person. There are two types of gambling: one is gentlemanly; the other is plebeian, greedy, the gambling for all sorts of riff-raff. The sharp distinction is strictly observed here and – how vile, in essence, is this distinction! A gentleman, for instance, may stake 5 or 10 louis d'or, rarely more than that; however, he may also stake a thousand francs if he is very rich, but simply for the sake of the game itself, simply for the sake of amusement, simply to observe the process of winning or losing; he must on no account show any interest in his winnings. When he wins he may, for instance, laugh out loud, or make a remark to one of the onlookers, and he may even stake again and then double it, but only out of curiosity, in order to observe the workings of chance, to calculate, but not for the plebeian desire to win. In a word, he must look upon all these gaming tables, roulette and *trente et quarante*,[4] only as an amusement organized solely for his pleasure. He must not even suspect the greed and traps on which the bank depends. And it would not at all be a bad thing if, for instance, he were of the opinion that all the other gamblers, all this scum trembling over a gulden, were precisely the same sort of rich men and gentlemen as he, and that they were playing solely for the sake of diversion and amusement. This utter ignorance of reality and innocent view of people would, of course, be extraordinarily aristocratic. I have seen how quite a few mamas push forward their daughters, innocent and elegant little misses of fifteen and sixteen, and after giving them a few gold coins, teach them how to play. The young lady wins or loses, is sure to be smiling and walks away very contented. Our general made his way to the table like a respectable and important gentleman; a lackey rushed to proffer him a chair, but he did not notice him; he very slowly took out his purse, very slowly took 300 francs in gold from his purse, staked it on black and won. He didn't pick up his winnings but left them on the table. Black came up again; he didn't pick them up this time either, and when it came up red the third time he lost 1,200 francs in one go. He walked away with a smile, retaining his composure. I am convinced that he felt torn-up inside and if the stake had been two or three times as much again, he would not have retained his composure, but would have let his emotions show. However, I witnessed a Frenchman win and then lose almost 30,000 francs cheerfully and without any sign of emotion. A true gentleman, even if he loses his entire fortune, must not show emotion. Money is supposed to be so far beneath a gentleman that it's almost not worth thinking about. Of course, it would have been exceedingly aristocratic not even to notice the filth of all this riff-raff and the whole milieu. But then, sometimes the opposite stratagem is no less aristocratic: that is, to have a close look, even to examine carefully, for example, all this riff-raff through a lorgnette; but only so as to view all this crowd and all this filth as an entertainment of some sort, as a performance arranged for gentlemen's amusement. Although you may be jostled in this crowd, you still look around with the absolute conviction that you are merely an observer and in no way a part of it. But then again, it wouldn't do to look too closely: that would not be gentlemanly, because this spectacle in any case does not merit great or too close observation. And in general, there are few spectacles worthy of a gentleman's very close attention. And yet it seemed to me personally that all this very much merited close attention, particularly for the person who had come not merely to watch, but who sincerely and conscientiously counted himself a member of all this riff-raff. As far as my most secret moral convictions are concerned, there is no place for them in my present deliberations. Be that as it may; I am speaking to clear my conscience. But I will make this observation: for some time now I have found it terribly repugnant to judge my actions and thoughts by any moral standard whatsoever. Something else was guiding me . . .

The riff-raff indeed play a very dirty game. I even would not object to the suggestion that the most ordinary sort of thievery takes place there at the table. The croupiers, who sit at the ends of the table, keep track of the stakes and settle up – it's a terrible lot of work. And what riff-raff they are as well – for the most part Frenchmen. However, I was watching and noting everything not so that I could describe roulette; I was acclimatizing myself so that I would know how to conduct myself in the future. I noticed, for example, that there is nothing more commonplace than when somebody's hand stretches out suddenly from the other side of the table and takes your winnings for himself. An argument ensues, sometimes shouting and – then just imagine finding witnesses and proving that the stake was yours.

At first this was all double Dutch to me; by guessing I had just somehow determined that the bets were placed on numbers, both odd and even, and on colours. I made up my mind to try my luck this evening with a hundred gulden of Polina Alexandrovna's money. The thought that I was about to begin gambling not for myself somehow threw me off track. It was an extraordinarily unpleasant sensation, and I wanted to have done with it as soon as possible. I kept thinking that by playing for Polina I was undermining my own luck. Is it really impossible to come into contact with the gaming table without at once becoming infected with superstition? I began by taking out five friedrichs d'or, that is, fifty gulden, and staked them on even. The wheel turned round and came up thirteen – I had lost. With a sickening sensation, solely somehow to have done with it and leave, I staked another five friedrichs d'or on red. And it came up red. I staked all ten friedrichs d'or – and it came up red again. I staked all one more time, and it came up red again. After receiving forty friedrichs d'or, I staked twenty on the twelve middle numbers, not knowing what would come of it. They paid out three times my stake. Thus from ten friedrichs d'or I suddenly had eighty. I was overcome by an unusual and strange sensation, which I found so unbearable that I decided to leave. It seemed to me that I would not have played at all like that if I had been playing for myself. However, I staked all eighty friedrichs d'or once more on even. This time it came up four; they counted out another eighty friedrichs d'or, and after gathering up the whole pile of 160 friedrichs d'or, I set off to find Polina Alexandrovna.

They were all out for a stroll somewhere in the park and I didn't manage to see her until dinner. This time the Frenchman wasn't there and the general was in an expansive mood: among other things, he thought it necessary to remark to me once again that he didn't wish to see me at the gaming tables. In his opinion, he would be greatly compromised if I were somehow to lose too much; 'but even if you were to win a great deal, even then I would be compromised too,' he added significantly. 'Of course, I do not have the right to dictate your actions, but you yourself must agree...' As was his wont, he didn't finish what he was saying. I answered him drily that I had very little money and that consequently I couldn't lose too noticeably even if I did play. As I was going upstairs to my room, I managed to deliver her winnings to Polina and informed her that I would not play for her another time.

'But why not?' she asked, alarmed.

'Because I want to play for myself,' I answered, scrutinizing her with surprise, 'and it holds me back.'

'So you absolutely continue to be convinced that roulette is your only way out and your salvation?' she asked sarcastically. I answered again very seriously that yes, I did; and as far as my certainty of winning without fail, though I agreed that it might be ridiculous, 'I wished to be left in peace.'

Polina Alexandrovna insisted that we divide today's winnings fifty–fifty, and she gave me eighty friedrichs d'or, suggesting that we continue playing on these terms in future. I refused the half share absolutely and finally, and informed her that I could not play for other people, not because I didn't wish to do so, but because I would certainly lose.

'And yet, no matter how silly it seems, I too have put almost all my hopes on roulette,' she said, deep in thought. 'And so you must without fail continue playing for me and go halves, and – it goes without saying – that you will do so.' At this point she walked away from me, without listening to my further objections.

Chapter 3

And yet, yesterday she did not say a word to me about gambling all day long. And in general she avoided talking to me yesterday. Her former manner with me had not changed. There was the same utter indifference in her treatment of me when we met, and even something scornful and hateful. In general, she makes no secret of her revulsion for me; I can see this. Nevertheless, she also makes no secret of the fact that she needs me for something and that she is saving me for something. A strange sort of relationship has developed between us, which in many ways I find incomprehensible – if one takes into consideration her pride and arrogance towards everyone. She knows, for example, that I love her to distraction, she even allows me to speak of my passion – and of course she could not have better expressed her scorn to me than this permission to speak of my love freely and unchecked. It is as if she were saying, 'You see, I take so little notice of your feelings that it's absolutely all the same to me what you talk about with me and what your feelings are towards me.' She had spoken to me about her own affairs before as well, but she had never been completely candid. Moreover, in her contempt for me there were, for example, such refinements as these: she knows, let's say, that I am aware of some circumstance in her life or something of the sort that worries her a great deal; she even tells me herself something of her circumstances if she needs to use me somehow for her purposes, like a slave, or to run some errand; but she always tells me only as much as a person who is being used to run an errand needs to know, and if I am still unaware of the entire chain of events, if she herself sees how I am tormented and worried by her torments and worries, she never deigns to reassure me with friendly candour, even though by frequently employing me for commissions that are not only bothersome but also dangerous, in my opinion she was obliged to be candid with me. But is it worth troubling about my feelings, about whether I am also worried, and perhaps am three times as concerned and tormented by her cares and failures as she is herself!

I knew about her intention to play roulette three weeks ago. She had even warned me that I must play in her stead, because it would be unseemly for her to do so herself. I had noticed then by her tone of voice that she had some serious concern, not merely a desire to win some money. What is money to her in and of itself! There must be a purpose, there must be some circumstances, which I might guess, but which so far I do not know. It goes without saying that the humiliation and the slavery in which she keeps me might have given me (it very often does) the opportunity to question her myself rudely and directly. Since I am her slave and so insignificant in her eyes, she has no reason to take offence at my rude curiosity. But the fact of the matter is that, while she allows me to ask questions, she doesn't answer them. Sometimes she doesn't even notice them at all. That's how it is between us!

Yesterday there was a lot of talk among us about the telegram that had been sent to Petersburg four days ago and to which there had been no reply. The general is visibly worried and glum. It has to do with Grandmother, of course. The Frenchman is worried, too. Yesterday, for example, after dinner the two men had a long and serious talk. The Frenchman's tone with all of us was unusually arrogant and offhand. Just like in the proverb: 'Seat a pig at the table and he'll put his feet on it.' He was even offhand with Polina to the point of rudeness; however, he was happy to take part in the walks to the casino and in the cavalcades and rides into the country. I have known for a long time something of the circumstances that bind the Frenchman to the general: in Russia they were going to start up a factory together; I don't know whether their project went bust or whether there's still talk of it. Besides, by chance I came to know part of a family secret: last year the Frenchman did indeed come to the general's rescue and gave him 30,000 roubles to make up a deficit in the government funds when he retired from his post. And it goes without saying that the general is in his clutches; but now, right now, the main role in all this is nevertheless being played by Mlle Blanche, and I am certain that I am not mistaken in this.

Who is Mlle Blanche? They say that she's a French noblewoman, here with her mother, and that she has a colossal fortune. It is also known that she is somehow related to our marquis, only very distantly, some sort of cousin or second cousin. People say that before my trip to Paris relations between the Frenchman and Mlle Blanche were much more formal; they seemed to be on a more refined and delicate footing; but now their acquaintance, friendship and family ties appear somehow coarser, somehow more intimate. Perhaps our affairs appear to be in such a poor state that they don't consider it necessary to stand on ceremony with us or dissemble. The day before yesterday I had taken note of how Mr Astley would scrutinize Mlle Blanche and her mother. It seemed that he knew them. It even seemed that our Frenchman had met Mr Astley before as well. However, Mr Astley is so reserved, bashful and taciturn that one can almost certainly rely on him not to wash any dirty linen in public. In any case, the Frenchman barely speaks to him and almost never looks at him, which must mean that he's not afraid of him. That's understandable; but why does Mlle Blanche almost never look at him either? Particularly since the marquis let something slip yesterday: he suddenly said in the course of the general conversation, I don't remember in what connection, that Mr Astley was colossally rich and that he knew this for a fact; at this point Mlle Blanche might well have looked at Mr Astley! On the whole, the general is anxious. One can appreciate what a telegram about his aunt's death would mean to him now!

Although it seemed certain to me that Polina was avoiding conversation with me, to make some point, as it were, I assumed a cold and indifferent air myself; I kept thinking that she was about to come to me of herself. But then yesterday and today I turned all my attention, for the most part, to Mlle Blanche. The poor general, he's completely done for! To fall in love at the age of fifty-five with such strong passion, of course, is a misfortune. Additionally you need to take into account that he's a widower, his children, his utterly ruined estate, debts, and, finally, the woman with whom he happened to fall in love. Mlle Blanche is beautiful. But I don't know whether I'll be understood if I say that she has one of those faces that can be frightening. At least I've always been afraid of such women. She's probably about twenty-five years old. She's tall with sloping shoulders; her neck and bosom are magnificent; her skin is a dusky yellow colour, her hair is as black as India ink, and she has an awful lot of hair, enough for two coiffures. Her eyes are black, the whites of her eyes are yellowish, she has an insolent look, her teeth are very white, and her lips are always painted; she smells of musk. She dresses strikingly, richly, with *chic*, but with great taste. Her feet and hands are marvellous. Her voice is a husky contralto. She sometimes bursts into laughter and then she'll show all her teeth, but usually she looks on silently and insolently – at least when she's in the presence of Polina and Marya Filippovna. (A strange rumour: Marya Filippovna is leaving for Russia.) Mlle Blanche seems not to have had any education, perhaps she's not even very intelligent, but she is suspicious and cunning. Her life seems not to have been without its adventures. If one were to tell the whole truth, then perhaps the marquis is not related to her at all, and the mother is not her mother. But there is information that in Berlin, where we met them, she and her mother had some respectable acquaintances. As far as the marquis himself is concerned, even though I still have doubts that he is a marquis, the fact that he belongs to respectable society among us, for example, in Moscow and in some places in Germany, does not seem subject to doubt. I wonder what his standing is in France? They say he has a château. I thought that during these two weeks a lot of water would flow under the bridge, and yet I still don't know for certain whether anything definite has been said between Mlle Blanche and the general. On the whole, everything now depends on our fortune, that is, on whether the general can show them a lot of money. If, for instance, news comes that Grandmother is not dead, then I'm certain that Mlle Blanche will immediately disappear. I find it surprising and funny, however, what a gossip I've become. Oh, how it all disgusts me! What pleasure it would give me to wash my hands of everybody and everything! But can I really leave Polina, can I really quit spying on her? Spying, of course, is vile, but – what do I care!

Yesterday and today I've also been curious about Mr Astley. Yes, I'm convinced that he's in love with Polina! It's curious and ridiculous how much can sometimes be expressed in the look of a bashful and painfully chaste man, who has been touched by love, and precisely just when that man would rather vanish into thin air than say or express anything with a word or a look. Mr Astley quite often meets us on our walks. He takes off his hat and passes by, it goes without saying, dying with the desire to join us. If he's invited, then he immediately declines.

Whenever we stop to rest at the casino, at a concert or by the fountain, he without fail is to be found not far from our bench, and no matter where we are – in the park, in the forest or on the Schlangenberg – you need only raise your eyes, look around and without fail somewhere, either on a nearby path or behind a bush, a little piece of Mr Astley comes into view. It seems that he's looking for an opportunity to talk with me in private. This morning we met and exchanged a few words. At times he speaks extremely curtly. Without even a 'good morning', he began by saying: 'Ah, Mlle Blanche! . . . I've seen a great many women like Mlle Blanche!'

He fell silent, looking at me significantly. I don't know what he wanted to say by this, because when I asked him what he meant, he shook his head with a sly smile and added: 'So that's how it is. Is Mlle Pauline very fond of flowers?'

'I don't know, I really don't know,' I replied.

'What! You don't know that either!' he cried out in great amazement.

'I don't know, I've never really noticed,' I repeated, laughing.

'Hm, that gives me a special idea.' Then he nodded and walked on. He, however, had a satisfied air about him. He and I speak the most wretched French.

Chapter 4

Today was a ridiculous, outrageous and absurd day. It's now eleven o'clock at night. I'm sitting in my little closet of a room and remembering. It began with having to play roulette for Polina Alexandrovna this morning. I took all her 160 friedrichs d'or, but on two conditions: first of all, that I don't want to play for half, that is, if I win, I won't take anything for myself, and secondly, that this evening Polina will explain to me exactly why she needs to win and exactly how much money is necessary. All the same, I can by no means imagine that it's solely for the sake of the money. Clearly the money is needed and as soon as possible for some particular purpose. She promised to explain, and I set off. It was awfully crowded in the gaming rooms. They're all so insolent and so greedy! I elbowed my way through to the middle and stood right next to the croupier; then I timidly began to try my hand at the game, staking two or three coins. Meanwhile, I observed and took note; it seemed that calculation as such meant very little and did not at all have the importance that players attributed to it. They sit with slips of paper ruled into columns, note down the numbers that come up, count, figure their chances, calculate, finally place their stake and – lose precisely as much as we mere mortals who play without calculating. But I did draw one conclusion that seems to be correct: although there is no system in the course of random chance, there really does appear to be some sort of order, which, of course, is very peculiar. For example, it does happen that first the twelve middle numbers come up, followed by the twelve last ones; let's say these twelve last numbers come up twice and then it passes to the twelve first numbers. After landing on the twelve first numbers, it passes to the twelve middle numbers, they come up three or four times, and it again passes to the twelve last numbers, where again after landing there twice, it passes to the first numbers, and after landing on the first numbers it again lands on the middle numbers three times, and it goes on in this way for the course of half the morning or a couple of hours. One, three and two; one, three and two. It's very amusing. Another day or another morning it might, for example, happen that red is followed by black and back again almost without any order, constantly, so that it doesn't land more than two or three times in a row on either the red or the black. The very next day or next evening, red comes up time after time; and this might happen, for example, more than twenty-two times in a row and will certainly continue like this for some time, for instance, during a whole day. A great deal of this was explained to me by Mr Astley, who spent the morning at the gaming tables but who didn't place a stake himself even once. As for me, I lost absolutely everything and very quickly. I straightaway staked twenty friedrichs d'or on even and won, I staked five and again I won, and so it went for another two or three times. I think that about 400 friedrichs d'or came into my hands in some five minutes. At that point I should have walked away, but some strange sensation arose within me, some sort of challenge to fate, some desire to give it a flick on the nose or to stick my tongue out at it. I staked the largest sum allowed, 4,000 gulden, and lost. Then, flushed with excitement, I took out everything that I had left, staked my money on the same thing and lost again, after which I walked away from the table, stunned. I couldn't even understand what had happened to me and didn't inform Polina Alexandrovna of my losses until just before dinner. In the meantime I had been roaming about in the park.

At dinner I was again in an excited state, just as I had been three days earlier. The Frenchman and Mlle Blanche were again dining with us. It turned out that Mlle Blanche had been in the gaming halls that morning and had witnessed my exploits. This time she spoke to me somewhat more attentively. The Frenchman went a more direct route and simply asked me whether I had really lost my own money. I think he suspects Polina. In a word, there's something there. I lied and said at once that it was mine.

The general was extremely surprised: where did I get so

much money? I explained that I had begun with ten friedrichs d'or, that six or seven wins in a row, doubled, had brought me up to five or six thousand gulden, and that I had then squandered it all on two plays.

Of course, this was all plausible. As I was explaining it, I looked at Polina, but I couldn't detect anything in her face. However, she had allowed me to lie and didn't correct me; from this I concluded that I had needed to lie and conceal that I was playing for her. In any event, I thought to myself, she owes me an explanation and promised earlier to reveal a few things to me.

I thought that the general would make some remark to me, but he kept his silence; I observed agitation and uneasiness in his face. Perhaps in his straitened circumstances he simply found it difficult to hear that such a respectable pile of gold had come and gone in a quarter of an hour from such an improvident fool as I.

I suspect that he and the Frenchman had a heated falling out yesterday evening. They were talking for a long time and heatedly about something, behind closed doors. The Frenchman had walked out as if he were annoyed by something, but early this morning he visited the general again – probably to continue yesterday's conversation.

After hearing of my losses, the Frenchman observed to me caustically and even spitefully that one must be more prudent. I don't know why he added that although many Russians gamble, in his opinion Russians have no talent for gambling.

'But in my opinion, roulette is simply made for Russians,' I said, and when the Frenchman grinned contemptuously at my reply, I observed to him that of course the truth was on my side, because when I spoke of the Russians as gamblers, I was criticizing them a great deal more than I was praising them, and that consequently I could be believed.

'On what do you base your opinion?' the Frenchman asked.

'On the fact that the ability to acquire capital has entered the catechism of virtues and merits of the Western civilized man, and is practically the highest one. The Russian not only is incapable of acquiring capital, he even squanders it somehow scandalously and to no purpose. Nevertheless, we Russians also need money,' I added, 'and consequently, we are very glad of and very susceptible to such methods as roulette, for instance, where one can suddenly become wealthy in two hours effortlessly. We find this very attractive; and since we are playing to no purpose, without any effort, we lose!'

'To some extent that's true,' the Frenchman observed smugly.

'No, it's not true, and you should be ashamed to speak about your fatherland like that,' the general observed sternly and imposingly.

'I beg your pardon!' I answered him, 'really, then, which is more vile: shocking Russian behaviour or the German method of accumulating through honest work?'

'What a shocking idea!' the general exclaimed.

'What a Russian idea!' the Frenchman exclaimed.

I laughed; I wanted terribly much to provoke them.

'But I would rather spend my whole life roaming about in a Kirghiz[1] tent,' I cried, 'than bow down to the German idol.'

'What idol?' the general cried, now seriously angry.

'The German method of accumulating wealth. I've not been here long, but nevertheless, what I have managed to observe and establish rouses the indignation of my Tatar[2] blood. My God, I don't want those virtues! I managed yesterday to cover some ten versts[3] around here. Why, it's exactly the same as in those edifying little German picture books: every house everywhere you go has its

Vater,[4] who is terribly virtuous and unusually honest. In fact, so honest that it's frightening to approach him. I can't stand honest people whom it's frightening to approach. Each such *Vater* has a family, and in the evenings they all read instructive books out loud. Above their little house rustle elms and chestnut trees. The setting sun, a stork on the roof,[5] and everything is unusually poetic and touching...

'Now don't be angry, General, allow me to tell something even more touching. I remember myself how my late father, also under the lime trees in the front garden, in the evenings would read aloud to me and my mother similar little books... So I can well and truly judge this. Well, then, every such family here is in complete servitude and obedience to the *Vater*. They all work like oxen and save up money like Jews.[6] Let's say that the *Vater* has already saved so many gulden and is counting on giving his trade or little plot of land to his eldest son; in order to do this the daughter is not given a dowry and she becomes an old maid. And what's more, in order to do this the youngest son is sold into bondage or into the army, and the money is added to the family capital. Really, that's what's done here; I've asked around. All this is done for no other reason than honesty, from such an acute sense of honesty that the youngest son who is sold into servitude believes that he has been sold for no other reason than honesty – and that is the ideal, when the victim himself rejoices that he is being led to the slaughter. And what happens next? Next you find that the eldest son is none the better for it: he has his Amalchen, with whom his heart is one – but they cannot marry, because not enough gulden have been accumulated yet. They are also well behaved and sincere as they wait and then go to the slaughter with a smile. Amalchen's cheeks are already sunken and she's growing withered. Finally, in twenty years, their well-being has multiplied;

the gulden have been saved up honestly and virtuously. The *Vater* blesses his forty-year-old eldest son and the thirty-five-year-old Amalchen, with her withered breasts and red nose . . . As he does so, he weeps, moralizes and dies. The eldest son becomes a virtuous *Vater* himself, and the whole story begins all over again. In some fifty or seventy years the grandson of the first *Vater* really does possess considerable capital and leaves it to his son, and he to his, and he to his, and some five or six generations later he is a Baron Rothschild or Hoppe & Co.,[7] or the devil knows what. Well, sir, isn't that a majestic spectacle: a century or two of uninterrupted labour, patience, intelligence, honesty, character, firmness, calculation, and a stork on the roof! What else could you want, after all there's nothing loftier than this, and it's from this point of view that they begin to judge the entire world, and the guilty, that is, those who differ from them in the slightest respect, are immediately punished. Well, if that's the case, I'd rather kick up a row like a Russian or get rich at roulette. I don't want to be Hoppe & Co. in five generations. I need money for myself, and I don't consider myself simply to be merely something essential and subordinate to capital. I know that I have got terribly carried away, but so be it. Such are my convictions.'

'I don't know whether there's much truth in what you've said,' the general observed thoughtfully, 'but I know for certain that you begin to show off unbearably as soon as you're allowed to forget yourself just a little bit . . .'

As was his wont, he didn't finish saying what he had to say. If our general started talking about something just somewhat more significant than the usual everyday conversation, then he never finished saying what he had to say. The Frenchman was listening offhandedly, somewhat wide-eyed. He had understood almost nothing of what I had said. Polina looked at me with haughty indifference.

It seemed that she hadn't heard me or anything else that was said at the table this time.

Chapter 5

She was unusually pensive, but immediately upon leaving the table she ordered me to accompany her on a walk. We took the children and set off for the fountain in the park.

Since I was in a particularly excited state, I stupidly and rudely blurted out the question: Why is it that our Marquis des Grieux, our Frenchman, not only does not accompany her now, when she goes out somewhere, but does not even speak to her for days on end?

'Because he's a scoundrel,' she answered me strangely. I had never heard her voice such an opinion about des Grieux and fell silent, afraid to understand her irritability.

'But did you notice that he's not on good terms with the general today?'

'You want to know what's the matter,' she answered curtly and irritably. 'You know that the general has mortgaged everything to him, the entire estate is his, and if Grandmother doesn't die, then the Frenchman will soon take possession of everything that has been mortgaged to him.'

'Ah, so it's really true that everything has been mortgaged? I had heard that, but didn't know that it was absolutely everything.'

'But of course it is.'

'And if that's the case, goodbye Mlle Blanche,' I observed. 'She won't be the general's wife then! Do you know what: I think the general is so much in love that he might shoot himself if Mlle Blanche throws him over. It's dangerous to fall in love like that at his age.'

'I myself think that something will happen to him,' Polina Alexandrovna observed pensively.

'And how splendid that would be,' I cried, 'it would be impossible to express more coarsely that she had agreed to marry him only for his money. They're not even bothering to observe the niceties; it's happened without any sense of decorum. It's marvellous! And as for your grandmother, what could be more ridiculous and more sordid than sending telegram after telegram enquiring whether she's dead or not? Well? What do you think, Polina Alexandrovna?'

'It's all nonsense,' she said with disgust, interrupting me. 'I, on the contrary, am surprised that you're in such a cheerful mood. What are you so happy about? Surely not about losing my money?'

'Why did you give it to me to lose? I told you that I can't play for other people, much less for you. I'll obey you, no matter what you order me to do; but the result doesn't depend on me. You know, I warned you that nothing would come of it. Tell me, are you very crushed that you lost so much money? Why do you need so much?'

'Why these questions?'

'But after all, you promised to explain to me . . . Listen, I'm absolutely convinced that when I start playing for myself (and I have twelve friedrichs d'or), I'll win. Then you can take however much you need from me.'

A look of contempt crossed her face.

'Don't be angry with me,' I continued, 'for such a suggestion. I'm so very conscious of the fact that I am nothing before you; that is, in your eyes, so you can even accept money from me. You cannot take offence at a present from me. And besides, I lost yours.'

She glanced at me quickly and after seeing that I was speaking irritably and sarcastically, she again interrupted the conversation:

'There's nothing of interest to you in my circumstances. If you must know, I'm simply in debt. I borrowed some money and I want to pay it back. I had the mad, strange idea that I would be certain to win, here, at the gaming tables. Why I had this idea – I don't know, but I believed in it. Who knows, perhaps because I believed that I had no other choice.'

'Or because it was simply necessary for you to win? That's exactly like the drowning man who grasps at a straw. You must agree that if he weren't drowning, he wouldn't look upon a straw as a tree branch.'

Polina was surprised.

'But then,' she asked, 'aren't you hoping for the same thing? Once two weeks ago you yourself were talking to me, a great deal and for a long time, about how you were absolutely certain that you would win at roulette here, and you were trying to persuade me not to think you were a madman; or were you only joking then? But I recall that you were talking so seriously that it would be impossible to take it for a joke.'

'That's true,' I answered pensively, 'I am still absolutely certain that I will win. I'll even confess to you that you have just raised a question for me: Why has my senseless and shocking loss today not left me with any doubt whatsoever? I am still absolutely certain that I will win without fail as soon as I start playing for myself.'

'Why are you so very sure?'

'If you like – I don't know. I only know that I *need* to win, that it is also my only way out. And that's perhaps why I think that I will win without fail.'

'Therefore, you also *need* it too much if you are so fanatically certain?'

'I wager that you doubt that I'm in a position to feel a serious need?'

'It's all the same to me,' Polina answered quietly and

indifferently. 'If you like – *yes*, I doubt that anything could make you seriously suffer. You may suffer, but not seriously. You are an unsettled and insecure person. What do you need money for? I saw nothing serious in any of the reasons that you put forward to me then.'

'By the way,' I interrupted, 'you said that you needed to repay a debt. It must be quite a debt, then! Is it the Frenchman you owe?'

'What questions! You're particularly impertinent today. You're not drunk, are you?'

'You know that I allow myself to say anything, and sometimes ask very blunt questions. I repeat, I am your slave, and one is not ashamed before slaves, and a slave cannot give offence.'

'That's all nonsense! And I can't stand this "slave" theory of yours.'

'Note that I do not speak of my slavery, because I want to be your slave, but I simply speak of it as a fact that in no way is dependent upon me.'

'Speak plainly, why do you need money?'

'But why do you want to know?'

'As you like,' she answered and turned her head away proudly.

'You can't stand my "slave" theory, yet you demand slavery: "Answer and don't argue!" Fine, so be it. Why do I need money, you ask? What do you mean, why? Money is everything!'

'That I understand, but not falling into madness from wanting it! You, too, are approaching a state of frenzy, of fatalism. There's something here, some special purpose. Speak without beating about the bush. I want to know.'

She seemed to be getting angry and I was awfully pleased that she was questioning me so heatedly.

'Of course, there's a purpose,' I said, 'but I don't know

how to explain it. Nothing more than that money will make me a different person even for you, not a slave.'

'What? How will you achieve that?'

'How will I achieve it? What, you don't even understand how I could achieve your looking at me as anything but a slave! Well, that's just what I don't want, such surprise and bewilderment.'

'You said that you found this slavery pleasurable. And that's what I thought myself.'

'That's what you thought,' I cried with a strange sense of pleasure. 'Ah, such naivety is good coming from you! Well, yes, yes, my slavery to you is a pleasure to me. There is, there really is pleasure in the ultimate degree of submission and insignificance,' I went on, delirious. 'The devil knows, perhaps there is in the knout as well, when the knout is on your back and tears the flesh to shreds . . . But perhaps I want to experience some other pleasures as well. Recently at dinner the general, in your presence, admonished me on account of the 700 roubles a year, which I perhaps may even not receive from him. The Marquis des Grieux raises his eyebrows, stares and at the same time doesn't even see me. While perhaps I, for my part, passionately wish, in your presence, to take the Marquis des Grieux by the nose.'

'The talk of a milksop. One can behave with dignity in any situation. If there's a struggle, then it will elevate, not degrade.'

'That's right out of a copybook![1] You simply assume that I might not know how to behave with dignity. That is, though I may be a dignified person, I don't know how to behave as if I were. Do you understand that this may be possible? And all Russians are like that, and do you know why: because Russians are too richly endowed and versatile to find an appropriate form for themselves right away.

It's all a matter of form. For the most part, we Russians are so richly endowed that genius is needed to find the appropriate form. Well, and genius more often than not is lacking, because it is generally seldom to be found. Only among the French and perhaps some other Europeans has the form been so well defined that one can look extremely dignified and yet be the most undignified person. That's why form matters so much with them. A Frenchman will suffer insult, a real, serious insult without blinking, but he won't suffer a flick on the nose for anything, because that would be a breach of the accepted and time-honoured form of decorum. That's why our young ladies fall so easily for the French, because their form is so good. In my opinion, however, they don't have any form at all – it's nothing more than the cockerel – *le coq gaulois*.[2] However, I don't understand these things, I'm not a woman. Perhaps, cockerels are fine. And besides I've been leading you up the garden path, but you don't stop me. Stop me more often; when I talk to you I want to say everything, everything, everything. I lose all sense of form. I'll even agree that not only do I not have form, but I do not have any virtues whatsoever. I declare that to you. I won't even worry about any virtues. Everything within me has now come to a stop. You yourself know why. I don't have a single human thought in my head. For a long time now I have not known what is happening in the world, neither here nor in Russia. I've just been through Dresden and I don't remember what Dresden was like. You yourself know what has swallowed me up. Since I have no hope and am nothing in your eyes, I can speak my mind: everywhere I look I see only you, nothing else matters. Why and how I love you – I don't know. Do you know, maybe you're not good at all? Just imagine, I don't even know whether you're good or not – or even good-looking. Your heart most likely isn't good; your mind is ignoble; that's very likely the case.'

'Perhaps that's why you're counting on buying me with money,' she said, 'because you don't believe in my nobleness.'

'When did I count on buying you with money?' I cried.

'You've been letting your tongue get away from you so that you've lost the thread of what you were saying. You were thinking of buying my respect with your money, if not me.'

'Oh, no, that's not it at all. I told you that I found it difficult to explain myself. You're overwhelming me. Don't be angry with my chatter. You understand why you can't be angry with me: I'm simply mad. But then, it's all the same to me, even if you do get angry. All I need to do up there, in my little closet of a room, is remember and imagine merely the rustling of your dress, and I'm ready to gnaw my hands off. And why are you angry with me? Because I called myself your slave? Make use of my slavery, make use of it! Do you know that some day I will kill you? I won't kill you because I have stopped loving you or because I'm jealous of you, but I'll kill you simply because sometimes I want to devour you. You laugh . . .'

'I'm not laughing at all,' she said angrily. 'I order you to be silent.'

She stopped, breathless with anger. My God! I don't know whether she was pretty or not, but I have always liked looking at her when she would stop like that in front of me, and that was why I often liked to provoke her anger. Perhaps she had noticed this and became angry on purpose. I told her this.

'What filth!' she exclaimed with disgust.

'It's all the same to me,' I continued. 'Do you also know that it's dangerous for the two of us to walk together: many times I have been irresistibly tempted to beat you, disfigure you, strangle you. And do you think that it won't come to that? You'll drive me mad. You can't think that I'm afraid of a scandal? Or your anger? What's your anger to me? I love without hope, and I know that after this I will love you a thousand times more. If I kill you some day, I'll have to kill myself as well, you know; but I'll put off killing myself as long as possible so that I can feel the unbearable pain of being without you. Do you want to know something incredible? I love you *more* with every passing day, and that's all but impossible, you know. And how can I not be a fatalist after that? Do you remember the day before yesterday, on the Schlangenberg, I whispered to you, after being provoked by you: "Say the word and I'll jump into the abyss." If you had said the word, I would have jumped then. Do you really not believe that I would have jumped?'

'What foolish chatter!' she cried.

'I don't care whether it's stupid or clever,' I cried. 'I know that when I'm with you I need to talk, talk, talk – and I do talk. I lose all self-respect when I'm with you – and I don't care.'

'Why should I make you jump off the Schlangenberg?' she said coldly, and in a particularly insulting manner. 'It would be absolutely of no use to me.'

'Splendid!' I cried, 'you uttered that splendid "no use" on purpose, in order to crush me. I can see through you. No use, you say? But, you know, pleasure is always useful, and a wild boundless power – even over a fly – is also a pleasure, you know, in its own way. Man is a despot by nature and loves to be a tormentor. You like it terribly.'

I remember that she was scrutinizing me particularly intently. My face must have expressed all my incoherent and absurd feelings then. I recall that our conversation then really went almost word for word as I have described it here. My eyes had become bloodshot. Foam caked the corners of my mouth. And as for the Schlangenberg, I swear on my honour even now: if she had ordered me to throw myself down, I would have done it! If she had said it simply as a joke, or with scorn, or if she had said it with a jeer, even then I would have jumped!

'No, why, I believe you,' she pronounced, but in a way that only she knows how sometimes to speak, with such scorn and malice, with such arrogance that, my God, at that moment I could have killed her. She was taking a chance. I had not lied when I told her about that.

'You're not a coward?' she asked me suddenly.

'I don't know, perhaps I am a coward. I don't know . . . I haven't thought about that for a long time.'

'If I were to say to you: kill this man – would you kill him?'

'Who?'

'Whomever I want.'

'The Frenchman?'

'Don't ask questions, but answer me – whomever I tell you. I want to know: were you speaking seriously just now?' She waited for her answer so seriously and with such impatience that I started feeling somehow strange.

'But will you tell me, finally, what's going on here!' I cried. 'What's wrong, are you afraid of me? I can see for myself that everything's in a muddle here. You're the stepdaughter of a man who's ruined and gone mad, poisoned by passion for that she-devil – Blanche; then there's that Frenchman, with his mysterious influence on you and – now you are seriously asking me . . . a question like that. At least let me know; otherwise I'll go mad here and do something. Or are you ashamed to confer upon me such candour? But surely you can't be ashamed with me?'

'That isn't at all what I'm talking to you about. I asked you a question and am waiting for your answer.'

'It goes without saying, I'd kill,' I cried, 'whomever you ordered me to, but surely you can't . . . surely you won't order me to do that?'

'And what do you think, that I'll spare you? I'll give the

order and remain on the sidelines. Could you bear that? But of course not, how could you! You perhaps would kill if ordered to do so, but then you would come and kill me for daring to send you.'

It was as if something had hit me on the head when I heard those words. Of course, even then I considered her question to be something of a joke, a challenge; but nevertheless she had uttered it too seriously. Nevertheless, I was struck that she had spoken out like that, that she maintained such rights over me, that she would consent to wield such power over me, and say so frankly: 'Go to your ruin, while I remain on the sidelines.' There was something so cynical and candid in these words that, in my opinion, it went too far. Was that, then, how she regarded me now? It had already gone beyond slavery and being a nonentity. A view like that raises a person to your own level. And however absurd, however improbable our whole conversation may have been, my heart was pounding.

Suddenly she burst out laughing. We were sitting on a bench then, the children playing before us, just opposite the place where carriages would stop and let people off in the avenue in front of the casino.

'Do you see that fat baroness?' she cried. 'That's Baroness Wurmerhelm.[3] She only arrived the day before yesterday. Do you see her husband: the tall, gaunt Prussian holding a walking stick? Do you remember how he looked us over the day before yesterday? Off you go now, walk up to the baroness, take off your hat and say something to her in French.'

'But why?'

'You swore that you would jump off the Schlangenberg; you swear that you are prepared to kill if I give the order. Instead of all these killings and tragedies I just want to have a laugh. Off you go now – no excuses. I want to see the baron beat you with his stick.'

'Are you challenging me: do you think that I won't do it?'

'Yes, I'm challenging you; off you go, it's what I want!'

'As you wish, I'm going, though it's a preposterous fancy. There's only one thing – won't there be some unpleasantness for the general, and through him for you as well? By God, I'm not worrying about myself, but about you – well and about the general too. And what sort of fancy is this to insult a woman for no reason?'

'No, I can see you're nothing but a chatterbox,' she said scornfully. 'Your eyes just now were bloodshot, but perhaps that was from drinking too much wine at dinner. Do you really think that I don't understand myself that it's both stupid and vulgar and that the general will be furious? I simply want to have a laugh. Well, I want to and that's all there is to it! And why should you insult a woman? So that you get beaten with a stick all the sooner.'

I turned around and set off in silence to carry out her commission. Of course it was stupid and of course I didn't know how to get myself out of it, but when I started walking towards the baroness, I remember, it was as if something were egging me on; to wit, the idea of acting like a naughty schoolboy. And I was terribly overwrought, as if I were drunk.

Chapter 6

Two days have passed now since that stupid day. And what shouts, rows, explanations, rumbles! And what a brouhaha it's all been, what wrangling, stupidity and vulgarity – and I'm the cause of it all. But then again, sometimes it is funny – at least to me. I'm unable to comprehend what has happened to me; am I in fact in a state of frenzy or have I simply lost my bearings and am I going to wreak havoc until they tie me up? At times it seems that I'm losing my mind. At times it seems that I'm not all that far removed from childhood, from the school desk, and that I'm simply behaving like a naughty schoolboy.

It's Polina, it's all Polina! Perhaps there wouldn't be any schoolboy pranks if it weren't for her. Who knows, perhaps I do all this out of despair (no matter how stupid it is to think like that). And I don't understand, I don't understand what's good about her! Yes, she's rather good-looking; I think she's good-looking. After all, she drives other men out of their mind. She's tall and svelte. Only she's very thin. I think you could tie her in a knot or bend her double. Her footprint is very narrow and long – it's tormenting. Truly tormenting. Her hair has a reddish tint. Her eyes are real cat's eyes, but how proudly and haughtily she can use them. One evening about four months ago, when I had just come here, she was talking heatedly and for a long time in the drawing room with des Grieux. And she looked at him in such a way . . . that later when I went to my room to go to bed, I could imagine that she had given him a slap – that she had just done it to him, and stood there in front of him looking at him . . . It was from that evening that I loved her.

However, to business.

I walked down the path to the avenue, stood in the middle of it and waited for the baroness and baron. At a distance of five paces, I took off my hat and made a bow.

I remember that the baroness was dressed in a light-grey silk dress of immense circumference, with flounces, a crinoline and a train. She is quite short and exceptionally fat, with a double chin so terribly fat you can't see her neck at all. Her face is crimson. Her eyes are small, malevolent and insolent. She walks as though she were bestowing an honour on everyone. The baron is gaunt, tall. His face, as is usual with Germans, is lopsided and covered with a thousand tiny wrinkles; he wears glasses; he's about forty-five years old. His legs begin practically right from his chest; that means he has breeding. He's as proud as a peacock. A bit clumsy. There's something sheep-like about his face, which in its own way might pass for profundity.

All this flashed before my eyes in a matter of three seconds.

My bow and my hat in my hands at first scarcely caught their attention. Only the baron arched his eyebrows slightly. The baroness kept sailing straight at me.

'*Madame la baronne,*' I pronounced loudly and clearly, rapping out each word, '*j'ai l'honneur d'être votre esclave.*'[1]

Then I made a bow, put on my hat and walked past the baron, politely turning my face to him and smiling.

I had been ordered to take off my hat, but bowing and playing the naughty schoolboy was my own idea. The devil only knows what urged me on. It's as if I was hurtling down from a mountain.

'*Hein!*'[2] the baron cried, or rather, wheezed, turning towards me with angry surprise.

I turned around and came to a stop in polite expectation, as I continued to look at him and smile. He was evidently perplexed and raised his eyebrows *nec plus ultra*.[3] His face grew darker and darker. The baroness also turned in my direction and also looked at me in furious bewilderment. Some of the passers-by began to gawk. Some even stopped.

'*Hein!*' the baron wheezed again, with a redoubled wheeze and with redoubled fury.

'*Jawohl,*' I drawled, as I continued to look him straight in the eye.

'*Sind Sie resend?*'[4] he shouted, waving his stick and, it seems, beginning to cower a bit. Perhaps he was baffled by my clothes. I was very decently, even foppishly, dressed, like a man who clearly belongs to the most respectable society.

'*Jawo-o-ohl!*' I shouted suddenly with all my might, drawing out the 'o' like Berliners do, who constantly use the word *jawohl* in conversation, drawing out the letter 'o' more or less, to express different nuances of ideas and feelings.

The baron and the baroness quickly turned around and almost ran away from me in fright. Some of the onlookers began to talk, while others looked at me in bewilderment. However, I don't remember it very clearly.

I turned around and started walking at my normal pace towards Polina Alexandrovna. But when I was still about a hundred paces from her bench, I saw that she had got up and set off to the hotel with the children.

I caught up with her on the porch.

'I carried out ... your folly,' I said, as I came up beside her.

'Well, what of it? Now get yourself out of it,' she answered, without even a glance in my direction, and went up the stairs.

I spent all that evening walking in the park. I even walked across the park and then through a forest into another principality. In a cottage I ate some fried eggs and drank wine – for this idyll they extorted a whole thaler and a half from me.

I didn't return home until eleven o'clock. I was immediately summoned to the general.

Our party occupies two suites in the hotel; they have four rooms in all. The first, a large room, is the salon and has a piano. Adjacent to it is another large room, which is the general's study. He was waiting for me there, standing in the middle of his study in an extremely majestic pose. Des Grieux was sprawled out on the sofa.

'Allow me to ask you, my dear sir, what have you been up to?' the general began, addressing me.

THE GAMBLER

'I would like you to get straight to the point, General,' I said. 'You no doubt wish to speak about my encounter today with a certain German?'

'A certain German?! That German is Baron Wurmerhelm and a very important person, sir! You have behaved rudely to him and the baroness.'

'Not at all.'

'You frightened them, my dear sir,' the general shouted.

'Not in the least. When I was in Berlin my ears started ringing with this *jawohl* that they repeat after every word and which they drawl out so disgustingly. When I came upon them in the avenue, this *jawohl* suddenly came to mind, I don't know why, and made me irritable ... And besides that the baroness, as she has already done three times upon meeting me, has a habit of making straight for me, as if I were some worm that can be trampled underfoot. You must agree that I, too, may have my pride. I took off my hat and politely (I assure you that it was politely) said: "*Madame, j'ai l'honneur d'être votre esclave.*" When the baron turned around and shouted, "*Hein!*" – suddenly something induced me to also shout "*Jawohl!*" I shouted it twice: the first time in a normal voice, and the second time I drawled it out with all my might. And that's all there is to it.'

I must confess that I was terribly happy with this extremely childish explanation. I myself was surprised how much I wanted to spin out this story with as many absurdities as possible.

And the further along I went, the more I developed a taste for it.

'Are you making fun of me, is that it?' the general shouted. He turned to the Frenchman and explained in French that I was definitely asking for a scandal. Des Grieux grinned contemptuously and shrugged his shoulders.

'Oh, don't think anything of the kind, it wasn't that at

all!' I exclaimed to the general. 'Of course, I behaved badly, and I admit that to you in all sincerity. My behaviour might even be called a stupid and unseemly schoolboy's prank, but nothing more. And you should know, General, that I very much repent my actions. But there is one circumstance here that in my view almost absolves me even from repentance. Recently, for the last two or even three weeks, I have not been feeling well: I'm sick, nervous, irritable, fantastic, and on certain occasions I've completely lost all self-control. Indeed, sometimes I've wanted terribly to turn to the Marquis des Grieux suddenly and ... However, there's no point in finishing what I was going to say; he might take offence. In a word, these are symptoms of an illness. I don't know whether Baroness Wurmerhelm will take this circumstance into consideration when I apologize to her (because I do intend to apologize). I don't suppose she will, all the more so because as I understand it lawyers have started abusing this circumstance of late in the courts: in criminal trials they all too often have begun justifying their clients – the criminals – by the fact that they didn't remember anything at the moment the crime was committed and that it was apparently some kind of illness. "He beat him," they say, "but he doesn't remember a thing." And just imagine, General, medicine supports them – our medical men actually attest to the fact that there is an illness like this, a temporary insanity, when a person remembers almost nothing, or remembers only half, or a quarter. But the baron and baroness are people of the old generation, and Prussian *junkers*[5] and landowners at that. They probably are still unaware of this progress in the legal and medical worlds, and therefore they won't accept my explanation. What do you think, General?'

'Enough, sir!' the general uttered sharply and with restrained indignation. 'Enough! I will try, once and for all, to rid myself of your schoolboy pranks. You will not apologize to the baron and baroness. Any dealings with you, even though it were to consist solely of your asking their forgiveness, would be too degrading for them. The baron, upon learning that you belong to my household, has already had a talk with me in the casino, and I must admit that had it gone a little further he would have demanded satisfaction from me. Do you understand what I – I – have been subjected to, my dear sir? I, sir, was forced to apologize to the baron and gave him my word that you would immediately, as of today, cease to be a member of my household...'

'Excuse me, General, excuse me, so it was he who categorically demanded that I cease to be a member of your household, as you are pleased to put it?'

'No, but I considered myself obliged to give him that satisfaction, and, it goes without saying, the baron was gratified. We are parting, my dear sir. I still owe you these four friedrichs d'or and three florins in the local money. Here's the money, and here's the paper with the account; you may check the figures. Goodbye. From this time forth we are strangers. I have had nothing from you but bother and unpleasantness. I'll call the attendant now and inform him that as of tomorrow I am not responsible for your hotel expenses. I have the honour to remain your humble servant.'

I took the money and the paper on which the account had been written in pencil, bowed to the general and said to him very seriously:

'General, the matter cannot end like this. I am very sorry that you have been subjected to unpleasantness by the baron, but – I beg your pardon – you yourself are to blame. Why did you take it upon yourself to answer for me to the baron? What is the meaning of the expression that I belong to your household? I am merely a tutor in your household, and nothing more. I am not your son, I am not under your guardianship and you cannot answer for my actions. I am a legally competent person. I am twenty-five years old, I am a university graduate, I am a nobleman and I am a complete stranger to you. Only my unbounded respect for your merits prevents me from demanding satisfaction from you right now and a further explanation for the fact that you took it upon yourself to answer for me.'

The general was so stunned that he flung up his hands, then suddenly turned towards the Frenchman and hurriedly recounted to him that I had practically challenged him to a duel just now. The Frenchman roared with laughter.

'But I do not intend to let the baron off,' I continued with complete composure, not in the least embarrassed by Monsieur des Grieux's laughter, 'and since, General, by consenting to listen to the baron's complaint today and thus entering into his interests, you have made yourself a participant, as it were, in this whole affair, then I have the honour of informing you that no later than tomorrow morning I will demand from the baron, in my own name, a formal explanation of his reasons for addressing another person instead of me, when his business was with me, as if I were unable or unworthy of answering him myself.'

My hunch proved right. Upon hearing this new bit of nonsense, the general became terribly frightened.

'What, do you really intend to continue this damned business!' he cried. 'But what are you doing to me, good Lord! Don't you dare, don't you dare, my dear sir, or I swear!... There are authorities here, too, and I... I... In a word, with my rank... and the baron's, too... In a word, you'll be arrested and sent away from here under police escort so that you don't make a row! Understand that, sir!' And although he was choking with rage, nevertheless he was terribly frightened.

'General,' I answered with a calmness that he found unbearable, 'one cannot be arrested for making a row before the row happens. I have not yet begun my explanations with the baron, and you are completely in the dark as to how and on what grounds I intend to set about the business. I wish only to clear up the offensive assumption that I am under the guardianship of a person who supposedly has power over my free will. You are becoming alarmed and worried for no reason.'

'For God's sake, for God's sake, Alexey Ivanovich, abandon this senseless undertaking!' the general muttered, suddenly changing his wrathful tone for a pleading one, and even grabbing me by the hands. 'Well, just imagine what will come of it. More unpleasantness! You will agree that I must behave in a particular way, particularly now! . . . Particularly now! . . . Oh, you don't know, you don't know all my circumstances! . . . I am prepared to take you back when we leave this place. It's only now that, well, in a word – after all, you understand the reasons!' he cried in despair. 'Alexey Ivanovich, Alexey Ivanovich! . . .'

As I was making my way to the door, I once more earnestly asked him not to worry; I promised that everything would turn out well and properly, and hurried to leave.

Sometimes Russians abroad are too cowardly and are terribly afraid of what people will say, how they will be regarded and whether this or that is the proper thing to do – in a word, they behave as if they were wearing a corset, particularly those who lay claim to being of some importance. Their favourite thing is some sort of preconceived, established form, which they follow slavishly – in hotels, on walks, at meetings, while travelling . . . But the general had let slip that apart from everything else there were some particular circumstances, that he needed 'to behave particularly'. And that was why he suddenly became so faint-hearted and frightened and changed his tone with me. I took this into consideration and made a note of it. And, of course, tomorrow he could without thinking what he was doing apply to some authorities, so that indeed I must be careful.

I did not at all wish to make the general himself angry, however; but I did want to make Polina angry now. Polina had treated me so cruelly and had pushed me on to such a stupid path that I very much wanted to drive her to the point where she would ask me to stop. My schoolboy's prank, after all, might compromise her, too. Besides, some different feelings and desires were taking shape within me; if I, for instance, should disappear of my own accord into nothingness in her presence, that does not at all mean that I am a wet chicken in the presence of other people, and of course it's certainly not for the baron 'to beat me with his stick'. I wanted to have a good laugh at them all, and come out of it a splendid fellow. Let them watch me. I dare say that she'll be frightened of a scandal and call me to her side once more. And if she doesn't, then she'll nevertheless see that I'm not a wet chicken...

(An astonishing bit of news: I've just heard from our nanny, whom I met on the stairway, that Marya Filippovna left today for Karlsbad, all alone on the evening train, to visit her cousin. What does this mean? The nanny says that she had been planning it for some time; but how is it that nobody knew? However, perhaps I'm the only one who didn't know. Nanny let slip to me that Marya Filippovna had a talk with the general the day before yesterday. I understand, sir. It's probably – Mlle Blanche. Yes, something decisive is coming.)

THE GAMBLER

Chapter 7

In the morning I called the attendant and informed him that I wished to be billed separately. My room was not so expensive to alarm me and make me leave the hotel altogether. I had sixteen friedrichs d'or, and there ... and there perhaps lay wealth! Strange as it may seem, I still hadn't won, but I was acting, feeling and thinking like a wealthy man, and I couldn't imagine myself any other way.

I had intended, despite the early hour, to go at once to see Mr Astley in the Hotel d'Angleterre, which was quite near us, when suddenly des Grieux came to see me. This had never happened before, and besides, my relations with this gentleman of late had been very aloof and very strained. He clearly hadn't been bothering to conceal his contempt for me, hadn't even tried to conceal it; while I – I had my own reasons for not regarding him with favour. In a word, I loathed him. His arrival surprised me very much. I at once grasped that something special was brewing.

He was very amiable when he entered and even complimented me on my room. Seeing that I had my hat in my hand, he enquired whether I was really going out for a walk so early. When he heard that I was going to see Mr Astley on business, he thought it over for a moment, reflected and his face assumed an extremely anxious look.

Des Grieux was like all Frenchmen, that is, gay and amiable when necessary and expedient, and unbearably boring when being gay and amiable had ceased to be necessary. The Frenchman is rarely naturally amiable; he is always amiable on command, as it were, or when it is to his advantage. If, for example, he sees the necessity to be fantastic, original, a bit out of the ordinary, then his fantasy, of the most stupid and unnatural kind, is pieced together from earlier accepted forms that have long since become vulgar. The natural Frenchman consists of the most plebeian, petty and ordinary positivism – in a word, he's the most boring being in the world. In my opinion, only novices and, in particular, Russian young ladies find Frenchmen attractive. Any respectable being notices at once and finds unbearable the conventionalism of the established forms of salon amiability, familiarity and gaiety.

'I've come to see you on business,' he began extremely unceremoniously, though politely, 'and I won't conceal the fact that I come to you as an ambassador, or rather, as a mediator from the general. As I know very little Russian, I understood almost nothing yesterday; but the general explained it to me in detail, and I confess...'

'But listen, Monsieur des Grieux,' I interrupted him, 'here you've undertaken to be a mediator in this business. Of course, I am "*un outchitel*" and have never laid claim to being a close friend of this household or to any other especially intimate relations, and therefore I do not know all the circumstances; but explain to me, are you now really a member of this family? Because, in the end, you take such an interest in everything, and without fail you are the mediator in everything...'

He didn't like my question. It was too transparent for him, and he didn't want to say more than he had to.

'I am bound to the general in part through business, in part through *certain special* circumstances,' he said drily. 'The general sent me to ask you to abandon your intentions of yesterday. Everything you concocted, of course, is very clever; but he particularly asked me to convey to you that you will fail utterly; moreover, the baron won't receive you; and, finally, in any event, he has the means by which to forestall any further unpleasantness from you. You must see that. Tell me, what is the purpose of continuing? The general has promised you that he will certainly take you back into his household again at the first opportunity and until that time will pay your salary, *vos appointements*.[1] Now that's rather handsome, don't you think?'

I very calmly raised the objection that he was somewhat mistaken; that perhaps the baron wouldn't send me packing, but on the contrary, would hear me out, and that he had probably come to try to discover how exactly I intended to pursue the matter.

'Good heavens! Since the general is so interested, then it goes without saying that he would like to know what you're going to do and how you're going to do it. That's only natural!'

I proceeded to explain and he began to listen, sprawled out with his head inclined somewhat towards me and a suggestion of overt and unconcealed irony in his face. I tried with all my might to pretend that I was regarding the matter very seriously. I explained that since the baron had turned to the general with his complaint about me, as if I were the general's servant, then, first of all, he had deprived me of my post, and secondly, he had slighted me, as though I were a person who was not in a position to answer for myself and to whom it was not even worth talking. Of course, I was justified in feeling offended; however, considering the difference in our ages, positions in society and so on and so forth (I could hardly keep from laughing at this point), I did not want to commit another act of thoughtlessness, that is, by challenging the baron directly or merely offering him satisfaction. Nevertheless, I considered myself fully within my rights in offering him, and the baroness in particular, my apologies, all the more so because of late I have indeed felt ill, out of sorts and, so to speak, fantastic and so on and so forth. However, the baron himself, with his insulting appeal to the general yesterday and his insistence that the general dismiss me from my position, had put me in such a position that now I could no longer offer him and the baroness my apologies, because both he and the baroness and all of society would certainly think that I had come with my apologies out of fear and in order to regain my post. From all this it follows that I now find myself forced to ask the baron that he apologize to me first, in the most moderate terms – for example, he might say that he did not wish to offend me in any way. And when the baron says this, then I, my hands now untied, will extend to him my heartfelt and sincere apologies. In a word, I concluded, I ask only that the baron untie my hands.

'Ugh! What scruples and what refinement! And why should you apologize? Well, you must admit, *monsieur* . . . *monsieur* . . . that you are undertaking all this on purpose, in order to annoy the general . . . but perhaps, you have some ulterior motive . . . *mon cher monsieur, pardon, j'ai oublié votre nom, monsieur Alexis? . . . n'est ce pas?*'[2]

'But excuse me, *mon cher marquis*, what business is it of yours?'

'*Mais le général . . .*'[3]

'And what of the general? Yesterday he said something, that he needed to maintain a certain footing . . . and he was so worried . . . but I didn't understand a thing.'

'There is here, there exists here a particular circumstance,' des Grieux picked up in a pleading tone, in which vexation was heard more and more. 'You know Mlle de Cominges?'

'That is, Mlle Blanche?'

'Well, yes, Mlle Blanche de Cominges . . . *et madame sa mere*[4] . . . You must admit, the general . . . In a word, the general is in love and even . . . perhaps the marriage will even take place here. And just imagine that at the same time there are all sorts of scandal and talk.'

'I don't see any scandal or talk that have any bearing on the marriage.'

'But *le baron est si irascible, un caractère prussien, vous savez, enfin il fera une querelle d'Allemande.*'[5]

'But that will be with me, and not you, since I no longer belong to the household ...' (I purposely tried to be as thick-headed as possible.) 'But excuse me, so is it settled that Mlle Blanche is marrying the general? What are they waiting for? I mean to say – why conceal this, at any rate, from us, the members of the household?'

'I can't tell you ... however, it's not yet completely ... however ... you know that they are waiting for news from Russia; the general needs to put his affairs in order ...'

'Ah, yes, *la baboulinka*!'

Des Grieux looked at me with hatred.

'In a word,' he interrupted, 'I rely completely on your innate kindness, your intelligence, your tact ... You, of course, will do this for the family in which you have been received as one of their own, in which you have been loved and respected ...'

'Pardon me, I've been thrown out! Here you've just been claiming that it was all for the sake of appearances; but you must admit that if you're told: "Of course, I don't want to box your ears, but for the sake of appearances let me box your ears" ... Isn't that practically the same thing?'

'If that's the way it is, if no entreaties can have any influence over you,' he began severely and haughtily, 'then allow me to assure you that measures will be taken. There are authorities here, you'll be sent away today – *que diable! un blanc-bec comme vous*[6] wants to challenge a person like the baron to a duel! And do you think that you'll be left in peace? Believe me, nobody here is afraid of you! If I have made a request, it was more on my own account, because you have caused the general worry. And do you really think, do you really think that the baron won't simply order you thrown out by his lackey?'

'But, you see, I'm not going myself,' I answered with extraordinary calm, 'you are mistaken, Monsieur des Grieux, all this will be managed much more properly than you think. I'm going to see Mr Astley now and ask him to be my go-between, in a word, to be my second. This man likes me and will certainly not refuse. He will go to the baron and the baron will receive him. If I am *un outchitel* and seem to be some sort of *subalterne*,[7] well and, finally, defenceless – then Mr Astley is the nephew of a lord, a real lord, everybody knows that, Lord Pibroch, and that lord is here. Believe me, the baron will be courteous to Mr Astley and will hear him out. And if he doesn't hear him out, then Mr Astley will regard that as a personal offence (you know how persistent the English are) and send a friend to the baron, and he has some good friends. Consider now that things might not turn out as you had supposed.'

The Frenchman was definitely frightened; indeed, all this looked very much like the truth and, as a result, it turned out that I really was in a position to instigate a scandal.

'But I beg you,' he began in an utterly pleading voice, 'drop all this! It's as though you are pleased that a scandal will come of it! It's not satisfaction that you require, but a scandal! I said that it all would come out amusing and even clever, which perhaps is what you're aiming for, but in a word,' he concluded, seeing that I had risen and was taking my hat, 'I came to you to give you these few words from a certain person; read them – I was told to wait for an answer.'

Having said this, he took from his pocket a little note, folded and sealed, and gave it to me.

In Polina's handwriting was written:

I gather that you intend to continue with this business. You're angry and you're starting to act like a schoolboy. But there are particular circumstances here, which perhaps I will explain to you later; meanwhile, please, stop and calm yourself. How stupid it all is! I need you and you promised to obey me. Remember the Schlangenberg. I ask you to be obedient and, if necessary, I order it.

Yours, P.

PS If you are angry with me about what happened yesterday, then forgive me.

Everything seemed to be swimming before my eyes as I read these lines. My lips turned white and I began to tremble. The damned Frenchman looked on with an earnestly reticent pose, having averted his eyes from me, as if to avoid witnessing my embarrassment. It would have been better if he had burst out laughing at me.

'Fine,' I answered, 'tell *mademoiselle* that she may rest easy. Allow me, however, to ask you,' I added sharply, 'why is it that you withheld the note for so long? Instead of nattering about trifles, it seems you should have begun with that . . . if you came expressly on that errand.'

'Oh, I wanted . . . In general, this is all so strange that you will forgive my natural impatience. I wanted to learn from you myself as quickly as possible what your intentions are. However, I do not know what is in the note and thought that there would always be opportunity to give it to you.'

'I understand; you were quite simply ordered to give it to me only as a last resort, but not to do so if everything was settled by talking it out. Isn't that so? Tell me plainly, Monsieur des Grieux!'

'*Peut-être*,'[8] he said, assuming an air of some particular reserve and regarding me with some sort of particular look.

I took my hat; he nodded and left. I thought I saw a sarcastic smile on his lips. And how could it be otherwise?

'You and I still have a score to settle, Frenchy; we'll see how you measure up!' I muttered as I went down the stairs. I still couldn't take anything in; it was as if I had been hit over the head. The fresh air revived me a bit.

A couple of minutes later, when I was just barely beginning to take things in, two thoughts presented themselves to me clearly: *first*: that such trifles as some schoolboyish pranks and improbable threats uttered by a mere boy in passing yesterday could raise such a *general* alarm! And the *second* thought: what is the nature of this Frenchman's influence on Polina? Just a word from him – and she does everything he asks, writes a note and even *begs* me. Of course, their relationship had always been a riddle to me from the very beginning, from the time that I first knew them; however, during these past few days I have observed in her a definite loathing and even contempt for him, while he didn't even look at her, was even simply rude to her. I have observed this. Polina herself spoke to me of her loathing; she's come out with some extremely significant admissions... That means he simply has her in his power, he has her in fetters of some sort...

Chapter 8

On the promenade, as they call it here, that is, the chestnut avenue, I met my Englishman.

'Oh, oh!' he began, when he caught sight of me, 'I was on my way to see you and you're coming to see me. So, have you already parted company from your people?'

'Tell me, first of all, how is it that you know all about it?' I asked in astonishment. 'Does everybody really know all about it?'

'Oh, no, not everybody; and it's not worth their knowing. Nobody's talking about it.'

'Then how is it that you know about it?'

'I know, that is, I chanced to learn. Now where are you going from here? I like you and that's why I came to see you.'

'You're a good fellow, Mr Astley,' I said (however, I was terribly surprised: how did he find out?), 'and since I haven't had my coffee yet and you probably didn't have a proper cup, let's go to the cafe in the casino, and we can sit there, have a smoke, and I'll tell you everything, and . . . you'll tell me too.'

The cafe was a hundred paces away. They brought us our coffee, we sat down, I lit a cigarette, Mr Astley didn't smoke but having fixed his gaze on me, he prepared to listen.

'I'm not going anywhere, I'm staying here,' I began.

'And I was certain that you would stay,' Mr Astley replied approvingly.

On my way to see Mr Astley I did not at all intend and particularly did not want to tell him anything about my love for Polina. All this time, I had hardly said a single word to him about it. Moreover, he was very shy. I had observed from the first that Polina made an extraordinary impression on him, but that he never mentioned her name. But strangely enough, suddenly, now, no sooner had he sat down and fixed upon me his intent, lustreless gaze than I felt for no reason at all the desire to tell him everything, that is, all about my love in all its particulars. I talked for a full half-hour, and I found it extraordinarily pleasant to be talking about it for the first time! Noticing, however, that he would become embarrassed at certain, particularly passionate places, I purposely intensified the passion of my story. I regret one thing: perhaps I said a bit more than I should have about the Frenchman . . .

Mr Astley listened, seated across from me, motionless, not uttering a word or a sound and looking me in the eyes; but when I started talking about the Frenchman, he suddenly cut me short and asked severely: Did I have the right to bring up this extraneous circumstance? Mr Astley always asked questions very strangely.

'You're right, I'm afraid I don't,' I answered.

'You can say nothing definite about this marquis and Miss Polina apart from mere conjectures?'

I again was surprised by such a categorical question from such a shy person as Mr Astley.

'No, nothing definite,' I answered, 'nothing, of course.'

'If that's the case, then you have done wrong not only by speaking about it with me, but even by thinking of it yourself.'

'All right, all right! I admit it, but that's not the point now,' I interrupted, keeping my surprise to myself. Then I proceeded to tell him all about what happened yesterday, with all the details: Polina's bit of mischief, my adventure with the baron, my dismissal, the general's unusual cowardice; and, finally, I gave a detailed account of today's visit by des Grieux, in all its particulars; in conclusion I showed him the note.

'What do you deduce from this?' I asked. 'I came precisely to learn your thoughts. As far as I'm concerned, I think I could kill that little Frenchy and perhaps I will.'

'And I as well,' Mr Astley said. 'As far as Miss Polina is concerned, then . . . you know, we enter into relations even with people whom we loathe if necessity so dictates. There may be relations here of which you are ignorant, which depend on extenuating circumstances. I think that you can set your mind at rest, to a certain extent, of course. As far as her conduct yesterday is concerned, of course, it's strange – not because she wanted to be rid of you and sent you to brave the baron's cudgel (which he didn't use, I don't understand why, since he was holding it), but because such an escapade for such a . . . for such an exceptional miss[1] is unseemly. It goes without saying that she couldn't foresee that you would carry out her taunting wish literally . . .'

'Do you know what?' I cried suddenly, as I peered intently at Mr Astley. 'It's just occurred to me that you have already heard about everything, and I know from whom? – from Miss Polina herself!'

Mr Astley looked at me with surprise.

'Your eyes are sparkling and I read suspicion in them,' he said, having at once regained his composure. 'But you have no right whatsoever to divulge your suspicions. I cannot recognize that right and absolutely refuse to answer your question.'

'Well, enough! There's no need,' I cried out, strangely agitated and not understanding where that idea had come from! And when, where and how could Mr Astley have been chosen by Polina to be her confidant? Of late, however, I had somewhat lost sight of Mr Astley, while Polina had always been something of a mystery for me, so much so that now, for example, having launched into the whole story of my love to Mr Astley, I was suddenly struck, as I was telling it, by how I could say almost nothing precise and positive about my relationship with her. On the contrary, everything was fantastic, strange, unfounded, and unlike anything else.

'Well, all right, all right; I've lost the thread and there's a great deal that I am unable to grasp right now,' I answered, as if I was out of breath. 'However, you're a good man. Now to another piece of business, and I will ask not for your advice, but for your opinion.'

I was silent for a moment and began:

'Why do you think that the general got so scared? Why have they all made such a fuss over my very stupid practical joke? Such a fuss that even des Grieux himself found it necessary to get involved (and he gets involved only in the most important matters), pay me a visit (and what a visit!), beg, plead with me – he, des Grieux, begs me! Finally, take note, he came at nine o'clock, just before nine, and he already had Miss Polina's note in his hands. So when, one wants to know, was it written? Perhaps Miss Polina was roused out of bed for this! Moreover, from this I see that Miss Polina is his slave (because she even asks me for my forgiveness!); moreover, what is all this to her, to her personally? Why is she so interested? Why are they so afraid of some baron? And what if the general is marrying Mlle Blanche de Cominges? They say that they have to behave in some *particular* way as a result of this circumstance – but this is all too particular, you must agree! What do you think? I'm convinced by your look that you know more than I do here as well!'

Mr Astley grinned and nodded.

'Indeed, it seems that I do know a great deal more about this than you,' he said. 'The whole matter concerns Mlle Blanche alone, and I am certain that this is the absolute truth.'

'Well, what about Mlle Blanche?' I cried in impatience (I suddenly hoped that now something would be revealed about Mlle Polina).

'I think that at the present moment Mlle Blanche has a particular interest in avoiding in any way possible an encounter with the baron and baroness – even more so an unpleasant encounter, and even worse a scandalous one.'

'Well! Well!'

'Mlle Blanche was here in Roulettenburg during the season the year before last. And I was here as well. Mlle Blanche then was not called Mlle de Cominges, nor did her mother Madame *veuve*[2] Cominges exist then. At least there was no mention of her. Des Grieux – there was no des Grieux either. I am deeply convinced that not only are they not related, but also that they were not even acquainted until quite recently. Des Grieux also became a marquis only quite recently – I'm convinced of that by a certain circumstance. One might even presume that he took the name des Grieux only recently. I know here a certain individual who has met him under a different name.'

'But he really does have a respectable circle of acquaintance, doesn't he?'

'Oh, that may be. Even Mlle Blanche may have. But the year before last Mlle Blanche, owing to a complaint from this same baroness, received an invitation from the local police to quit the city and she did so.'

'How is that?'

'She made her first appearance here then with a certain Italian, some sort of prince, with a historic name, something like Barberini[3] or something of the sort. The man was all rings and diamonds, and not fake ones either. They drove around in a marvellous carriage. Mlle Blanche played *trente et quarante*, at first very well, but then her luck took a sharp turn for the worse, as I recall. I remember that she lost a considerable sum one evening. But worst of all, *un beau matin*[4] her prince vanished no one knows where; the horses and carriage vanished as well – everything vanished. The hotel bill was frightful. Mlle Zelmá (instead of Barberini she had suddenly become Mlle Zelmá) was in the utmost despair. She wailed and screamed for the whole hotel to hear and rent her clothes in a fit of rage. A certain Polish count (all travelling Poles are counts) was staying there in the hotel, and Mlle Zelmá, rending her clothes and scratching her face like a cat with her beautiful hands washed in perfume, made something of an impression on him. They talked things over and by dinner she had consoled herself. In the evening he appeared with her on his arm in the casino. Mlle Zelmá laughed, as was her wont, very loudly, and her manner had become somewhat more composed. She had entered right into the ranks of those ladies who, when they play roulette, walk up to the table and elbow for all they're worth for a place for themselves among the gamblers at the table. This is considered particularly chic among these ladies. You have, of course, noticed them?'

'Oh, yes.'

'They're not worth noticing. To the annoyance of the respectable patrons, they are not asked to leave, at least those who change thousand-franc notes at the table every day. However, as soon as they stop changing notes, they're immediately asked to move on. Mlle Zelmá still continued to change notes, but her luck was worse than ever. Note that these ladies very often are lucky when they gamble; they have marvellous self-control. However, my story is at an end. One day, the count vanished just as the prince had done. Mlle Zelmá made her appearance that evening alone; this time nobody presented himself to offer his arm. In two days' time she had lost absolutely everything. After betting her last louis d'or and losing it, she looked around and saw next to her Baron Wurmerhelm, who was scrutinizing her very carefully and with profound indignation. But Mlle Zelmá didn't detect his indignation, and turning to the baron with her celebrated smile asked him to stake ten louis d'or on red for her. As a result, following a complaint from the baroness, she received an invitation by evening not to make any further appearances in the casino. If you're surprised at my knowing all these petty and utterly indecent details, it's only because I've heard them at length from Mr Feeder, a relation of mine, who that very evening drove Mlle Zelmá in his carriage from Roulettenburg to Spa.[5] Now do you understand? Mlle Blanche wants to become the general's wife, probably so that in future she will not receive any more invitations like the one she did the year before last from the casino police. She no longer plays now; but that's because now, to all appearances, she has capital that she lends at interest to the gamblers here. That's much shrewder. I even suspect that the unfortunate general owes her money, too. Perhaps des Grieux does as well. Perhaps des Grieux is her partner. You must agree that at least until the wedding she would not wish to attract the attention of the baroness and baron for any reason. In a word, nothing could be less to her advantage than a scandal. And you are connected with their household, and your actions might cause a scandal, all the more so since she daily appears in public on the general's arm or with Miss Polina. Now do you understand?'

'No, I don't understand!' I cried, banging the table so hard that the *garçon*[6] came running in alarm.

'Tell me, Mr Astley,' I repeated in a frenzy, 'if you knew this whole story, and consequently, you know by heart what Mlle Blanche de Cominges is, why didn't you warn me at least, or the general himself, or finally, and most importantly, Miss Polina, who has appeared here in public at the casino arm in arm with Mlle Blanche. How could you?'

'There wasn't any point in warning you, because you couldn't have done anything,' Mr Astley answered calmly. 'And indeed what was there to warn you about? The general perhaps knows even more about Mlle Blanche than I do, and nevertheless he accompanies her and Miss Polina on their walks. The general is an unfortunate man. Yesterday I saw Mlle Blanche galloping on a splendid horse with Monsieur des Grieux and that little Russian prince, while the general galloped behind them on a chestnut. He had said that morning that his feet were aching, but he rode well. And just at that very moment it suddenly occurred to me that he is an utterly ruined man. Moreover, all this is none of my business, and I only recently had the honour of getting to know Miss Polina. However,' (Mr Astley remembered suddenly), 'I've already told you that I cannot recognize your right to ask certain questions, despite the fact that I sincerely like you...'

'Enough,' I said, as I got up, 'now it's clear to me as day that Miss Polina also knows everything about Mlle Blanche, but that she can't part with her Frenchman, and therefore she reconciles herself to the idea of taking walks with Mlle Blanche. Believe me, no other influence would force her to walk with Mlle Blanche and to implore me in a note not to touch the baron. This must be the influence before which everything must bow. And yet it was she herself who set me loose on the baron! The devil take it, you can't make heads or tails of it!'

'You're forgetting, first of all, that this Mlle de Cominges is the general's fiancée and, secondly, that Miss Polina, the general's stepdaughter, has a little brother and a little sister, the general's own children, who have been completely abandoned by this madman and who seem to have been robbed by him as well.'

'Yes, yes! That's so. To leave the children would mean to abandon them completely, to remain would mean protecting their interests and perhaps saving some scraps of the estate. Yes, yes, all that's true! But still, still! Oh, I understand now why they all take such an interest in Granny!'

'In whom?' Mr Astley asked.

'In that old witch in Moscow, who won't die and about whom they wait for a telegram, saying that she's dead.'

'Well, yes, of course, all their interests are tied to her. It's all a matter of the inheritance! If the inheritance is announced, then the general marries; Miss Polina will also be free, and des Grieux...'

'Well, and what of des Grieux?'

'Des Grieux will be paid his money; that's all he's waiting for here.'

'Is that all? Do you think he's only waiting for that?'

'I don't know any more,' Mr Astley fell into a stubborn silence.

'But I know, I know!' I repeated, enraged. 'He's also waiting for the inheritance, because Polina will receive a dowry, and once she receives the money, she'll immediately throw herself on his neck. All women are like that! And those that are the proudest turn out to be the most pathetic slaves. Polina is capable only of loving passionately and nothing more! That's my opinion of her! Just take a look at her, particularly when she's sitting alone, deep in thought: it's something destined, fated, cursed! She's capable of all the horrors of life and passion... she... she... but who is that calling me?' I suddenly exclaimed. 'Who's shouting? I heard someone shout in Russian: "Alexey Ivanovich!" A woman's voice, listen, listen!'

At this moment we were approaching our hotel. We had left the cafe long ago now, almost without noticing it.

'I heard a woman shouting, but I don't know who is being called; it was in Russian; now I see where the shouts are coming from,' Mr Astley was pointing, 'it's that woman who's shouting, the one sitting in the large chair and who has just been carried on to the porch by all those lackeys. They're carrying up suitcases behind her, which means that the train has just arrived.'

'But why is she calling me? She's shouting again; look, she's waving to us.'

'I can see that she's waving,' Mr Astley said.

'Alexey Ivanovich! Alexey Ivanovich! Oh, my heavens, what a blockhead!' desperate cries resounded from the hotel porch.

We almost ran to the entrance. I stepped on to the porch and... I stopped dead in my tracks in amazement, my legs rooted to the ground.

Chapter 9

At the top of the steps of the hotel's wide porch, carried up the stairs in a chair and surrounded by footmen, maidservants and numerous obsequious hotel staff, and in the presence of the hotel manager himself, who had come out to greet the exalted guest arriving with such fuss and noise, with her own servants and with so many trunks and cases, sat – *Grandmother!* Yes, it was she herself, the formidable and rich, seventy-five-year-old Antonida Vasilyevna Tarasevichev, landowner and grand lady of Moscow, *la babulinka*, about whom telegrams had been dispatched and received, who was dying and did not die, and who suddenly, in person, appeared among us out of the clear blue sky. Although she had lost the use of her legs and was carried in a chair, as always these last five years, she was her usual animated, quick-tempered, complacent self, sitting up straight, loudly and commandingly shouting, scolding everybody – well, she was exactly the same as the couple of times I had the honour of seeing her after entering the general's household as tutor. Naturally, I stood before her dumbstruck with amazement. She had made me out with her lynx eyes a hundred paces away, when she was being carried in her chair, and she had recognized me and hailed me by name and patronymic,[1] which, as was usually the case with her, she had remembered once and for all. 'And this is the woman they had expected to see in her coffin, buried and leaving behind an inheritance,' flashed through my mind, 'but she'll outlive us all and the whole hotel! But, my God, what's going to happen to them now, what's going to happen to the general! She'll turn the whole hotel upside down!'

'Well, my dear fellow, why are you standing there, just staring at me with big eyes!' Grandmother continued to shout at me. 'Don't you know how to bow and say hello? Or have you become too proud and don't want to? Or maybe you don't recognize me? Do you hear that, Potapych,' she turned to a grey old man, in tails with a white tie and a rosy bald spot, her butler, who had accompanied her on the journey, 'do you hear that, he doesn't recognize me! They've buried me! They sent telegram after telegram: is she dead or not? I know everything, you see! And, as you see, I am alive and kicking.'

'For heaven's sake, Antonida Vasilyevna, why would I wish you any harm?' I answered gaily, after coming to my senses. 'I was merely surprised . . . And how could one not be surprised, it's so unexpected . . .'

'And what's there for you to be so surprised about? I got on the train and off I went. It's comfortable on the train, there's no jolting. Have you been out for a walk or something?'

'Yes, I took a walk to the casino.'

'It's nice here,' Grandmother said, as she had a look around, 'it's warm and the trees are lush. I like that! Are our people at home? Is the general?'

'Oh, at this hour everybody is certain to be at home.'

'So they have customary hours and all the ceremonies? They set the tone. I hear that they keep a carriage, *les seigneurs russes*![2] They fritter away all their money and then go abroad! And is Praskovya[3] with them?'

'And Polina Alexandrova as well.'

'And the Frenchy? Well, I'll see them all for myself. Alexey Ivanovich, show me the way, straight to him. So, are you comfortable here?'

'So-so, Antonida Vasilyevna.'

'And you, Potapych, tell that blockhead of a manager to give me a comfortable suite, a good one, not too high up, and take my things there at once. Why are they all crowding round to carry me? Why are they all clambering? What servility! And who is that with you?' she turned to me once again.

'This is Mr Astley,' I answered.

'And who is Mr Astley?'

'A traveller, a good friend of mine; he's acquainted with the general.'

'An Englishman. That's why he stares at me with his teeth clenched. However, I like the English. Well, haul me upstairs, right to their rooms; where are they?'

They carried Grandmother; I led the way up the hotel's wide staircase. Our procession created quite an effect. Everyone whom we met stopped and stared. Our hotel was considered the very best, the most expensive and the most aristocratic at the spa. On the staircase and in the corridors one always met magnificent ladies and important Englishmen. A number made enquiries downstairs of the manager, who, for his part, was deeply impressed. He, of course, answered all who asked that she was an important foreign lady, *une russe, une comtesse, grande dame* and that she was taking the very same suite that had been occupied a week ago by *la grande duchesse de N*.[4] Grandmother's commanding and imperious appearance as she was being carried in her chair, was the cause of the great effect. Upon meeting any new face she at once took their measure with a curious glance and questioned me loudly about them all. Grandmother was a large woman, and although she never got up from her chair, one could sense, by looking at her, that she was quite tall. She sat as straight as a board and did not lean against her chair. She held high her large, grey head with its broad and sharp features; she had a somewhat arrogant and even defiant look about her; and it was plain to see that her carriage and gestures were completely natural. Despite her seventy-five years, her complexion was rather fresh-looking and even her teeth were in fairly good shape. She was dressed in a black silk dress and a white cap.

'I find her extremely interesting,' Mr Astley whispered to me, as we walked up the stairs together.

'She knows about the telegrams,' I thought, 'and she's heard about des Grieux, but it seems that she still hasn't heard much about Mlle Blanche.' I at once communicated this to Mr Astley.

Sinner that I am! My first surprise had just passed and I was terribly delighted by the thunderbolt that we would set off now at the general's. It was as if I was being egged on, and I led the way extremely cheerfully.

Our party had taken rooms on the third floor; I did not announce our arrival and did not even knock on the door, but simply threw it open and Grandmother was carried in in triumph. They were all, as if on purpose, gathered together in the general's study. It was twelve o'clock and the entire party seemed to be planning some sort of excursion – they were going together as a group, some by carriage, others on horseback; moreover, some of their acquaintances had been invited. In addition to the general, Polina and the children and their nanny, there were in the study: des Grieux, Mlle Blanche, again in riding habit, her mother Madame *veuve* Cominges, the little prince as well as some travelling scholar, a German, whom I saw with them for the first time. The chair with Grandmother was set down in the middle of the study, three paces away from the general. My goodness, I shall never forget the effect this had! Before our entrance the general had been telling some story, and des Grieux was correcting him. It should be noted that Mlle Blanche and des Grieux for two or three days now for some reason had been very solicitous of the little prince – *à la barbe du pauvre general*,[5] and the tone set by the assembled company, though perhaps artificial, was that of a most cheerful and cordial family. At the sight of Grandmother the general suddenly was struck dumb, gaped and stopped short in mid-sentence. He looked at her, wide-eyed, as though he had been bewitched by the gaze of a basilisk. Grandmother also looked at him in silence, without stirring – but what a triumphant, defiant and mocking look it was! They looked at each other like that for a full ten seconds, amidst the profound silence of all those around them. Des Grieux at first froze, but soon feelings of extraordinary anxiety could be glimpsed on his face. Mlle Blanche arched her eyebrows, opened her mouth and stared wildly at Grandmother. The prince and the scholar contemplated the whole scene in profound bewilderment. Polina's face expressed extreme surprise and bewilderment, but suddenly she went as white as a sheet; a minute later the blood quickly rushed to her face and coloured her cheeks. Yes, it was a catastrophe for everyone! All I could do was turn my eyes from Grandmother to the others and back again. Mr Astley stood to the side, as was his wont, calm and proper.

'Well, here I am! Instead of a telegram!' Grandmother burst out at last, breaking the silence. 'What, weren't you expecting me?'

'Antonida Vasilyevna ... Auntie ... However in the world ...' muttered the unfortunate general. If Grandmother had waited a few seconds longer before speaking, he might have had a stroke.

'What do you mean, how in the world? I got on the train and off I went. After all, what's the railroad for? And you all were thinking that I had already turned up my toes and left you my inheritance? You see, I know that you've been sending telegrams from here. I think you must have paid a lot of money for them. It's not cheap from here. So I threw my legs over my shoulders and came. Is that the Frenchman? Monsieur des Grieux, I believe?'

'*Oui, madame*,' des Grieux rejoined, '*et croyez, je suis si enchanté . . . votre santé . . . c'est un miracle . . . vous voir ici, une surprise charmante . . .*'[6]

'*Charmante*, my eye; I know you, you clown; I don't believe even this little bit of what you say!' and she showed him her little finger. 'And who's this?' she turned, pointing to Mlle Blanche. She was apparently impressed by the striking Frenchwoman in riding habit, holding a whip. 'Is she from here?'

'That's Mlle Blanche de Cominges, and this is her mother, Madame de Cominges; they have taken rooms in this hotel,' I reported.

'Is the daughter married?' Grandmother asked, not standing on ceremony.

'Mlle de Cominges is not married,' I answered as respectfully as I could, having purposely lowered my voice.

'Is she fun to be with?'

At first I didn't understand her question.

'You don't find her company dull? Does she understand Russian? Des Grieux there picked up some bits and pieces when he was in Moscow.'

I explained to her that Mlle de Cominges had never been to Russia.

'*Bonjour!*'[7] Grandmother said, after suddenly turning to Mlle Blanche.

'*Bonjour, madame*,' Mlle Blanche dropped a formal and elegant curtsey, making haste, under the cover of extraordinary modesty and respect, to show with all the expression of her face and figure her extreme surprise at such a strange question and mode of address.

'Oh, she's lowered her eyes, she's all hoity-toity and puts on airs; you can see what sort of bird she is; some sort of actress. I'm staying here in the hotel downstairs,' she suddenly turned to the general, 'I'll be your neighbour; does that make you happy or not?'

'Oh, Auntie! Do believe in the sincere feeling... of my pleasure,' the general rejoined. He had already somewhat regained his senses, and since when the opportunity presented itself he knew how to speak well, importantly and with pretensions to a certain effect, he proceeded to grow expansive now. 'We were so worried and alarmed by the news of your illness... We have received such despairing telegrams, and suddenly...'

'Well, lies, lies!' Grandmother interrupted him at once.

'But how,' the general also interrupted quickly and raised his voice, trying not to notice that 'lies'. 'Nonetheless, how did you decide to undertake such a journey? You must agree, that at your age and with your health... at the very least, it's all so unexpected, so our surprise is understandable. But I'm so glad... and we all' (he began to smile ingratiatingly and with rapture) 'will try as best we can to make your season here a most pleasant stay...'

'Well, enough idle chatter; a lot of mindless blather, as usual; I'm quite capable of taking care of myself here. However, I don't have anything against you; I don't bear grudges. How, you ask. But what's so surprising about it? It was the simplest thing imaginable. And why are they all so surprised? How are you, Praskovya. What do you do here?'

'How do you do, Grandmother,' Polina said, as she approached her. 'Was it a long journey?'

'Well, this one asked something more intelligent than the lot of you – with you it's all "oh" and "ah". You see, it was bedrest and bedrest, doctors and more doctors, so I chased the doctors away and summoned the sacristan from St Nicholas's. He had cured one old woman of the same illness with hay-dust. Well, he helped me; on the third day I was all in a sweat and I got up. Then my

Germans gathered round again, put on their spectacles and began to lay down the law: "If you were to go abroad now," they said, "and take the waters, all your obstructions would be eliminated." And why ever not, I thought. Then those fools, the Zazhigins, started with their sighing: "You'll never make it!" they said. Well, and how do you like that! I got ready in a day and on Friday last week I took my maid, and Potapych, and Fyodor the footman, but I sent Fyodor packing in Berlin, because I saw that he wasn't at all necessary, and I could have made the trip all on my own ... I took a private carriage, and there are porters at every station who will carry you wherever you want for twenty kopecks. My, what a suite you've taken!' she concluded, taking a look around. 'Whose money is paying for this, my dear? After all, everything you have is mortgaged. What a pile of money you must owe this Frenchy alone. You see, I know everything, everything!'

'I, Auntie ...' the general began, all embarrassed, 'I'm surprised, Auntie ... I think I can without anybody's supervision ... and moreover, my expenses don't exceed my means, and we are here ...'

'They don't exceed your means? Listen to him! Then you must have robbed the children of every last kopeck, and you their guardian!'

'After that, after such words ...' the general began indignantly, 'I just don't know ...'

'I dare say, you don't know! And you most likely don't ever leave the roulette table? Have you squandered everything?'

The general was so astonished that he nearly choked on the surge of his agitated feelings.

'Roulette! Me? With my standing ... Me? Come to your senses, Auntie, you must still be ill ...'

'Well, lies, lies; most likely they can't drag you away; it's all lies! I'll have a look and see what this roulette is all about this very day. You, Praskovya, tell me where to go and what to see, and Alexey Ivanovich here will show me, and you, Potapych, write down all the places we should go. What is there to see here?' she suddenly turned to Polina again.

'Nearby there are the ruins of a castle, and then there's the Schlangenberg.'

'What is this Schlangenberg? A grove or something?'

'No, it's not a grove, it's a mountain; there's a *pointe*...'[8]

'What sort of *pointe*?'

'The highest point on the mountain, it's an enclosed place. The view from there is superb.'

'Haul my chair up the mountain? Will they manage it?'

'Oh, porters can be found,' I answered.

At this moment Fedosya, the nanny, came up to say hello to Grandmother, and she brought the general's children.

'Well, there's no need to start kissing. I don't like kissing children: all children have snotty noses. Well, how do you like it here, Fedosya?'

'It's very, very good, Antonida Vasilyevna, ma'am,' Fedosya answered. 'How have you been, ma'am? We've been so worried about you.'

'I know, you're a simple soul. So who are these people here, all guests?' she turned again to Polina. 'Who is that shabby little creature, the one with the glasses?'

'Prince Nilsky, Grandmother,' Polina whispered to her.

'A Russian? And here I thought he wouldn't understand! Perhaps he didn't hear! Mr Astley I've already seen. And here he is again,' Grandmother had caught sight of him again. 'How do you do?' she turned to him suddenly.

Mr Astley made a bow to her in silence.

'Well, have you something nice to say to me? Say something! Translate for him, Polina.'

Polina translated.

'Only that I look at you with great pleasure and rejoice

in your good health,' Mr Astley answered seriously, but with great readiness. It was translated for Grandmother and she evidently liked it.

'The English always answer so nicely,' she observed. 'For some reason I've always liked the English, there's no comparison with the little Frenchies! Come and pay me a visit,' she again turned to Mr Astley. 'I will try not to trouble you too much. Translate that for him, and tell him that I am downstairs, downstairs – do you hear, downstairs,' she repeated to Mr Astley, pointing down with her finger.

Mr Astley was extremely pleased by the invitation.

With an attentive and satisfied gaze Grandmother examined Polina from head to foot.

'I could love you, Praskovya,' she said suddenly, 'you're a fine girl, better than all of them, and what a temper you have – my, my! Well, and I have a temper, too; turn around, please; is that a hairpiece you have in your hair?'

'No, Grandmother, it's my own.'

'Quite right. I don't like the stupid fashion nowadays. You're very beautiful. I would fall in love with you if I were a young gentleman. Why don't you get married? However, it's time for me to be going. I want to get some air, because it's been nothing but the train and the train . . . Well, are you still angry?' she turned to the general.

'Please, Auntie, enough!' the general took heart as he recollected himself, 'I understand, at your age . . .'

'*Cette vieille est tombée en enfance*,'[9] des Grieux whispered to me.

'I want to have a look at everything here. Will you let me have Alexey Ivanovich?' Grandmother continued to the general.

'Oh, as much as you like, but I myself . . . and Polina and Monsieur des Grieux . . . we all, we would all consider it a pleasure to accompany you . . .'

'*Mais, madame, cela sera un plaisir*,'[10] des Grieux chimed in with a charming smile.

'*Plaisir*, I'm sure. I think you're ridiculous, sir. By the way, I won't give you any money,' she added suddenly to the general. 'Well, now, to my room. I must have a look, and then we'll go round all those places. Well, lift me up.'

They lifted Grandmother up again and a crowd of us all started off, following the chair down the staircase. The general walked, stunned, as if he had been hit over the head with a cudgel. Des Grieux was pondering something. Mlle Blanche wanted to remain, but for some reason also decided to go with everyone. The prince at once set off right behind her, and up above, in the general's room, only the German and Madame *veuve* Cominges remained.

Chapter 10

At spas – and, it seems, throughout Europe – hotel administrators and managers, when assigning rooms to their guests, are guided not so much by their guests' demands and wishes, as by their own personal view of them; and, one should note, they are rarely mistaken. But Grandmother, goodness knows why, was assigned such an opulent suite that it even went too far: four magnificently appointed rooms, with bath, servants' quarters, a special room for the lady's maid and so on and so forth. Indeed, a week ago some *grande duchesse* had stayed in these rooms, which of course was announced at once to the new guests, thus raising the price for the suite. Grandmother was carried through, or rather, wheeled through all the rooms, and she examined them attentively and sternly. The manager, an elderly man with a bald head, respectfully accompanied her during this first inspection.

I don't know who they all took Grandmother for, but

apparently for some extremely important and, more importantly, incredibly wealthy individual. They at once entered into the book: *'Madame la générale princesse de Tarassevitcheva,'*[1] though Grandmother had never been a princess. Her own servants, a private compartment on the train and the profusion of unnecessary trunks, cases and even chests that arrived with Grandmother probably gave rise to this prestige; while the chair, Grandmother's curt tone and voice, and her eccentric questions asked in the most uninhibited manner that brooked no objections, in a word, the sum total of Grandmother's appearance – erect, curt, imperious – put the finishing touches to the universal reverence she commanded. During the inspection Grandmother would suddenly order that they stop pushing her chair, point to something in the furnishings and address the most unexpected questions to the respectfully smiling, but already cowering, manager. Grandmother put her questions in French, which, however, she spoke rather poorly, so I would usually translate. By and large, she was not pleased by the manager's answers and found them unsatisfactory. And she kept asking things, which seemed pointless, and were about God knows what. Suddenly, for example, she stopped before a painting – a rather bad copy of some well-known original with a mythological subject.

'Whose portrait is that?'

The manager stated that it was probably some countess or other.

'How is it that you don't know? You live here, and don't know. Why is it here? Why is she cross-eyed?'

The manager could not answer all these questions satisfactorily and even became flustered.

'Oh, what a blockhead!' Grandmother remarked in Russian.

She was carried further on. The same story repeated

itself with a certain Saxon statuette, which Grandmother examined for a long time and then ordered that it be taken away, no one knew why. Finally, she badgered the manager about how much the carpets in the bedroom cost and where they had been woven. The manager promised to find out.

'Oh, what asses!' Grandmother grumbled and turned all her attention to the bed.

'What a magnificent canopy! Strip the bed.'

They did so.

'More, more, strip off everything. Take off the pillows, the pillowcases, lift up the feather bed.'

They turned everything over. Grandmother examined it all attentively.

'It's a good thing that they don't have bedbugs. Take all the bed linen away. Make up the bed with my linen and my pillows. However, this is all too magnificent; what do I, an old woman, need with such a suite – it's boring to be all alone. Alexey Ivanovich, you must come and visit me often, after the children have finished their lessons.'

'As of yesterday I am no longer in the general's employ,' I answered, 'and I'm staying in the hotel quite on my own.'

'How is that?'

'A few days ago a certain distinguished German baron and the baroness, his wife, arrived here from Berlin. Yesterday, when I was out for a walk, I spoke to him in German without adhering to the Berlin pronunciation.'

'Well, and so what?'

'He thought I was being impertinent and complained to the general, and the general dismissed me the same day.'

'And what, did you swear at this baron? (Although even if you had sworn at him, it wouldn't matter!)'

'Oh, no. On the contrary, the baron raised his stick at me.'

'And you, you snivelling fool, you allowed him to treat

your tutor like that,' she suddenly turned to the general, 'and even sacked him! You simpletons – you're all simpletons, I can see that.'

'Don't worry, Auntie,' the general replied with a certain note of arrogant familiarity, 'I know how to conduct my affairs. Moreover, Alexey Ivanovich has not told it all to you very accurately.'

'And so you just put up with it?' she turned to me.

'I wanted to challenge the baron to a duel,' I answered as modestly and calmly as possible, 'but the general was opposed.'

'And why were you opposed?' Grandmother again turned to the general. 'And you, sir, off with you, come when you're called,' she turned to the manager, 'there's no point in you standing there gaping. I can't abide that Nuremberg mug!' He bowed and left, of course without understanding Grandmother's compliment.

'For goodness' sake, Auntie, are duels really possible?' the general asked with a grin.

'But why are they impossible? Men are all cocks; you should have fought. You're all simpletons, I can see that; you don't know how to stand up for your country. Well, lift me up! Potapych, see to it that two porters are always on hand, hire them and settle on the terms. I don't need more than two. They only need to carry me on the stairs, because on level ground, outside, I can be wheeled around, tell them that; and pay them in advance, it's more respectful. You, of course, will always be at my side, and you, Alexey Ivanovich, will point out for me this baron when we go out for our walk – what sort of person is this von baron, I want to at least have a look at him. Well, and where's the roulette?'

I explained that the roulette tables were to be found in the gaming rooms inside the casino. Then came the questions: Were there a lot of them? Did many people play? Do they play all day long? How is it set up? I answered finally that it would be better to see them with her own eyes, because it's rather difficult to describe.

'Well, then take me there straight away! You lead the way, Alexey Ivanovich!'

'What, Auntie, aren't you even going to have a rest after your journey?' the general asked solicitously He was a bit flustered; indeed they all seemed somehow embarrassed and began to exchange glances. They probably found it a bit ticklish, even shameful, to accompany Grandmother straight to the casino, where, it goes without saying, she might do something eccentric, and in public; and yet, they all volunteered to accompany her.

'But why should I rest? I'm not tired; and I've been sitting for almost five days straight. Then we'll have a look around and see what kind of springs and healing waters they have and where they are. And then . . . what is it you called it, Praskovya – *pointe*, is that it?'

'*Pointe*, Grandmother.'

'Well, *pointe* it is. But what else is there here?'

'There's lots of things, Grandmother,' Polina said after a moment's hesitation.

'Why, you don't even know yourself! Marfa, you'll come with me as well,' she said to her maid.

'But why ever do you need her, Auntie,' the general suddenly bestirred himself, 'and what's more it's impossible, and it's unlikely that Potapych will be allowed into the casino itself.'

'What nonsense! I should abandon her just because she's a servant! She's also a living person; it's already a week that we've been on the road, and she wants to see something, too. Who can she go with besides me? She wouldn't dare show her nose on the street all by herself.'

'But, Grandmother . . .'

'Are you ashamed to be with me, is that it? Then stay

home, nobody's asking you. My, what a general! I'm a general's widow myself. And really why should you all trail after me? I'll have a look at everything with Alexey Ivanovich...'

But des Grieux firmly insisted that we all escort her and launched into the most polite phrases regarding the pleasure of accompanying her and so forth. Everyone set off.

'*Elle est tombée en enfance,*' des Grieux repeated to the general, '*seule elle fera des bêtises...*'[2] I didn't catch anything else, but he evidently had some sort of plan, and perhaps his hopes had even returned.

The casino was half a verst away. Our route ran through the chestnut avenue to the square, which we skirted and ended up right at the entrance to the casino. The general had calmed down somewhat, because even though our procession was rather eccentric, it was nevertheless orderly and respectable. And there wasn't anything surprising in the fact that a person who was ill and weak and who did not have the use of her legs should make an appearance at a spa. But the general was clearly afraid of the casino: why should an invalid, without the use of her legs, and what's more an old lady, go to the roulette tables? Polina and Mlle Blanche walked on either side of the chair as it was wheeled along. Mlle Blanche laughed, was modestly cheerful and would sometimes even quite kindly dance attendance on Grandmother, so that in the end she was praised. Polina, on the other hand, was obliged to answer Grandmother's constant and innumerable questions, such as: Who is that who walked by? Who was that woman who rode by? Is the town large? Are the gardens large? What kind of trees are those? What mountains are those? Do eagles fly here? What's that funny roof? Mr Astley walked beside me and whispered to me that he expected a lot from this morning. Potapych and Marfa followed, walking right behind the chair – Potapych in his tailcoat and white tie, but wearing a peaked cap, and Marfa, the ruddy-faced, forty-year-old maid, who was beginning to turn grey, wearing a bonnet, a cotton dress and squeaky goatskin shoes. Grandmother quite frequently would turn around and talk to them. Des Grieux and the general had fallen behind a bit and were talking about something with great fervour. The general was very downcast; des Grieux spoke with a look of determination. Perhaps he was bucking the general up; evidently he was giving him some advice. But Grandmother had already uttered the fateful phrase: 'I won't give you any money.' Perhaps des Grieux found this statement to be incredible, but the general knew his Auntie. I noticed that des Grieux and Mlle Blanche continued to wink at each other. I could just make out the prince and the German traveller at the far end of the avenue: they had fallen behind and were going somewhere else.

We arrived in the casino in triumph. The porters and lackeys exhibited the same deference as the hotel staff. They looked on, however, with curiosity. Grandmother at first ordered that she be carried through all the rooms; some she praised, to others she remained absolutely indifferent; she asked questions about everything. Finally, we came to the gaming rooms. The lackey standing guard at the closed doors, seemingly taken aback, suddenly flung them wide open.

The appearance of Grandmother at the roulette table created a profound impression on the public. There were perhaps a hundred and fifty or two hundred gamblers, several rows deep, crowding round the roulette tables and at the other end of the room where the table for *trente et quarante* was situated. Those who had managed to push their way through to the table, as was their custom, stood firm and did not cede their place until they had lost all their money; it was not allowed to stand there as a mere observer and occupy a place at the gambling table for nothing. Although chairs are placed all around the table, only a few of the gamblers sit down, particularly when there is a great crush of people, because standing they can crowd in closer together and, consequently, take up less space, and it's more convenient for placing a bet. The second and third rows crowded behind the first, waiting and watching for their turn; but sometimes a hand would thrust its way through in impatience, in order to place a large stake. They even managed to thrust through in this way from the third row to place bets; as a result not ten minutes would pass, and sometimes only five, before some 'scene' would ensue over disputed stakes at one end or the other of the table. The casino police, however, are quite good. Of course, it's impossible to avoid crowding; on the contrary, they're glad of the flood of people, because it's profitable; but the eight croupiers sitting around the table watch the stakes with an eagle eye; it's they who tally up the winnings and settle any disputes that might arise. In extreme cases the police are called in, and the matter is over in a minute. Police are stationed right there in the gaming rooms, among the players in plain clothes so that it's impossible to recognize them. They keep a particular look out for petty thieves and professional crooks, who are particularly plentiful at the roulette tables, given its unusual suitability to their trade. Indeed, everywhere else you have to steal from pockets or a place under lock and key, and in the event of failure this can end in a lot of trouble. But here it's all very simple: you only need to walk up to the roulette table, start playing and then suddenly, plainly for all to see, take somebody else's winnings and put them in your pocket; if a dispute should ensue, the swindler insists loud and clear that the stake was his. If the thing is done deftly and the witnesses hesitate, then the thief very often succeeds in keeping the money for himself, if the sum, of course, is not a very considerable one. In the latter instance it most likely would have been noticed earlier by the croupiers or one of the other gamblers. But if the sum is not so very considerable, then the real owner, embarrassed by the thought of a scene, sometimes even simply declines to engage in a dispute and walks away. But if they succeed in exposing the thief, they make a big scene of turning him out at once.

Grandmother looked at all this from a distance, with wild curiosity. She very much liked that the petty thieves were turned out. *Trente et quarante* did not excite much interest in her; she liked roulette more and how the little ball rolled about. She voiced a desire, finally, to have a closer look at the game. I don't understand how it happened, but the lackeys and some other bustling agents (primarily little Poles who had lost all their money and who were foisting their services on the fortunate gamblers and all the foreigners) at once found and cleared a place for Grandmother, despite the crush, at the very centre of the table, next to the head croupier, and they wheeled her chair there. A number of people who were not playing, but observing the play from the sidelines (primarily Englishmen and their families), at once crowded closer to the table to watch Grandmother from behind the gamblers. A great many lorgnettes were turned in her direction. The croupiers nourished new hopes: such an eccentric player truly seemed to promise something unusual. A seventy-year-old woman without the use of her legs and who wished to play, of course, was not an everyday occurrence. I also pushed my way through to the table and made a place for myself next to Grandmother. Potapych and Marfa remained somewhere far off to the side, among the crowd. The general, Polina, des Grieux and Mlle Blanche also took their places to the side, among the spectators.

Grandmother began by first scrutinizing the players.

She asked me abrupt, curt questions in a half-whisper: Who's that man? Who's that woman? She particularly liked a certain very young fellow at the end of the table who was playing for very big stakes, betting thousands at a time, and who, as they were whispering all around, had already won as much as 40,000 francs, which lay before him in a heap of gold and banknotes. He was pale; his eyes sparkled and his hands were shaking; he was placing his bets now without even counting, by the handful, and meanwhile he kept winning and winning, and raking in more and more. The attendants were making a fuss over him, they found a chair for him, they cleared a space around him so that he would have more room, so that he wouldn't be crowded – all of this in expectation of a generous reward. Some players will tip from their winnings without counting, but just like that, out of sheer delight, taking the money out of their pockets by the handful. Next to the young man a little Pole had settled in, who was fussing over him with all his might, and whispering something to him politely and continually, more than likely telling him how to place his stake, advising and directing the game – it goes without saying, also in expectation of a tip afterwards. But the player hardly looked at him, placed his bets as luck would have it and kept raking it in. He had become visibly flustered.

Grandmother observed him for several minutes.

'Tell him,' Grandmother suddenly began fussing, poking me, 'tell him that he should quit, that he should take his money quickly and walk away. He'll lose everything, he's going to lose everything now!' she began pleading, almost breathless with emotion. 'Where's Potapych? Send Potapych over to him! Well, tell him, tell him,' she nudged me, 'but really, where can Potapych be! *Sortez, sortez!*'[3] she began shouting to the young man. I bent down to her and whispered firmly that shouting like that was not allowed here and that even raising one's voice was not permitted, because it interfered with keeping count and they would throw us out immediately.

'What a shame! The man is done for, it's his own fault... I can't look at him, it makes me sick. What a blockhead!' and Grandmother quickly turned to look in the other direction.

There, on the left, on the other side of the table, among the players could be seen a young lady with some sort of dwarf beside her. I don't know who the dwarf was – whether he was a relative or whether she had brought him along for the effect. I had noticed this young lady before; she would make her appearance at the gaming table every day at one o'clock in the afternoon and would leave exactly at two; every day she played for an hour. She was already known here and was offered a chair at once. She took from her pocket some gold and some thousand-franc notes and began to place her bets quietly, coolly, with deliberation, writing down the numbers on a slip of paper with a pencil and trying to work out a system by which chance fell into different groups at a given moment. She staked significant sums of money. Every day she would win one, two, at most three thousand francs – no more, and she would leave as soon as she had won. Grandmother scrutinized her for a long time.

'Well, that one won't lose! That one there won't lose! What kind of woman is she? Do you know? Who is she?'

'A Frenchwoman most probably, of a certain kind,' I whispered.

'Ah, you can tell a bird by the way it flies. You can see that her claws are sharp. Now explain to me what each turn means and how you stake.'

I explained to Grandmother as best I could the innumerable combinations of stakes – *rouge et noir, pair et impair, manque et passe*[4] – and, finally, the various subtleties in the system of numbers. Grandmother listened attentively, remembered them, asked me to repeat them and learned them by heart. One could immediately point to an example for each system of staking, so she learned a lot and committed it to memory very quickly and easily. Grandmother was quite pleased.

'But what is this *zéro*? That croupier there, the one with the curly hair, the head one, I think, just shouted *zéro*. And why did he rake in everything that was on the table? Such a pile, why did he take it all for himself? What's the meaning of that?'

'*Zéro*, Grandmother, means the bank wins all. If the ball falls on *zéro*, then everything on the table goes to the bank without even counting it. True, you're given another chance to win your money back, but the bank doesn't pay anything out.'

'How do you like that! So I get nothing?'

'No, Grandmother, if you had staked on *zéro*, then when *zéro* comes up you're paid thirty-five times to one.'

'What, thirty-five times more and does it come up often? Why don't they stake on it, the fools?'

'There are thirty-six chances against it, Grandmother.'

'What nonsense! Potapych! Potapych! Wait, I have some money with me – here!' She pulled out of her pocket a tightly stuffed purse and took from it one friedrich d'or. 'Here, stake it on *zéro* right away.'

'Grandmother, *zéro* just came up,' I said, 'so it stands to reason that it won't come up now for a long time. You'll lose your stake; wait just a bit.'

'You're talking nonsense, now stake!'

'All right, but it might not come up until evening; you can lose thousands, it has happened.'

'Well, rubbish, rubbish! Don't walk in the forest if you're afraid of wolves. What? We lost? Stake again!'

A second friedrich d'or was lost as well; a third was

staked. Grandmother could hardly sit still; she had fixed her burning eyes on the ball as it bounced along the spokes of the spinning wheel. The third one lost as well. Grandmother was beside herself; she couldn't sit still, she even banged her fist on the table when the croupier announced '*trente-six*'[5] instead of the *zéro* she was waiting for.

'For goodness' sake!' Grandmother was becoming angry, 'when will that confounded little *zéro* come up? For the life of me I'm going to sit here until *zéro* comes up! It's that confounded little curly-haired croupier that's doing it, he never lets it come up! Alexey Ivanovich stake two gold pieces at once! Otherwise, you've staked so much and lost that when *zéro* does come up you won't get anything.'

'Grandmother!'

'Stake, stake! It's not your money.'

I staked two friedrichs d'or. The ball flew around the wheel for a long time, and at last began to bounce along the spokes. Grandmother froze and squeezed my hand, and suddenly – bang!

'*Zéro*,' the croupier proclaimed.

'You see, you see!' Grandmother quickly turned around towards me, all aglow and pleased. 'You see, I told you, I told you! The Lord himself gave me the idea of staking two gold pieces. Well, how much do I get now? Why aren't they paying it out? Potapych, Marfa, where in the world are they? Where have all our people gone? Potapych, Potapych!'

'Grandmother, later,' I whispered, 'Potapych is by the door, they won't let him in here. Look, Grandmother, they're paying out your money, take it!' They tossed over towards Grandmother a heavy roll of fifty friedrichs d'or wrapped in blue paper and counted out another twenty friedrichs d'or that weren't wrapped. I shovelled all this to Grandmother.

THE GAMBLER

'*Faites le jeu, messieurs! Faites le jeu, messieurs! Rien ne va plus?*'[6] the croupier cried, inviting stakes and getting ready to spin the wheel.

'My Lord! We're too late! He's going to spin it right now! Stake, stake!' Grandmother pleaded, 'and don't dawdle, be quick about it.' She was beside herself and kept poking me with all her might.

'But where should I put the stake, Grandmother?'

'On *zéro*, on *zéro*! On *zéro* again! Stake as much as possible. How much do we have all together? Seventy friedrichs d'or? No reason to spare them, stake twenty friedrichs d'or at a time.'

'Come to your senses, Grandmother! Sometimes it doesn't come up once in two hundred spins! I assure you, you'll lose all your capital.'

'Oh, you're talking nonsense, nonsense! Stake! How he wags his tongue! I know what I'm doing,' Grandmother was even shaking with excitement.

'According to the rules, you're not allowed to stake more than twelve friedrichs d'or on *zéro*, Grandmother – well, and that's what I've staked.'

'What do you mean, not allowed? You're not lying, are you? Monsieur! Monsieur,' she began poking the croupier sitting next to her on her left, who was getting ready to spin, '*Combien zéro? Douze? Douze?*'[7]

I quickly explained the question in French.

'*Oui, madame,*' the croupier politely confirmed, 'just as, according to the rules, no single stake may exceed 4,000 florins at a time,' he added by way of explanation.

'Well, nothing can be done about it, stake twelve.'

'*Le jeu est fait!*'[8] the croupier cried. The wheel began to spin and it came up thirteen. We lost!

'Again! Again! Again! Stake again!' Grandmother shouted. I no longer contradicted her and with a shrug of my shoulders, I staked another twelve friedrichs d'or. The wheel spun round and round for a long time. Grandmother simply trembled, as she followed the wheel. 'Does she really think that she'll win with *zéro* again?' I thought to myself, looking at her, surprised. The firm conviction of a win shone on her face, the certain expectation that in just a little while they would shout out: *zéro*! The ball bounced into the slot.

'*Zéro!*' the croupier cried.

'What!!!' Grandmother turned to me in frenzied triumph.

I was a gambler myself; I sensed it at that very moment. My hands and legs were trembling, my head was pounding. Of course, this was a rare occurrence that in some ten turns *zéro* came up three times; but there was nothing particularly surprising about it. I myself had been a witness the day before yesterday when *zéro* came up three times *in a row*, and one of the players, who was zealously writing down the numbers on a slip of paper, observed loudly that only yesterday this same *zéro* had come up only once in twenty-four hours.

They settled up with Grandmother particularly deferentially and respectfully, since she had won such an impressive amount. She received exactly 420 friedrichs d'or, that is, 4,000 florins and twenty friedrichs d'or. She was given the 20 friedrichs d'or in gold, and the 4,000 in banknotes.

But this time Grandmother didn't call Potapych; she was occupied by something else. She wasn't poking anyone and wasn't trembling outwardly. If one may put it like this, she was trembling inwardly. Her whole being was concentrated on something, and then she took aim:

'Alexey Ivanovich! He said that you could only stake 4,000 florins at a time, right? Here, take it, stake this entire 4,000 on red,' Grandmother decided.

THE GAMBLER

It was useless trying to talk her out of it. The wheel began spinning.

'*Rouge!*' the croupier proclaimed.

Again a win of 4,000 florins, that is, eight in all.

'Give me four, and stake four on red again,' Grandmother commanded.

I staked 4,000 again.

'*Rouge!*' the croupier proclaimed once again.

'Twelve in all! Put it all here. Pour the gold here, into the purse, and put away the notes.

'Enough! Home! Wheel the chair out!'

Chapter 11

The chair was wheeled to the door at the other end of the room. Grandmother was beaming. All our party at once crowded around her to offer their congratulations. However eccentric Grandmother's behaviour may have been, her triumph made up for a great many things, and the general was no longer afraid of being compromised in public by his family ties with such an odd woman. With a condescending and cheerfully familiar smile, he congratulated Grandmother as though he were indulging a child. He was, however, clearly impressed, like all the other onlookers. All around people were talking and pointing at Grandmother. Many walked past her in order to get a closer look at her. Mr Astley, standing off to the side, was explaining about her to two of his English friends. Some majestic spectators, ladies, were examining her with majestic bewilderment as though she were some sort of marvel. Des Grieux was profuse with his congratulations and smiles.

'*Quelle victoire!*' he said.

'*Mais, madame, c'était du feu!*'[1] Mlle Blanche added with a flirtatious smile.

'Yes, I've just gone and won 12,000 florins! What am I saying? Not twelve, what about the gold? With the gold it almost comes to thirteen. How much is that in our money? About 6,000 roubles, isn't it?'

I informed her that it amounted to more than seven, and that at the current exchange rate, it might even be as much as eight.

'You must be joking, 8,000! And here you sit, you simpletons, doing nothing! Potapych, Marfa, did you see?'

'My dear, how did you do it? Eight thousand roubles,' Marfa exclaimed, wriggling.

'Here you are, there's five gold pieces for each of you, there!'

Potapych and Marfa rushed to kiss her hands.

'And give the porters a friedrich d'or each. Give them a gold piece each, Alexey Ivanovich. Why is that lackey bowing, and the other one as well? Are they congratulating me? Give them each a friedrich d'or, too.'

'*Madame la princesse* ... *un pauvre expatrié* ... *Malheur continuel* ... *les princes russes sont si généreux*,'[2] someone dressed in a worn frock coat, a florid waistcoat, sporting a moustache, holding a peaked cap in his outstretched hand and with a servile smile was hanging around the chair.

'Give him a friedrich d'or as well. No, give him two; well, that's enough, otherwise there'll be no end to them. Lift me up, carry me out! Praskovya,' she turned to Polina Alexandrovna, 'tomorrow I'll buy you a dress, and one for Mlle ... what's her name, Mlle Blanche, is that it? I'll buy her a dress as well. Translate that for her, Praskovya!'

'*Merci, madame*,' Mlle Blanche dropped an ingratiating curtsey, after distorting her mouth into a mocking smile, which she exchanged with des Grieux and the general. The general was somewhat embarrassed and was terribly happy when we reached the avenue.

'Fedosya, I was thinking how surprised Fedosya will be,' Grandmother said, remembering the general's nanny. 'I must make her a present of a dress as well. Hey, Alexey Ivanovich, give something to this beggar!'

Some hunchbacked ragamuffin was walking down the road and looked at us.

'But he might not be a beggar, but some sort of rogue, Grandmother.'

'Give! Give! Give him a gulden!'

I walked up to him and gave it to him. He looked at me with wild bewilderment; however, he took the gulden in silence. He smelled of spirits.

'And you, Alexey Ivanovich, have you tried your luck yet?'

'No, Grandmother.'

'But your eyes were on fire, I saw them.'

'I'll give it a try, Grandmother, I certainly will, but later.'

'And stake on *zéro* right away! You'll see! How much capital do you have?'

'Only twenty friedrichs d'or in all, Grandmother.'

'Not much. I'll give you fifty friedrichs d'or as a loan, if you like. Here, you can take this roll here, but you, my dear sir,' she suddenly turned to the general, 'all the same, you should not expect anything, I won't give you anything!'

The general winced, but kept his silence. Des Grieux frowned.

'*Que diable, c'est une terrible vieille!*'[3] he whispered to the general through clenched teeth.

'A beggar, a beggar, another beggar!' Grandmother cried out. 'Alexey Ivanovich, give this one a gulden, too.'

This time we had met an old grey man with a wooden leg, who was wearing some sort of long-skirted blue frock coat and holding a long walking stick. He looked like an old soldier. But when I held out the gulden to him, he took a step back and looked me over menacingly.

'*Was ist's der Teufel!*'[4] he cried, following this with another dozen oaths.

'What a fool!' Grandmother cried, with a wave of her hand. 'Let's go! I'm famished! We'll eat now, then I'll rest a bit, and we'll go back there again.'

'You want to play again, Grandmother?' I cried.

'And what did you think? That I would watch you while you all sit here and mope about?'

'*Mais, madame*,' des Grieux came nearer. '*Les chances peuvent tourner, une seule mauvaise chance et vous perdrez tout . . . surtout avec votre jeu . . . c'était terrible!*'

'*Vous perdrez absolument*,'[5] Mlle Blanche chirped.

'And what business is it of yours? I'm not losing your money, it's mine! But where's that Mr Astley?' she asked me.

'He stayed behind in the casino, Grandmother.'

'Too bad; now there's a fine man.'

Upon her arrival home, Grandmother was still on the stairs when she met the manager, beckoned to him and bragged of her winnings; then she summoned Fedosya, gave her three friedrichs d'or and ordered that dinner be served. During dinner Fedosya and Marfa could not say enough good things about her.

'I'm watching you, ma'am,' Marfa chattered, 'and I say to Potapych, what's our lady want to do? And there was so much money on the table, so much money, goodness gracious! I haven't seen that much money in all my born days, and gentlefolk all around, only gentlefolk sitting there. And wherever do all these gentlefolk come from, Potapych, I say. May the Mother of God herself help her, I think. I prayed for you, ma'am, but it was as if my heart had stopped beating, stopped beating, and I'm trembling,

trembling all over. May the Lord help her, I'm thinking, and then the Lord did help you. I'm still trembling, ma'am, I'm trembling all over.'

'Alexey Ivanovich, after dinner, at four o'clock, be ready and we'll go. But goodbye for now, and don't forget to send for some sort of doctor, I need to drink the waters as well. Or else you might forget.'

I left Grandmother's stupefied. I tried to imagine what would happen now to our people and what turn things would take. I clearly saw that they (the general in particular) had still not managed to come round from the first blow even. The fact of Grandmother's appearance instead of the telegram, expected with each passing hour about her death (and consequently about the inheritance), had so shattered the entire course of their plans and the decisions they had adopted that they regarded the further exploits of Grandmother at the roulette table with absolute bewilderment and a sort of stupor that had befallen them all. And yet, this second fact was almost more important than the first: Grandmother had repeated twice that she would not give the general any money, but who knows? – all the same, it was too early to lose hope. Even des Grieux, who was involved in all the general's affairs, had not lost hope. I'm certain that Mlle Blanche, who was also very involved (to put it mildly: becoming the general's wife and a considerable inheritance!), would not lose hope and would use all her coquettish seductions on Grandmother – in contrast to the stubborn and arrogant Polina who did not know how to play up to anyone. But now, now, when Grandmother had performed such feats at the roulette table, now when Grandmother's personality had shown itself to them so clearly and typically (an obstinate, power-loving old woman *et tombée en enfance*), now, it seemed likely, everything was lost: you see, she was as happy as a child that she had prevailed, and as usually happens, she would be utterly ruined. My God! I thought (and with a gloating laugh, may the Lord forgive me), my God, each friedrich d'or that Grandmother staked today lay like a sore on the general's heart, infuriated des Grieux and drove Mlle de Cominges into a frenzy as she saw the cup dashed from her lips. And here's another fact: even with her winnings, beside herself with joy, when Grandmother was giving money to everybody and took every passer-by to be a beggar, even then she had burst out at the general with: 'But I still won't give you anything!' That means that she had settled on this idea, dug her heels in, and made a promise to herself. There was danger! Danger!

All these thoughts were going through my head as I went up the grand staircase from Grandmother's rooms to the very top floor, to my little closet of a room. All this interested me a great deal; although, of course, I had been able even before this to guess the thickest of the main threads that connected the actors before me now, nevertheless I still did not know for certain all the links and mysteries of this game. Polina had never completely trusted me. Although it did happen, it's true, that at times she would open up her heart to me, unintentionally, as it were, I had observed that often, in fact almost always, after these revelations she would either turn everything she had said into a joke or would confuse the issue and try to put everything into a false light. Oh, she had concealed a great deal! In any event, I had sensed that the finale of this whole mysterious and strained situation was approaching. One more blow – and it would all be over and revealed. I gave scarcely any thought to my own fate, which was also tied up in all this. I was in a strange frame of mind: I had all of twenty friedrichs d'or in my pocket; I was far away from home in a foreign land, without a job and without the means for existence, without hopes, without plans – and I wasn't at all worried! If it hadn't been for the thought of Polina, I'd simply have given myself up wholly to the comic interest of the approaching denouement and would have doubled over with laughter. But I'm troubled about Polina; her fate is being decided, I had sensed that, but I must confess that it's not at all her fate that troubles me. I want to fathom her secrets; I would like her to come to me and say: 'I love you', and if not that, if such madness is inconceivable, then . . . well, what is there for me to wish for? Do I really know what I want? I'm done for; all I want is to be in her presence, in her light, in her radiance, for ever, always, my whole life. I don't know anything else! And can I really leave her?

On the third floor, in their corridor, somebody seemed to have nudged me. I turned around and, twenty paces away if not more, I saw Polina coming out the door. It was as if she had been waiting and looking for me, and she at once beckoned me to her.

'Polina Alexandrovna . . .'

'Quiet!' she warned.

'Just imagine,' I whispered, 'it was as if something had just nudged me in the side; I turn around – and it's you! It's as if some sort of electricity were flowing from you!'

'Take this letter,' Polina said, worried and frowning, probably without hearing what I had said, 'and deliver it immediately to Mr Astley in person. Quickly, I beg you. There's no need for an answer. He himself . . .'

She didn't finish.

'Mr Astley?' I repeated with surprise.

But Polina had already disappeared behind the door.

'Aha! So they correspond!' It goes without saying that I at once ran off in search of Mr Astley, first at his hotel, where I didn't find him, then to the casino, where I ran through all the rooms, and finally, as I was making my way back home, frustrated, almost in despair, I met him by chance, in a cavalcade of some English men and women on horseback. I beckoned to him, stopped him and handed him the letter. We hadn't even had time to exchange a glance. But I suspect that Mr Astley deliberately gave rein to his horse as quickly as possible.

Was I tormented by jealousy? My spirits were certainly shattered. I didn't even want to find out what they were writing to each other about. So then, he's her confidant! 'He may be her friend all right,' I thought, 'and that's clear (but when did he manage that), but is it a matter of love?' Of course not, my reason whispered. But then reason alone counts for so little in such situations. In any event, this too would need to be cleared up. The matter was becoming unpleasantly complicated.

But even as I entered the hotel, the porter and the manager, who had just come out of his room, informed me that I was wanted, that they were looking for me, that they had already called to enquire of my whereabouts three times – and that it had been requested that I make my way to the general's rooms as quickly as possible. I was in a most foul frame of mind. In the general's study I found, apart from the general himself, des Grieux and Mlle Blanche alone, without her mother. The mother was most definitely a blind, used only for show; but when it came to real *business*, then Mlle Blanche handled it all by herself. And in all likelihood the woman knew nothing about the affairs of her so-called daughter.

The three of them were heatedly conferring about something, and the door to the study was even locked, which had never been the case before. As I approached the door, I could make out loud voices – the impertinent and caustic speech of des Grieux, the brazenly abusive and furious cries of Mlle Blanche and the pitiful voice of the general, who was evidently trying to vindicate himself about something. Upon my appearance they all seemed to show more restraint and pulled themselves together. Des Grieux smoothed his hair and changed his face from angry to smiling – the sort of nasty, officially courteous French smile that I loathe so. The crushed and flustered general assumed a dignified air, but somewhat mechanically. Only Mlle Blanche scarcely changed the expression on her face, ablaze with anger, and merely fell silent, fixing her gaze upon me with impatient expectation. I will note that up to now she had been unbelievably offhand in her treatment of me, and would not even respond to my bows – she simply ignored me.

'Alexey Ivanovich,' the general began in a gently scolding tone of voice, 'allow me to state that it is strange, exceedingly strange . . . in a word, your conduct in regard to me and my family . . . is, in a word, exceedingly strange . . .'

'*Eh! ce n'est pas ça,*' des Grieux interrupted with annoyance and disdain. (He was definitely the boss here!) '*Mon cher monsieur, notre cher general se trompe,*[6] when he adopts such a tone,' (I will continue his speech in Russian), 'but he wished to say to you . . . that is, to warn you, or rather, to ask you most persuasively not to ruin him – yes, that's right, ruin! I use precisely this expression . . .'

'But how, how?' I cut him short.

'Good heavens, you're undertaking to become the guide (or what shall I call it?) of this old woman, *cette pauvre terrible vieille,*[7] des Grieux hemmed and hawed, 'but you know that she'll gamble away everything; she'll be ruined! You yourself have seen, you were a witness to how she plays! If she begins to lose, she won't leave the table out of stubbornness, out of fury, and she'll keep playing and playing, and in such cases one never wins back what has been lost, and then . . . then . . .'

'And then,' the general took over, 'then you will have ruined the entire family! My family and I, we are her heirs, she doesn't have any closer relations. I will tell you candidly that my affairs are in shambles, an absolute shambles. You know something of this yourself . . . If she were to lose a significant sum or even the entire fortune (God forbid!), then what will become of them, what will become of my children!' (The general glanced at des Grieux.) 'And of me!' (He looked at Mlle Blanche, who had turned away from him in disdain.) 'Alexey Ivanovich, save us, save us! . . .'

'But how, General, tell me, what can I do . . . What do I matter in all this?'

'Refuse to help her, refuse, leave her! . . .'

'Then someone else will be found!' I cried.

'*Ce n'est pas ça, ce n'est pas ça,*' des Grieux interrupted again, '*que diable!* No, don't forsake her, but at the very least appeal to her conscience, persuade her, distract her . . . Well, in the end, don't let her lose too much, distract her somehow.'

'And how am I going to do that? If you were to take it on yourself, Monsieur des Grieux,' I added as naively as I could.

At this point I noticed the quick, fiery, questioning glance Mlle Blanche gave des Grieux. Something peculiar, something unconcealed that he could not hold back was glimpsed fleetingly in des Grieux's own face.

'But that's just it, she won't have me now!' des Grieux cried out, with a wave of his hand. 'If only! . . . Later! . . .'

Des Grieux cast a quick and significant glance at Mlle Blanche.

'*O mon cher monsieur Alexis, soyez si bon,*'[8] Mlle Blanche *herself* stepped towards me with an enchanting smile, took me by both hands and clasped them firmly. The devil take it! That diabolical face was capable of changing in a single second. At that moment her face looked so imploring, so sweet, smiling like a child and even naughty; when she had finished speaking, she gave me a roguish wink, on the sly from everyone; did she want to knock me off my feet all at once, was that it? And it didn't come off badly – but it was so crudely done, however, terribly so.

The general leapt up, he positively leapt up after her.

'Alexey Ivanovich, forgive me for beginning with you like that just now, I didn't at all mean to say . . . Forgive me, I implore you, I bow down before you in the Russian manner – you alone, you alone can save us! Mlle de Cominges and I implore you – you understand, you do understand, don't you?' he implored, turning his eyes on Mlle Blanche. He was very pitiful.

At that moment three quiet, polite knocks on the door were heard; it was opened – the servant for that floor had knocked, and several steps behind him stood Potapych. The ambassadors were from Grandmother. She had ordered that I be found and delivered immediately. 'She's angry,' Potapych declared.

'But it's only half past three!'

'She couldn't fall asleep, she kept tossing and turning, then she suddenly got up, ordered the chair and sent for you. She's already on the porch, sir . . .'

'*Quelle mégère!*'[9] des Grieux cried out.

Indeed, I found Grandmother on the porch, running out of patience because I wasn't there. She couldn't wait until four o'clock.

'Well, lift me up!' she cried, and we set off once again for the roulette tables.

Chapter 12

Grandmother was in an impatient and irritable state of mind; clearly, she had become obsessed with roulette. To everything else she paid little attention and in general was extremely absent-minded. For example, as we made our way she didn't ask about anything as she had done earlier. Catching sight of an exceedingly opulent carriage that tore past us, she raised her hand and asked, 'What's that? Who does it belong to?' – but didn't seem to hear my reply; her brooding was constantly interrupted by abrupt and impatient movements and outbursts. When I pointed out Baron and Baroness Wurmerhelm in the distance, as we were approaching the casino, she absent-mindedly looked and said with complete indifference: 'Ah!' – and then quickly turning around to Potapych and Marfa, who were walking behind, snapped at them:

'Well, why are you dogging my every step? I'm not going to take you every time! Go home! You and I are enough,' she added for my benefit, after they hastily made their bows and turned for home.

They were already expecting Grandmother in the casino. They at once made room for her in the same place, next to the croupier. It seems to me that these croupiers, who are always so proper and who make themselves out to be ordinary functionaries, who are almost completely indifferent whether the bank wins or loses, are not at all indifferent to the bank's losses, and of course are given some instructions for attracting players and for the overall management of the firm's interests, for which they certainly receive rewards and bonuses. In any event, they looked upon Grandmother as their prey. Then what had been predicted did in fact take place.

Here's how it went.

Grandmother went straight for *zéro* and at once ordered that twelve friedrichs d'or be staked. We staked it once, twice, three times – *zéro* never came up.

'Stake, stake!' Grandmother poked me impatiently. I obeyed.

THE GAMBLER

'How many times have we staked and lost?' she asked finally, gnashing her teeth in impatience.

'That was the twelfth time, Grandmother. We've lost 144 friedrichs d'or. I'm telling you, Grandmother, it might go on like this until evening...'

'Be quiet!' Grandmother interrupted. 'Stake on *zéro* and stake a thousand gulden on red now. Here's a banknote, take it.'

Red came up, but *zéro* lost again; we got back a thousand gulden.

'You see, you see!' Grandmother whispered, 'we got back almost all that we lost. Stake on *zéro* again; we'll stake another ten times and then quit.'

But Grandmother was completely bored by the fifth time.

'The devil take that nasty little *zéro*. Here, stake all 4,000 gulden on red,' she ordered.

'Grandmother! That's a lot; what if it doesn't land on red?' I implored her; but Grandmother almost hit me. (But then she was poking me so hard that one might almost say that she was hitting me.) There was nothing to be done, I staked on red all 4,000 gulden that we had just won. The wheel began to spin. Grandmother sat quietly and proudly bolt upright, not doubting that she was certain to win.

'*Zéro*,' the croupier proclaimed.

At first Grandmother didn't understand, but when she saw that the croupier had gathered up her 4,000 gulden along with everything that was on the table and learned that *zéro*, which had not come up for so long and on which we had staked and lost almost 200 friedrichs d'or, had just turned up, as if on purpose when Grandmother had just been calling it names and given up on it, she exclaimed and threw up her hands for the whole room to see. The people around us even started laughing.

'Goodness gracious! That confounded thing turns up now!' Grandmother howled, 'what an accursed, accursed thing! It's your doing! It's all your doing!' she savagely fell to pummelling me. 'You were the one who talked me out of it.'

'Grandmother, I talked sense to you; how can I answer for all the odds?'

'I'll give you odds!' she whispered menacingly, 'get out of my sight.'

'Goodbye, Grandmother,' and I turned around to walk away.

'Alexey Ivanovich, Alexey Ivanovich, stop! Where are you going? Well, what's the matter, what's the matter? Look, he's angry! Fool! Come stay a bit, stay a bit more, come, don't be angry, I'm the fool! Come, tell me, what I should do now!'

'Grandmother, I won't take it upon myself to suggest anything to you, because you'll blame me. Play your own game; you tell me what to do and I'll stake for you.'

'Well, well! Then stake another 4,000 gulden on red! Here's my pocketbook, take it.' She took it from her pocket and gave it to me. 'Come, take it quickly, there's 20,000 roubles in cash there.'

'Grandmother,' I whispered, 'such large sums . . .'

'Life's not worth living if I don't win it back. Stake!'

We staked and lost.

'Stake, stake, stake all eight!'

'I can't, Grandmother, four is the largest sum! . . .'

'Then stake four!'

This time we won. Grandmother cheered up.

'You see, you see!' she began nudging me, 'stake four again!'

We staked – and lost; and then we lost again and again.

'Grandmother, all 12,000 are gone,' I reported.

'I see that it's all gone,' she uttered in a state of calm fury, if I may put it that way. 'I see, my dear fellow, I see,' she muttered, with a fixed stare as though she were pondering something. 'Eh! Life's not worth living, stake another 4,000 gulden!'

'But there isn't any money, Grandmother; there's some of our five per-cent notes in the pocketbook and some sort of money orders, but no money.'

'What about the purse?'

'Only some change, Grandmother.'

'Do they have exchange bureaus here? I was told that all our notes can be exchanged,' Grandmother asked with determination.

'Oh, as many as you like! But what you lose in the exchange is so much ... that even a Jew would be horrified!'

'Nonsense! I'll win it back! Take me. Call those blockheads!'

I wheeled the chair away, the porters turned up and we left the casino.

'Faster, faster, faster!' Grandmother commanded. 'Lead the way, Alexey Ivanovich, to the closest one ... is it far?'

'A stone's throw, Grandmother.'

But at the turn from the square into the avenue we ran into all our party: the general, des Grieux and Mlle Blanche with her mother. Polina Alexandrovna wasn't with them, nor was Mr Astley.

'Well, well, well! Don't stop!' Grandmother shouted. 'Well, what do you want? I don't have time for you now!'

I was walking behind; des Grieux came running up to me.

'She lost all of her earlier winnings and squandered 12,000 gulden of her own. We're off to exchange some five per-cent notes,' I whispered to him hastily.

Des Grieux stamped his foot and rushed to inform the general. We continued wheeling Grandmother.

'Stop her, stop her!' the general whispered to me in a frenzy.

'And you just try stopping her,' I whispered to him.

'Auntie!' the general said as he approached, 'Auntie . . . we're just now . . . we're just now . . .' (his voice was trembling and failing him) 'we're going to hire horses and take a ride in the country . . . There's a breathtaking view . . . the *pointe* . . . we were coming to invite you.'

'Oh, enough of you and your *pointe*!' Grandmother waved him away in exasperation.

'There's a village . . . we'll have tea there . . .' the general continued, now in complete despair.

'*Nous boirons du lait, sur l'herbe fraîche*,'[1] des Grieux put in with savage anger.

Du lait, de l'herbe fraîche – it's just what the Parisian bourgeois finds ideally idyllic; this constitutes, as we know, his view on '*nature et la vérité*'.[2]

'Oh, enough of you and your milk! Go swill it yourself, I get a bellyache from it. And why are you pestering me?!' Grandmother cried out, 'I told you, I don't have time!'

'Here we are, Grandmother!' I cried out, 'here it is!'

We had come to the building that housed the banker's office. I went in to change the notes; Grandmother remained waiting at the entrance; des Grieux, the general and Blanche, not knowing what to do, stood off to the side. Grandmother gave them an angry look and they walked down the road to the casino.

They offered me such an awful rate that I couldn't bring myself to do it and returned to Grandmother to ask for instructions.

'Ah, the robbers!' she cried out, clasping her hands. 'Well! There's nothing to be done. Change it!' she cried out with determination. 'Stop, ask the banker to come and see me!'

'Do you mean one of the clerks, Grandmother?'

THE GAMBLER

'Yes, a clerk, it doesn't make any difference. Ah, the robbers!'

The clerk agreed to come out, upon learning that he was being asked by an elderly, frail countess, who could not walk. Grandmother angrily and loudly reproached him for a long time for swindling her, and she haggled with him in a mixture of Russian, French and German, while I helped with the translation. The serious clerk kept looking at us both and shaking his head in silence. He even scrutinized Grandmother with a curiosity that was so intent that it was disrespectful; finally, he began to smile.

'Well, clear off!' Grandmother cried out. 'May you choke on my money! Change it with him, Alexey Ivanovich; there's no time, otherwise we could go somewhere else.'

'The clerk says that others give even less.'

I don't recall the exact exchange rate, but it was terrible. I exchanged close to 12,000 florins in gold and notes, took the receipt and gave it to Grandmother.

'Well, well, well! No need to count it,' she waved her hands. 'Quick, quick, quick!'

'I'll never stake on that confounded *zéro* or red either,' she uttered, as we approached the casino.

This time I tried with all my might to coax her to stake much smaller sums, attempting to persuade her that should her luck change there would always be time to stake a large sum. But she was so impatient that even though she did agree at first, it was impossible to hold her in check when she was playing. As soon as she began to win stakes of ten, twenty friedrichs d'or – 'Well, there you are! Well, there you are!' (she began poking me) 'Well, there you are! We won, you see – if we'd wagered 4,000 instead of ten, we would have won 4,000, but what do we have now? It's all your doing, your doing!'

And no matter the vexation I felt as I watched her play, I finally made up my mind to keep quiet and not give her any more advice.

Suddenly des Grieux hurried over. The three of them were nearby; I had noticed that Mlle Blanche was standing with her mother off to the side, exchanging pleasantries with the little prince. The general was clearly out of favour, almost shunned. Blanche wouldn't even look at him, although he was playing up to her with all his might. The poor general! He would grow pale and then turn red, tremble and was no longer even following Grandmother's game. Blanche and the little prince finally left; the general ran after them.

'*Madame, madame,*' des Grieux whispered to Grandmother in a honeyed voice, having pushed his way through so that he was standing by her ear. '*Madame*, a stake like that no work . . . no, no, no is possible . . .' he said in mangled Russian. 'No!'

'But how, then? Well, teach me,' Grandmother turned towards him.

Des Grieux suddenly began chattering away in French, offering advice, fussing, saying that she needed to wait for the chance, starting to make calculations on the basis of some numbers . . . Grandmother didn't understand a thing. He was constantly turning to me so that I would translate; he kept thumping the table with his finger and pointing; finally, he grabbed a pencil and was about to make some calculations on a slip of paper. Grandmother finally lost her patience.

'Well, off with you, off with you! You just keep talking nonsense! "*Madame, madame*," but he doesn't understand anything about it himself; off with you!'

'*Mais, madame,*' des Grieux chirped, and once again he began to nudge and point. He was in quite a state.

'Well, stake it once like he says,' Grandmother instructed me, 'let's see, perhaps something really will come of it.'

Des Grieux merely wanted to divert her from staking large sums – he proposed staking on numbers one by one and in combinations. I placed the stakes according to his instructions, one friedrich d'or on the odd numbers below twelve and five friedrichs d'or on groups of numbers from twelve to eighteen and from eighteen to twenty-four: in all we staked sixteen friedrichs d'or.

The wheel began spinning. '*Zéro*,' the croupier cried out. We had lost everything.

'What a blockhead!' Grandmother cried out, as she turned to des Grieux. 'What a disgusting little Frenchman you are! And he gives advice, the monster! Off with you, off with you! He doesn't understand a thing and yet he pokes his nose in!'

Des Grieux, terribly offended, shrugged his shoulders, looked at Grandmother with contempt and walked away. He was ashamed that he had gotten involved; he couldn't help himself.

An hour later, no matter how hard we tried, we had lost everything.

'Home!' Grandmother cried.

She didn't say a word until we reached the avenue. In the avenue, when we were coming up to the hotel, she began to fulminate:

'What a fool! What a little fool! You're an old, old fool, you are!'

As soon as we entered her suite:

'Tea!' Grandmother shouted. 'And start packing immediately! We're leaving!'

'And where is it you wish to go, ma'am?' Marfa began.

'And what business is it of yours? The cobbler should stick to his last! Potapych, pack up everything, all the luggage. We're going back, to Moscow! I'm ruined, I lost 15,000 roubles.'

'Fifteen thousand, ma'am! My dear God!' Potapych cried out, after touchingly flinging up his hands, probably supposing that was what was expected from him.

'Come, come, you fool! And now he's even started whimpering! Silence! Start packing! Get the bill, quickly, quickly!'

'The next train leaves at half past nine, Grandmother,' I informed her, in order to put a stop to the furore.

'And what time is it now?'

'Half past seven.'

'What a nuisance! Well, never mind! Alexey Ivanovich, I don't even have a kopeck. Here are two more notes, run over there and change these for me. Otherwise, I won't have anything for the journey.'

I set off. When I returned to the hotel half an hour later, I found all our party with Grandmother. They seemed to be even more startled to learn that Grandmother was leaving for Moscow for good than they were by her losses. Even supposing that her departure would save her fortune, what would become of the general now? Who would pay des Grieux? Mlle Blanche, it goes without saying, wasn't going to wait for Grandmother to die and most likely would steal away with the little prince or with someone else. They stood before her, comforting her, trying to talk her round. Polina again was missing. Grandmother shouted at them furiously.

'Leave me in peace, you devils! What business is it of yours? Why is that goat's beard butting into my business?' she shouted at des Grieux, 'and you, you little pipsqueak, what do you want?' she turned to Mlle Blanche. 'What are you making a fuss about?'

'*Diantre!*' Mlle Blanche whispered, her eyes flashing furiously, but then suddenly she burst into laughter and walked out.

Elle vivra cent ans![3] she cried out to the general as she walked out the door.

'Ah, so you were counting on my death?' Grandmother yelled at the general. 'Get out! Throw them all out, Alexey Ivanovich! It's none of your business. It was my own money that I squandered, not yours!'

The general shrugged his shoulders, bowed and went out. Des Grieux followed him.

'Call Praskovya,' Grandmother ordered Marfa.

Five minutes later Marfa returned with Polina. All this time Polina had been sitting in her room with the children and, it seems, had purposely made up her mind not to go out all day. Her face was serious, sad and anxious.

'Praskovya,' Grandmother began, 'is it true, what I've chanced to learn just now, that your fool of a stepfather wishes to marry that silly French flirt – an actress is she, or something worse? Tell me, is it true?'

'I don't know for certain, Grandmother,' Polina answered, 'but from the words of Mlle Blanche herself, who does not find it necessary to be discreet, I conclude . . .'

'Enough!' Grandmother broke in energetically, 'I understand everything! I've always thought him capable of this and have always thought him a most shallow and frivolous man. He swaggers about because he's a general (but he was really only a colonel, he got the promotion on his retirement), and he puts on airs. I know, my dear, how you sent telegram after telegram to Moscow – "Will the old lady turn up her toes soon?" You were waiting for the inheritance; without money that nasty wench – what's her name, de Cominges isn't it? – wouldn't take him on as a lackey, what with his false teeth and all. They say that she has piles of money, that she loans it on interest and has not done badly for herself. I don't blame you, Praskovya; you weren't the one sending the telegrams; and I don't want to bring up the past either. I know that you have a nasty little temper – just like a wasp! You sting and then it swells up so, but I feel sorry for you because I loved Katerina, your mother. Well, what's it to be? Drop everything here and come with me. After all, you have nowhere to go; and it's not decent for you to be with them now. Stop!' Grandmother interrupted Polina who was about to reply, 'I haven't finished. I will ask nothing of you. I have a house in Moscow, as you know, a mansion, take an entire floor if you like and don't see me for weeks on end if my temper isn't to your liking. Well, do you want to or not?'

'Allow me to ask you first: do you really mean to leave at once?'

'Did you think that I was joking, my dear girl? I said I was leaving and I'm leaving. Today I squandered 15,000 roubles on that damned roulette of yours. Five years ago I made a promise to rebuild a wooden church in stone on my estate, and instead of that I threw it away here. Now, my dear girl, I'm going to go and build that church.'

'And what about the waters, Grandmother? After all, you did come to drink the waters, didn't you?'

'Oh, you and your waters! Don't annoy me, Praskovya; are you doing it on purpose, is that it? Tell me, are you coming or not?'

'I am very, very grateful to you, Grandmother,' Polina began with feeling, 'for the refuge that you are offering me. To some extent, you have understood my situation. I am so grateful that, believe me, I will come to you and perhaps quite soon; but now there are reasons, important ones . . . and I cannot decide right now, this minute. If you were staying for two weeks even . . .'

'That means, you don't want to?'

'It means that I can't. Besides, in any event I can't leave my brother and sister behind, and since . . . since . . . since it really is possible that they might be abandoned, then . . . If you will take me and the little ones, Grandmother, then of course I will come and, believe me, I will repay you!' she added heatedly. 'But I cannot come, Grandmother, without the children.'

'Well, no whimpering!' (Polina had no intention of whimpering; in fact, she never cried.) 'And room will be found for the chicks; the hen house is a big one. Besides, it's time they were in school. Well, so you're not coming now? Well, Praskovya, take care! I only wish you well, but I know, you see, why you're not coming. I know everything, Praskovya! That little Frenchman will bring you no good.'

Polina blushed. I was simply taken aback. (Everybody knows! So, I'm the only one who knows nothing!)

'Come, come, don't frown. I won't spread it on thick. Only mind that it doesn't end badly, do you understand? You're a clever girl; I'd be sorry for you. Well, enough, I wish I'd never set my eyes on the lot of you! Go! Goodbye!'

'Grandmother, I'll see you off,' Polina said.

'There's no need; don't bother, I'm sick of you all.' Polina kissed Grandmother's hand, but the latter pulled it away and kissed her on the cheek.

As she walked past me, Polina gave me a quick glance and at once turned away her eyes.

'Well, goodbye to you, too, Alexey Ivanovich! It's only an hour till the train. And I think you're tired of my company. Here, take these fifty gold pieces.'

'Thank you so very much, Grandmother, but I'm ashamed . . .'

'Come, come!' Grandmother cried out, but so energetically and threateningly that I didn't dare try to stop her and took them.

'When you're running around in Moscow without a job – come and see me; I'll recommend you to someone. Well, off with you!'

I went to my room and lay down on the bed. I think I lay

there for half an hour on my back, with my hands behind my head. Catastrophe had struck; there was more than enough to think about. I decided to have an urgent talk with Polina tomorrow. Ah! The little Frenchman? So, then, it was true! However, what could it mean? Polina and des Grieux! Goodness gracious! What a contrast!

This was all simply unbelievable. Suddenly beside myself, I jumped up in order to go at once to look for Mr Astley and make him talk, come what may. Of course, he knows more than I about all this. Mr Astley? There's another riddle for me!

But suddenly there was a knock at my door. I look and it's Potapych.

'My good sir, Alexey Ivanovich, the mistress is asking for you!'

'What's the matter? Is she leaving? There's still twenty minutes till the train.'

'She's anxious, sir, she can scarcely sit still. "Quickly, quickly!" – you, that is, sir; for Christ's sake, don't delay.'

I ran downstairs at once. They had already brought Grandmother out into the corridor. She had her pocket-book in her hands.

'Alexey Ivanovich, lead the way, let's go! . . .'

'Where, Grandmother?'

'Life's not worth living unless I win it back! Well, march, no questions! They play until midnight there, don't they?'

I was dumbfounded, gave it a moment's thought, but made up my mind at once.

'As you please, Antonida Vasilyevna, but I'm not going.'

'And why is that? What's this all about? Have you all gone crazy!'

'As you please: I would reproach myself afterwards; I don't want to! I want to be neither a witness nor a participant; spare me, Antonida Vasilyevna. Here's your fifty friedrichs d'or back; goodbye!' And after putting down the roll of friedrichs d'or there on the table right next to Grandmother's chair, I bowed and walked away.

'What nonsense!' Grandmother cried out to me as I was leaving. 'So don't come, I'll find the way there by myself! Potapych, come with me! Well, lift me up, carry me.'

I didn't find Mr Astley and returned home. It was late, past midnight, when I learned from Potapych how Grandmother's day ended. She had lost everything that I had just changed for her, that is, another 10,000 roubles in our money. That very same little Pole, to whom she had earlier given two friedrichs d'or, attached himself to her and directed her play the entire time. In the beginning, before the little Pole turned up, she had Potapych place the stakes, but she soon got rid of him; and that's when the little Pole came running. As luck would have it, he understood Russian and could even jabber away in a mixture of three languages, so that they could understand each other enough. Grandmother abused him mercilessly the whole time, and though he constantly prostrated himself at his lady's feet, he 'couldn't compare with you, Alexey Ivanovich,' Potapych told me. 'She treated you *just like you were a gentleman*, but that one – I saw it with my own eyes, may God strike me dead, was stealing her money right there from the table. She caught him at it twice herself, and she gave him such a dressing down, she called him every name in the book, sir, and she even pulled him by the hair once, indeed she did, I wouldn't lie, so that everybody around started laughing. She lost everything, sir; everything she had, everything that you changed for her. We brought the mistress back here – she asked only for a little drink of water, crossed herself, and went straight to bed. She was exhausted, I suppose, and fell asleep right away. May God send her angelic dreams! Oh, I've had enough of this being abroad!' Potapych said by way of conclusion.

'I said that it would come to no good. And now we should get back to our own Moscow as soon as possible! You name it, we've got it back home in Moscow: a garden, flowers the likes of which they don't even have here, smells, apples ripening, space – but no, we had to come abroad! Oh-oh-oh! . . .'

Chapter 13

Almost a whole month now has passed since I touched these notes of mine, begun under the influence of impressions that were powerful, though chaotic. The catastrophe, whose approach I sensed even then, indeed did come, but a hundred times more violently and unexpectedly than I had thought. It was all somewhat strange, shocking and even tragic, at least as far as I was concerned. Certain things happened to me that were almost miraculous; at least that's how I still look upon them, although from another point of view and especially if one were to judge by the whirl in which I found myself then, they were only somewhat out of the ordinary. But the most miraculous thing for me is how I regarded all these events. I still don't understand it myself! And all this has flown by like a dream – even my passion – which after all had been strong and true, but . . . what has become of it now? Indeed, every once in a while, the idea flashes through my head: 'Was I out of my mind then or have I been in some madhouse all this time, and maybe I'm sitting there now – so that it all only *seemed* to have happened and to this day only *seems* . . .'

I have gathered my notes together and reread them. (Who knows, perhaps in order to convince myself that I didn't write them in a madhouse?) Now I'm absolutely all alone. Autumn is coming, the leaves are turning yellow. I sit in this forsaken little town (oh, these little German towns are so forsaken!), and instead of weighing my next step, I am living under the influence of sensations that have only just passed, under the influence of fresh memories, under the influence of all this recent whirlwind, which pulled me then into its vortex and then threw me aside again. At times it still seems as though I were still whirling around in that same vortex, as though this storm is about to come tearing by again, to carry me away on its wing in passing, and I will again lose my sense of order and proportion, and I will spin, spin, spin...

However, perhaps I'll settle down somehow and stop spinning, if I give myself as precise an account as possible of all that happened this month. I feel drawn to my pen again; and sometimes there's absolutely nothing to do in the evenings. It's funny, but in order to have something to keep me busy I take out from the rotten little library here the novels of Paul de Kock[1] (in German translation!), which I can hardly stomach, but I read them and – marvel at myself: it's as if I were afraid of destroying the enchantments of the recent past with a serious book or some other serious occupation. It's as if this shocking dream and all the impressions that it left behind were so dear to me that I'm afraid even to have it touched by anything new in case it goes up in smoke! Is it really all so dear to me? Yes, of course it is; perhaps I will remember it even after forty years...

So then, let's get down to writing. However, I can now tell only part of the story and briefly at that: the impressions were quite different...

First of all, to finish up with Grandmother. The next day she lost every last thing. It was bound to happen: once someone like her starts down that road, it's like riding a sled down a snowy mountain, you go faster and faster. She played all day until eight o'clock in the evening; I wasn't there when she played and know about it only from what I've been told.

Potapych stood by her side all day long in the casino. The little Poles who were acting as Grandmother's guides changed several times during the course of the day. She began by banishing the little Pole from the day before, whom she had pulled by the hair, and took on another who turned out to be even worse. After banishing him and taking on the first one again, who had not left and who kept shoving up right against her chair and constantly thrusting his head forward during the entire time of his exile, she finally fell into absolute despair. The second little Pole whom she had banished did not intend to leave either; one planted himself on the right, the other on her left. They quarrelled and abused each other the entire time over the stakes and strategies, calling each other *łajdak*[2] and other Polish compliments, then they made up again, threw money around willy-nilly and gave worthless orders. When they quarrelled, they would each put down a stake from his own side: one, for example, on red, and the other immediately on black. It all ended with them making Grandmother so dizzy and confused that she finally turned to the old croupier almost in tears, asking that he protect her and have them banished. They were in fact immediately banished, despite their clamour and protests: they both shouted at once and tried to prove that Grandmother owed them money, that she had somehow deceived them and dealt with them dishonestly, basely. The unfortunate Potapych told me all this with tears that same evening, after she'd lost everything, and complained that they stuffed their pockets with money, that he himself had seen how they had been stealing shamelessly and constantly thrusting it in their pockets. For example, one would ask Grandmother for five friedrichs d'or for his trouble and immediately start staking it, right next to

Grandmother's stakes. Grandmother would win, but he'd cry out that it was his stake that had won and Grandmother's had lost. As they were being shown the door, Potapych came forward and reported that their pockets were full of gold. Grandmother at once asked the croupier to look into it, and despite the little Poles' screeching (they were just like two roosters that had been snatched up barehanded), the police did come and their pockets were emptied out at once in Grandmother's favour. Grandmother commanded the respect of the croupiers and the entire casino staff, for that matter, for the whole day, until she lost everything. Little by little, news of her spread throughout the town. All the visitors to the spa, of all nations, the ordinary and the most exalted, thronged to have a look at *'une vieille comtesse russe, tombée en enfance'*, who had already lost 'several million'.

But Grandmother gained very, very little from being rid of the two Poles. In their place a third Pole appeared at once to offer his services; he spoke absolutely perfect Russian, was dressed like a gentleman, but there was still something of the flunkey about him with his enormous moustache and his arrogance. He also kissed the *'pani*'s feet' and 'prostrated himself at the *pani*'s feet', but he behaved arrogantly to those around him, managed things like a despot – in a word, he immediately became Grandmother's master rather than her servant. He constantly turned to her, at every move, and swore by the most dreadful oaths that he was a most *'honourable pan'* and that he wouldn't take a single kopeck of Grandmother's money. He repeated these oaths so often that she became positively frightened. But since in the beginning this *pan* did in fact seem to improve her game and she started winning, Grandmother couldn't give him up. An hour later, both of the other little Poles, who had been turned out of the casino, reappeared behind Grandmother's chair, again offering their services, even if it were just running errands. Potapych swore that the *honourable pan* had winked at them and even handed them something. Since Grandmother had not had dinner and had hardly left her chair, one of the little Poles in fact did come in handy: he ran next door to the casino dining room and got her a cup of bouillon, and later some tea. Both of them, however, ran errands for her. But by the end of the day, when it had already become clear to everyone that she was losing her last banknote, there were as many as six little Poles standing behind her chair, none of whom had been seen or heard of earlier. And when Grandmother was gambling away her last coins, not only did they not listen to her, but they didn't even take any notice of her, but clambered right over her to reach the table, snatched up the money themselves, gave directions and staked, quarrelled and shouted, conferred confidentially with the *honourable pan*, while the *honourable pan* all but forgot about Grandmother's existence. Even when Grandmother had lost absolutely everything and was returning to the hotel that evening at eight o'clock, three or four little Poles still had not made up their minds whether to leave her or not but ran alongside her chair, shouting with all their might and claiming in a rapid-fire patter that Grandmother had somehow swindled them and must give them something. And that's how she made her way to the hotel, where they were finally driven away by force.

Potapych reckoned that Grandmother had lost as much as 90,000 roubles in all that day, not counting the money she had lost the day before. She had exchanged all her banknotes one after the other – five per-cent notes, the domestic bonds, all the shares that she had with her. I wondered how she endured sitting for those seven or eight hours in her chair, almost never leaving the table, but Potapych told me that she did in fact start to win considerably on three occasions; and carried away again by hope, she couldn't bring herself to leave. But gamblers know how a person can sit for almost an entire day over cards in the same spot, without taking his eyes off them.

Meanwhile, very decisive things were also taking place all day long in the hotel. That morning, before eleven o'clock, when Grandmother was still at home, our people, that is, the general and des Grieux, decided on the final step. Upon learning that Grandmother had no intention of leaving, but on the contrary was setting out again for the casino, they all (except Polina) went for a conclave, to talk things over finally and even *openly*. The general, trembling and with sinking heart in view of the awful consequences in store for him, even went a bit too far: after half an hour of prayers and entreaties, and even openly admitting everything, that is, all his debts and even his passion for Mlle Blanche (he had become completely flustered), the general suddenly adopted a threatening tone and even began to shout and stamp his feet at Grandmother; he shouted that she was bringing shame on the family, that she had become a scandal all over town and, finally... finally: 'You have disgraced the name of Russia, madam!' the general shouted, 'and we have the police for that sort of thing!' Grandmother at last chased him out with a stick (a real stick). The general and des Grieux conferred once or twice more that morning, and what interested them precisely was whether in actual fact they could make use of the police. In effect that the unfortunate but respectable old lady had lost her mind, was gambling away the last of her money and so forth. In a word, wouldn't it be possible to obtain some sort of order of protection or injunction?... But des Grieux merely shrugged his shoulders and laughed in the general's face, when the latter began talking utter nonsense as he darted back and forth in his study. Finally, des Grieux threw up his hands and vanished somewhere. That evening I learned that he had left the hotel altogether, after a decisive and mysterious discussion with Mlle Blanche. As for Mlle Blanche, she had already taken final measures that morning: she had completely thrown over the general and would not allow him in her sight. When the general ran to the casino after her and found her arm in arm with the little prince, neither she nor Madame *veuve* Cominges acknowledged him. Nor did the little prince return his bow. All that day Mlle Blanche made an effort with the prince, working on him so that he would at last speak his mind once and for all. But alas! She was cruelly deceived in her designs on the prince! This little catastrophe took place in the evening: it suddenly came to light that the prince was as poor as a church mouse and that he had been counting on borrowing money from her in exchange for his promissory note so that he could play roulette. Blanche indignantly sent him packing and locked herself in her room.

On the morning of that same day I went to see Mr Astley or, to be more precise, I had spent all morning trying to track him down, but wasn't able to do so. He wasn't at home, or in the casino, or in the park. He hadn't dined at his hotel that day. It was going on five o'clock when I suddenly caught sight of him making his way from the railroad platform straight for the Hotel d'Angleterre. He was in a hurry and very preoccupied, although it was difficult to detect signs of worry or any other sort of distress on his face. He cordially held out his hand to me with his usual exclamation of 'Ah!', but without stopping and continuing on his way down the road at a rather fast clip. I tagged along behind him; but somehow he managed to answer me in such a way that I didn't succeed in asking him about anything. Besides, for some reason I was terribly embarrassed to bring up Polina; he himself didn't ask a word about her. I told him about Grandmother; he heard me out attentively and seriously and shrugged his shoulders.

'She'll lose everything,' I observed.

'Oh, yes,' he answered. 'You see, she had just gone to play when I was leaving, and I knew for certain that she would lose everything. If there's time, I'll stop by the casino, because it will be interesting to have a look...'

'Where have you been?' I exclaimed, amazed that I hadn't asked yet.

'I was in Frankfurt.'

'On business?'

'Yes, on business.'

Well, what else could I ask? However, I kept walking beside him, until he suddenly turned into the Hotel de Quatre Saisons, situated there beside the road, nodded to me and disappeared inside. As I was making my way back home, I came to realize, little by little, that even if I had talked with him for two hours I would still not have learned anything at all, because... because I had nothing to ask him! Yes, of course, that's it! There was no way for me to formulate my question now.

All that day Polina was either strolling with the children and nanny in the park, or at home. She had been avoiding the general for a long time now and hardly spoke to him, at least about anything serious. I had noticed that a long time ago. But knowing the situation the general found himself in today, I thought that he wouldn't be able to avoid her, that is, they would have to have some sort of important family discussions. However, upon returning to the hotel after my conversation with Mr Astley, I met Polina and the children, and her face showed the most serene tranquillity, as if of all the family the storms had bypassed her. She nodded in answer to my bow. I arrived at my room quite angry.

Of course, I had been avoiding talking to her and we

hadn't seen each other since the incident with the Wurmerhelms. For all that, to some degree it amounted to swagger and posing on my part; but the more time went on, the more I seethed with genuine indignation. Even if she didn't love me at all, she shouldn't trample my feelings like that and receive my declarations with such scorn. After all, she knows that I truly love her; after all, she herself has allowed me to speak like that to her! True, it all began somewhat strangely between us. For some time now, from about two months ago, I had begun to notice that she wanted to make me her friend, her confidant, and that she was even testing me to some degree. But for some reason it didn't work between us; and instead we were left with the present strange relationship; and that's why I started talking to her like that. But if she finds my love repellent, why doesn't she forbid me outright to speak of it?

I'm not forbidden; on occasion she has even contrived for me to begin the conversation and . . . of course, she did this as a joke. I know for certain, I have distinctly noticed that – she found it pleasant after hearing me out and then irritating me to the point of pain, suddenly to disconcert me with some outburst of the greatest scorn and lack of consideration. And she knows, you see, that I can't live without her. It's been three days now since the incident with the baron, and I can't endure our *separation* any longer. When I saw her just now at the casino, my heart began to pound so that I turned white. But, you see, she can't live without me either! She needs me and – surely, surely not only to play the buffoon like Balakirev.[3]

She has a secret – that's clear! Her conversation with Grandmother had been an agonizing wrench to my heart. You see, I'd appealed to her a thousand times to be open with me, and she knew, you see, that I really was prepared to lay down my life for her. But she had always regarded this lightly, almost with scorn – or instead of the sacrifice of my life, which I had offered her, she asked for escapades like the one with the baron! Isn't that an outrage? Can that Frenchman really mean the whole world to her? And what about Mr Astley? But here the matter becomes decidedly incomprehensible; meanwhile, my God! how I have suffered!

Upon my arrival home, in a fit of rage, I seized my pen and dashed off the following:

> Polina Alexandrovna, I see clearly that things are coming to a head, and, of course, this will affect you as well. I repeat for the last time: do you need my life or not? If you need it, for *anything at all* – it's at your disposal; meanwhile, I'll stay in my room, at least for the most part, and won't go anywhere. If you need me – then write or send for me.

I sealed this note and sent it with the floor attendant, with instructions that it be delivered straight into her hands. I did not expect an answer, but three minutes later the attendant returned with the news that she 'sends her compliments'.

It was after six when I was summoned to the general's.

He was in his study, dressed as though he was just about to go out. His hat and stick lay on the sofa. I had the impression when I entered that he had been standing in the middle of the room, with his legs planted apart, his head lowered, and talking out loud to himself. But as soon as he caught sight of me, he rushed towards me almost shouting, so that I involuntarily took a step backwards and wanted to run away; but he grabbed me by both hands and dragged me towards the sofa; he sat down on it himself, and seated me directly across from him in an armchair, and, without letting go of my hands, with trembling lips, with tears suddenly glistening on his eyelashes, he uttered in an imploring voice:

'Alexey Ivanovich, save me, save me, have mercy on me!'

For a long time I couldn't understand a thing; he kept talking, talking, talking and repeating: 'Have mercy on me! Have mercy on me!' Finally, I guessed that he was expecting some sort of advice from me; or rather, abandoned by everybody, anxious and alarmed, he suddenly thought of me and summoned me just so that he could talk, talk, talk.

He had lost his mind, or at the very least he was utterly at his wits' end. He clasped his hands together and was ready to fall down before me on his knees so that (what do you think?) – so that I would immediately go to see Mlle Blanche and beg her, appeal to her to come back and marry him.

'For pity's sake, General,' I cried out, 'Mlle Blanche most likely is not even aware of my existence. What can I do?'

But my objections were made in vain; he didn't understand what was said to him. And then he launched into talking about Grandmother as well, but it was all terribly incoherent; he was still in favour of the idea of sending for the police.

'Back home, back home,' he began, suddenly seething with indignation, 'in a word, back home, in a well-ordered state, where there are authorities, old ladies like that would be fixed up at once with a guardian! Yes, my dear sir, yes,' he continued, suddenly adopting a reproving tone, jumping up from his seat and pacing up and down the room; 'you still don't know that, my dear sir,' (he was addressing some imaginary dear sir in the corner), 'well, you'll find out now . . . yes, sir . . . back home old women like that are made to knuckle under, under, under, yes, sir . . . Oh, the devil take it!'

And he threw himself on the sofa again, and a minute later, almost sobbing, gasping for breath, he hurriedly told me that Mlle Blanche would not marry him because

Grandmother had come instead of a telegram and that now it was clear that he wouldn't come into the inheritance. He seemed to think that I didn't know about any of this. I began to speak about des Grieux; he waved his hand:

'He's gone! I've mortgaged everything I have to him; I'm as poor as a church mouse! The money you brought ... that money – I don't know how much there is, perhaps 700 francs remain and – enough, sir, that's all there is, but after that – I don't know, sir, I don't know! ...'

'How will you pay your hotel bill?' I cried out in alarm. 'And ... what's to happen afterwards?'

He looked around pensively, but didn't seem to understand anything and perhaps didn't even hear me. I tried to bring the conversation around to Polina Alexandrovna and the children; he replied hastily: 'Yes, yes!' – but at once started talking about the prince again, about how he would now leave with Blanche and then ... and then ... 'What am I to do, Alexey Ivanovich?' he turned to me suddenly. 'I swear to God! What am I to do – tell me, what ingratitude! Isn't this ingratitude?'

Finally, he burst into floods of tears.

There was nothing to be done with a man like this; it was dangerous to leave him alone; something might happen to him. However, I somehow managed to get away from him, though I let the nanny know that she should look in on him frequently, and, on top of that, I spoke with the floor attendant, a very sensible fellow; he also promised that he would keep an eye on him.

I had scarcely left the general when Potapych came to me with a summons from Grandmother. It was eight o'clock and she had just come back from the casino after her final losses. I went to see her: the old woman was sitting in an armchair, utterly exhausted and visibly ill. Marfa had given her a cup of tea which she almost forced her to drink. Both Grandmother's voice and tone had noticeably changed.

'Good evening, Alexey Ivanovich,' she said, bowing her head slowly and imposingly. 'Forgive me for disturbing you again, please forgive an old woman. I, my friend, left there everything I had, almost a hundred thousand roubles. You were right not to go with me yesterday. I have no money now, not a kopeck. And I do not wish to linger here another minute, I'm leaving at half past nine. I've sent for your Englishman – his name is Astley, isn't it? – and I want to ask him to loan me 3,000 francs for a week. Please persuade him, won't you, and don't let him think anything's wrong and refuse. I'm still quite rich, my friend. I have three villages and two houses. And besides that there's still some money, I didn't bring it all with me. I'm telling you this so that he will not have any doubts . . . Ah, and here he is! One can see he's a good man.'

Mr Astley had hurried over at Grandmother's first summons. Without giving it a great deal of thought and without saying much, he immediately counted out 3,000 francs against a promissory note which Grandmother signed. After the business was finished, he took his leave and hurried out.

'And now you go as well, Alexey Ivanovich. There's just over an hour left – I want to lie down, my bones ache. Don't be hard on me, old fool that I am. Now I will no longer accuse young people of being frivolous, and it would also be a sin for me to blame that unhappy general of yours. All the same, I won't give him the money he wants, because, in my opinion, he's a complete nincompoop, but then I'm not any smarter than he is, old fool that I am. Truly, God calls the old to account as well and punishes them for their pride. Well, goodbye. Marfusha, help me up.'

I, however, wished to see Grandmother off. Besides, I

was in a state of some expectation; I kept waiting for something to happen at any minute. I couldn't bear staying in my room. I went out into the hallway, and even went for a bit of a walk on the avenue. My letter to her was clear and decisive, and the present catastrophe, of course, was final. I had heard about des Grieux's departure at the hotel. In the end, if she rejects me as a friend, then perhaps she won't reject me as a servant. You see, she does need me, if only to run errands; and I might be of use, how could it be otherwise!

When it was time for the train, I ran to the platform and helped Grandmother to her seat. They were all seated in a private family carriage.[4] 'Thank you, my dear, for your unselfish concern,' she said at parting with me. 'And mention to Praskovya again what I told her yesterday – I'll be expecting her.'

I went home. As I walked past the general's room, I met the nanny and asked about the general. 'Oh, sir, he's fine,' she answered cheerlessly. I went in, however, but in the doorway to the study I stopped in absolute amazement. Mlle Blanche and the general were roaring with laughter about something. *Veuve* Cominges was sitting right next to them on the sofa. The general, clearly beside himself with joy, was babbling all sorts of nonsense and would burst into prolonged nervous peals of laughter, which transformed his whole face into a myriad of tiny wrinkles, and his eyes would disappear from sight altogether. Later I learned from Blanche herself that, after banishing the prince and learning about the general's tears, she took it into her head to console him and stopped by to see him for a minute. But the poor general did not know at that moment that his fate had already been decided and that Blanche had begun packing so that she could rush off to Paris on the first morning train.

After standing on the threshold of the general's study

for a bit, I thought better of entering and left unnoticed. After going up to my room and opening the door, I suddenly noticed in the half-darkness the figure of someone sitting on the chair in the corner, by the window. The figure did not get up when I appeared. I quickly walked over, looked and – my breath was taken away: it was Polina!

Chapter 14

I actually cried out.

'What is it? What is it?' she asked strangely. She was pale and looked gloomy.

'What do you mean "what is it?" You? Here in my room!'

'If I come, then I do so *wholeheartedly*. That's my way. You'll see that in a moment; light a candle.'

I lit a candle. She got up, walked over to the table and placed before me a letter that had been unsealed.

'Read it,' she ordered.

'This – this is des Grieux's handwriting,' I cried out, seizing the letter. My hands were shaking, and the lines danced before my eyes. I have forgotten the letter's exact turns of phrase, but here it is – if not word for word, then at the very least, thought for thought.

Mademoiselle – des Grieux wrote – unfortunate circumstances compel me to leave immediately. You, of course, have noticed that I have deliberately avoided a final explanation with you until all the circumstances became clear. The arrival of your old relation (*de la vieille dame*) and her ridiculous conduct have put an end to all my uncertainties. My own affairs are in disarray, and this forbids me once and for all from nourishing any further the sweet hopes which I had allowed myself to entertain for some time now. I regret the past, but I hope you will not find anything in my conduct unworthy of a gentleman and an honest man (*gentilhomme et honnête homme*).[1] After losing almost all my money in loans to your stepfather, I find myself in urgent need of making use of what I have left: I have already let my friends in Petersburg know that they should immediately arrange for the sale of the property mortgaged to me; knowing, however, that your frivolous stepfather has squandered your own money, I have decided to forgive him 50,000 francs and am returning to him mortgage deeds on his property in that amount, so that you are now in a position to return all that you have lost, after laying claim to your property from him through legal channels. I hope, *Mademoiselle*, that my action will prove to be quite advantageous for you in the present circumstances. I also hope that with this action I am fulfilling in every respect the duty of an honest and noble man. Rest assured that the memory of you is forever imprinted on my heart.

'Well then, it's all clear,' I said, turning to Polina. 'Did you really expect anything different?' I added indignantly.

'I didn't expect anything,' she answered, to all appearances calmly, although there was something of a quaver in her voice. 'I made up my mind long ago; I read his thoughts and knew what he was thinking. He thought that I was looking for . . . that I would insist . . .' (She stopped, without finishing what she was saying, bit her lip and fell silent.) 'I deliberately doubled my scorn for him,' she began again, 'I waited to see what he would do. If a telegram had come about the inheritance, I would have flung at him what was owed by that idiot (my stepfather) and sent him packing! I have found him loathsome for a long, long time now. Oh, he was not the same man as before, a thousand times not the same one, but now, but now! . . . Oh, how happy I would be to throw at him now, into his vile face, that 50,000 and spit at him . . . and rub it in!'

'But the document, the mortgage deed for 50,000 that he returned, the general must have it now, right? Take it and give it to des Grieux.'

'Oh, it's not the same thing, not the same thing at all! . . .'

'Yes, true, true, it's not the same thing! Besides, what can the general do now? What about Grandmother?' I cried suddenly.

Polina looked at me somewhat absent-mindedly and impatiently.

'Why Grandmother?' Polina said with vexation. 'I can't go to her . . . And I don't want to ask anybody's forgiveness,' she added irritably.

'What's to be done!' I cried. 'And how, well, how could you have loved des Grieux! Oh, the scoundrel, scoundrel! Well, if you want, I'll kill him in a duel! Where is he now?'

'He's in Frankfurt and will stay there for three days.'

'Just one word from you and I'll be gone, tomorrow, on the first train!' I said in some sort of foolish enthusiasm.

She laughed.

'What if he were to say, first return the 50,000 francs. And why should he fight? . . . What nonsense!'

'Well then, where, where are you going to get these 50,000 francs?' I repeated, grinding my teeth, just as though one might suddenly pick them up from the floor. 'Look here – what about Mr Astley?' I asked, turning to her with the beginning of a strange idea.

Her eyes began to sparkle.

'What, do *you* really want me to leave you for that Englishman?' she said, looking me straight in the face with a piercing stare and a bitter smile. It was the first time that she had addressed me with the familiar *'you'*.

I think that at that moment her head began spinning from the excitement, and she suddenly sat down on the sofa, as if she were utterly exhausted.

THE GAMBLER

It was as if I had been struck by lightning; I stood there and didn't believe my eyes, I didn't believe my ears! Why, that means she loves me! She came *to me*, and not to Mr Astley! She, alone, a girl, had come to my room, in a hotel – which means that she had compromised herself in society's eyes – and I, I was standing before her and still didn't understand!

A wild idea flashed through my head.

'Polina! give me just one hour! Wait here for just an hour and . . . I will return! This . . . this is essential! You'll see! Stay here, stay here!'

And I ran out of the room, without answering her surprised, questioning look; she cried out something after me, but I didn't turn back.

Yes, sometimes the wildest idea, which looks like the most impossible idea, becomes so firmly entrenched in your head that in the end you take it to be something realizable . . . Moreover, if the idea is combined with a strong, passionate desire, then perhaps sometimes you take it in the end to be something fated, necessary, predestined, something that cannot but exist and come to be! Perhaps there's some reason here as well, some sort of combination of presentiments, some unusual force of will, that is becoming poisoned by your own fantasy or something else – I don't know; but something miraculous happened to me that evening (which I will never forget as long as I live). Even though it is completely supported by simple arithmetic, nevertheless I still find it to be something miraculous. And why, why had this certainty lodged itself inside me then so deeply, and for such a long time? To be sure, I used to think about it – I repeat – not as about an event that might happen among other things (and consequently, that might not happen), but as something that could not but come about!

It was a quarter past ten; I entered the casino with such

firm hopes and at the same time such agitation, the likes of which I had never experienced. There were still rather a lot of people in the gaming rooms, though less than half as many as in the morning.

After ten o'clock it's the genuine, desperate gamblers who remain at the gaming tables, those for whom roulette is the only thing that exists at the spa, who came only for that, who hardly notice what's happening around them, and who are interested in nothing else all season long, but only play from morning till night, and who very likely would be more than ready to play all night long until dawn, if that were possible. And they always leave with annoyance when the roulette closes at midnight. And when the head croupier calls out around twelve o'clock before the roulette closes: *'Les trois derniers coups, messieurs!'*,[2] they are sometimes prepared to stake on those three last turns everything they have in their pockets – indeed, this is when they lose most of their money. I made my way over to the same table where Grandmother had sat earlier. It wasn't very crowded, so I soon found a place to stand at the table. Directly in front of me, on the green cloth, was written the word *'passe'*. *'Passe'* is the series of numbers from nineteen to thirty-six inclusive. The first series, from one to eighteen inclusive, is called *'manque'*. But what did I care about that? I wasn't making any calculations, I didn't hear what number had come up in the last round nor did I even ask when I began playing, as the least shrewd gambler would have done. I took all my twenty friedrichs d'or from my pocket and threw them down on *passe*, which happened to lay before me.

'Vingt-deux!' the croupier called out.

I'd won – and once again I staked everything: both what I had before and my winnings.

'Trente et un,'[3] the croupier trumpeted. Another win! That meant I now had eighty friedrichs d'or in all! I moved

all eighty to the twelve middle numbers (I'd triple my winnings, but with the odds two to one against me) – the wheel started spinning and it came up twenty-four. They spread before me three rolls of 50 friedrichs d'or each and ten gold coins; all in all, counting what I had before, I now found myself with 200 friedrichs d'or.

Feeling as though I had a fever, I moved this entire pile of money on to red – and suddenly I came to my senses! And only this once during the whole of the evening, during all the time that I was playing, did fear course through me like a chill and cause my arms and legs to tremble. I sensed with horror and for an instant realized: what it would mean for me to lose now! My whole life was at stake!

'*Rouge!*' the croupier cried – and I took a deep breath, fiery pins and needles ran up and down my body. I was paid in banknotes; that meant I already had 4,000 florins and 80 friedrichs d'or! (I could still keep track of the total at this time.)

Next, I remember, I staked 2,000 florins on the middle twelve numbers again and I lost; I staked my gold and 80 friedrichs d'or and lost. I was consumed with rage: I snatched up the last remaining 2,000 florins and staked them on the first twelve numbers – haphazard, on the off chance, to no purpose, without any calculation! However, there was one moment of anticipation, similar perhaps to the sensation experienced by Madame Blanchard in Paris as she plummeted to the earth from a balloon.[4]

'*Quatre!*'[5] the croupier cried. In all, with my previous stake, I again found myself with 6,000 florins. I already looked like a conqueror, I was afraid of nothing, absolutely nothing, and I flung down four 4,000 florins on black. Some nine others, following my example, also rushed to stake black. The croupiers exchanged glances and conferred with one another. All around me people were talking and waiting.

It came up black. I no longer remember my calculations or the sequence of my stakes after this. I only remember, as if in a dream, that I had already won, I believe, some 16,000 florins; suddenly, after three unlucky rounds I squandered twelve of them; then I moved the last 4,000 to *passe* (but feeling almost nothing as I did so; I merely waited, somehow mechanically, without thinking) – and I won again; then I won another four times in a row. I remember only that I was raking in money by the thousands; I also recall that the twelve middle numbers came up more frequently than the rest, and I kept to them. They came up with some sort of regularity – without fail three or four times in a row, and then would disappear for two times, and then start up once again three or four times in a row. This astonishing regularity is sometimes encountered in streaks – and it's this that confuses inveterate gamblers who tot up their calculations with pencil in hand. And what terrible mockeries of fate sometimes take place here!

I don't think that more than half an hour had passed since my arrival. Suddenly the croupier informed me that I had won 30,000 florins, and since the bank could not be responsible for more than that at one time, this meant that the table would be closed until the following morning. I snatched up all my gold and dropped it into my pockets, I snatched up all the banknotes and immediately moved to another table in another room where there was another game of roulette; the whole crowd surged after me; a place was immediately cleared for me, and I once again began staking haphazardly and without calculating. I don't know what saved me!

Sometimes, however, glimmerings of calculation began to flash through my head. I would become attached to some numbers and odds, but I would soon abandon them and was staking again almost unconsciously. I must have been very absent-minded; I remember that the croupiers corrected the way I was playing several times. I made outrageous mistakes. My temples were wet with sweat and my hands were shaking. Some little Poles came running up to offer their services, but I didn't listen to anybody. My luck was holding! Suddenly loud talk and laughter broke out all around me. 'Bravo, bravo!' everybody shouted, some even clapped. I broke the bank here as well with 30,000 florins, and it too was closed until the following day!

'Leave, leave,' somebody's voice whispered to me on my right. It was a Frankfurt Jew; he had been standing next to me the whole time and, I think, had sometimes helped me play.

'For goodness' sake, leave,' another voice whispered in my left ear. I glanced around quickly. It was a quite modestly and decently dressed lady, about thirty, with a somewhat sickly-pale and weary face, but which even now bore traces of its former marvellous beauty. At that moment I was stuffing my pockets with banknotes, which I simply crumpled up, and gathering up the remaining gold coins from the table. When I picked up the last roll of fifty friedrichs d'or, I managed, completely unobserved, to thrust it into the pale lady's hand; I wanted terribly to do this then, and her slender, thin little fingers, I remember, pressed my hand firmly in token of warmest gratitude. All this happened in an instant.

After gathering up everything, I quickly moved over to the *trente et quarante*.

The aristocratic clientele plays *trente et quarante*. This is not roulette, but cards. Here the bank is responsible for a hundred thousand thalers at once. The largest stake is also 4,000 florins. I did not know the game at all and hardly knew a single stake, besides red and black, which they have here as well. And so I stuck to those. The whole casino crowded round. I don't remember whether I even once gave a thought to Polina all this time. I felt then an irresistible delight in grabbing and raking up the banknotes which were piling up in front of me.

Indeed, it was as if fate were urging me on. This time, as if on purpose, a circumstance occurred that, however, happens rather frequently in gambling. Chance becomes attached, say, to red and doesn't drop it for ten times, even fifteen times in a row. The day before yesterday I had heard that the previous week red came up twenty times in a row; nobody could even recall that happening in roulette and it was talked about with amazement. It goes without saying, everybody immediately drops red, and after the tenth time, say, almost nobody risks placing a stake on it. But none of the experienced gamblers stakes on black, the opposite of red, either. The experienced gambler knows what 'the caprice of chance' means. For example, it would seem that after coming up red sixteen times the seventeenth time without fail will come up black. And all the novices rush forward in crowds to double and triple their stakes, and lose terribly.

But on account of some sort of strange wilfulness, after observing that red had come up seven times in a row, I deliberately stuck with it. I'm convinced that pride was half responsible; I wanted to amaze the onlookers with this senseless risk, and – oh, the peculiar sensation – I distinctly remember that I really was suddenly overcome with a terrible craving for risk without any encouragement on the part of my pride. Perhaps when it undergoes so many sensations, the soul is not satiated, but merely irritated by them and demands still more sensations, stronger and stronger ones, until it reaches utter exhaustion. And I'm really not lying when I say that if the rules of the game allowed me to stake 50,000 florins at a time, I would certainly have done so. All round they were shouting that it was madness, that red had already come up fourteen times!

'*Monsieur a gagné déjà cent mille florins*,'[6] someone's voice next to me rang out.

I suddenly came to my senses. What? That evening I had won 100,000 florins! Whatever did I need more for? I fell upon the banknotes, crumpled them into my pocket without counting them, raked up all my gold coins and all the rolls, and ran out of the casino. Everybody around laughed as I made my way through the halls, looking at my bulging pockets and my unsteady gait from the weight of the gold. I think that it was well over half a pood.[7] Several hands stretched out towards me; I doled it out by the handful, as much as I happened to grab. Two Jews stopped me by the exit.

'You are bold! You are very bold!' they said to me. 'But you must leave tomorrow morning without fail, as early as possible, otherwise you will lose absolutely everything . . .'

I didn't listen to them. The avenue was so dark that you couldn't make out your hands in front of your face. It was half a verst to the hotel. I had never been afraid of thieves or robbers before, even when I was little; I didn't give them any thought now. I don't remember though what I was thinking about as I made my way; I had no thoughts about anything. I felt some sort of terrible delight at my good fortune, victory, power – I don't know how to express it. I also glimpsed Polina's image fleetingly; I remembered and was conscious of one fact: that I was going to her, that I would meet her now and tell her, show her . . . but I scarcely recalled what she had said to me earlier or why I had gone, and all of those recent sensations, which I had experienced just an hour and a half ago, now seemed something long past, remedied, superseded – something we would no longer remember, because now everything would begin anew. Almost at the end of the avenue I was seized by fear: 'What if I'm robbed and murdered right now?' My fear doubled with each step. I was almost running. Suddenly at the end of the avenue our hotel flashed into view all at once, illuminated by innumerable lights. Thank God – home!

I ran up to my floor and quickly opened the door. Polina was there, sitting on my sofa, arms folded, with a lighted candle in front of her. She looked at me with amazement and, to be sure, at that moment I looked rather strange. I stopped in front of her and began tossing my money on to the table in a pile.

Chapter 15

I remember she looked in my face with a terrible intensity, but without moving from where she was sitting, without even changing her position.

'I won 200,000 francs,' I cried, as I tossed down the last roll. An enormous pile of banknotes and rolls of gold coins took up the whole table; I couldn't take my eyes off it; there were moments when I completely forgot about Polina. Now I'd start putting these heaps of banknotes in order by making a stack of them, then I'd separate all the gold coins into one general pile; then I'd stop all that and begin pacing quickly about the room, then fall deep into thought, and then suddenly I'd walk over to the table again, and begin counting my money all over again. Suddenly it was as if I had come to my senses, and I rushed to the door and quickly locked it, turning the key around twice. Then I paused to reflect in front of my suitcase.

'Should I put it in my suitcase tomorrow?' I asked, suddenly turning to Polina, and suddenly remembering about her. She was still sitting, without moving, in the same place, but she was watching me intently. The expression

THE GAMBLER

on her face was somehow strange; I didn't like that look! I would not be wrong if I were to say that there was hatred in it.

I quickly walked over to her.

'Polina, here's 25,000 florins – that's 50,000 francs, even more. Take it, throw it in his face tomorrow!'

She didn't answer me.

'If you want, I'll take it myself, early in the morning. Shall I?'

She suddenly burst out laughing. She laughed for a long time.

I looked at her with surprise and a sorrowful feeling. This laughter was very much like her recent, frequent, mocking laughter at me, which had always attended my most passionate declarations. Finally, she stopped and frowned; she looked at me sternly from under her brows.

'I won't take your money,' she uttered scornfully.

'Why? What's the matter?' I cried. 'Polina, for goodness' sake, why?'

'I don't take money for nothing.'

'I offer it to you as a friend; I am offering you my life.'

She looked at me with a prolonged, searching look, as if she wanted to pierce me through.

'You're giving too much,' she uttered with a smile. 'Des Grieux's mistress isn't worth 50,000 francs.'

'Polina, how can you talk to me like that!' I exclaimed reproachfully. 'I'm not des Grieux, am I?'

'I hate you! Yes... yes!... I don't love you any more than I do des Grieux,' she exclaimed, her eyes suddenly beginning to flash.

And then she covered her face with her hands and went into hysterics. I rushed to her.

I understood that something had happened to her in my absence. She was not at all in her right mind.

'Buy me! Is that what you want? Is it? For 50,000 francs,

like des Grieux?' she burst into convulsive sobs. I embraced her, kissed her hands and feet; I fell to my knees before her.

Her hysterics were subsiding. She placed both her hands on my shoulders and scrutinized me intently; it seemed that she wanted to read something in my face. She listened to me, but evidently did not hear what I was saying. Her face assumed a worried and brooding look. I was afraid for her; it definitely seemed that she was losing her mind. Now she would suddenly start to draw me to her; a trusting smile wandered across her face; and then suddenly she would push me away and once again take to peering at me with a darkened look.

Suddenly she rushed to embrace me.

'But you do love me, don't you, don't you?' she said. 'After all you, after all you... you wanted to fight the baron for my sake!' And suddenly she burst out laughing, as if the memory of something funny and nice had suddenly come to her. She both wept and laughed – at the same time. Well, what was I to do? I seemed to be in a fever myself. I remember that she began saying something to me, but I could understand hardly a thing. It was a sort of delirium, a babbling – as if she wanted to tell me something as quickly as possible – a delirium that at times was interrupted by the most cheerful laughter, which began to frighten me. 'No, no, you're a dear, a dear!' she repeated. 'You're my faithful one!' and once again she would place her hands on my shoulders, and once again she would peer at me and continue to repeat: 'You love me... love me... will you love me?' I didn't take my eyes off of her; I had never before seen her in these paroxysms of tenderness and love; true, this of course was delirium, but... noticing the passionate look on my face, she suddenly began to smile cunningly; out of the blue she suddenly began talking about Mr Astley.

However, she had been talking about Mr Astley

constantly (particularly when she had been making such efforts to tell me something earlier), but what precisely she was trying to say, I could not fully grasp; I think she was even laughing at him; she kept constantly repeating that he was waiting... and did I know that he was probably standing under the window now? 'Yes, yes, under the window – well, open it, take a look, take a look, he's here, here!' She was pushing me towards the window, but as soon as I made the move to go, she burst into peals of laughter, and I would remain by her side, and she rushed to embrace me.

'Are we leaving? We're leaving tomorrow, aren't we?' suddenly occurred to her uneasy mind. 'Well...' (and she fell into thought) 'well, but will we catch up with Grandmother, what do you think? I think we'll catch up with her in Berlin. What do you think she'll say when we catch up with her and she sees us? And Mr Astley?... Well, that one won't jump off the Schlangenberg, do you think?' (She burst out laughing.) 'Well, listen: do you know where he's going next summer? He wants to go to the North Pole for scientific research and he invited me to go with him, ha-ha-ha! He says that we Russians wouldn't know anything without the Europeans and that we aren't capable of anything... But he's also a kind man! Do you know that he excuses the "general"; he says that Blanche... that passion – well, I don't know, I don't know,' she suddenly repeated as if she'd lost her train of thought while she was speaking. 'The poor things, I feel so sorry for them, and Grandmother... Well, listen, listen, how could you kill des Grieux? And did you really, really think that you would kill him? Oh, you silly fool. Did you really think that I would let you go to fight des Grieux? And you won't kill the baron either,' she added, after a sudden burst of laughter. 'Oh, how ridiculous you were with the baron then; I watched you both from the bench; and how loath you were to go then, when I sent you. And how I laughed, how I laughed then,' she added, roaring with laughter.

And suddenly she kissed and embraced me again, she passionately and tenderly pressed her face to mine again. I no longer thought about anything else and no longer heard anything. My head was spinning...

I think that it was around seven o'clock in the morning when I came to my senses; the sun was shining into the room. Polina sat beside me and looked about strangely, as if she were emerging from some sort of gloom and collecting her thoughts. She, too, had only just woken up and was looking intently at the table and at the money. My head was heavy and ached. I wanted to take Polina by the hand; she suddenly pushed me away and jumped up from the sofa. The dawning day was overcast; it had rained before daybreak. She walked over to the window, opened it, thrust out her head and shoulders and, leaning on the windowsill with her hand, her elbows resting on the frame, she stayed there for about three minutes, without turning around towards me or listening to what I was saying. I dreaded to think what would happen next and how it would all end. Suddenly she got up from the window, walked over to the table, and, looking at me with an expression of infinite hatred, her lips trembling with fury, she said to me:

'Well, now give me my 50,000 francs!'

'Polina, again, again!' I began.

'Or have you changed your mind? Ha-ha-ha! Perhaps you already regret it?'

The 25,000 florins, which I had already counted out last night, lay on the table; I picked the packet up and gave it to her.

'They're mine now, right? Isn't that right? Isn't it?' she asked me spitefully, holding the money in her hands.

'But it was always yours,' I said.

'Well, so here's your 50,000 francs!' She made a sweeping gesture with her arm and hurled them at me. The packet hit me painfully in the face and scattered all over the floor. After doing this, Polina ran out of the room.

I know, of course, that she was not in her right mind at that moment, although I don't understand this temporary insanity. True, to this day, a month later, she is still ill. However, what was the cause of this condition and, the main point, of this outburst? Wounded pride? Despair that she had resolved on coming to me? Had I given her the impression that I was relishing my good fortune and that when all was said and done I was just like des Grieux, wanting to get rid of her by making her a present of 50,000 francs? But, you see, that wasn't the case; my conscience is clear. I think her vanity was partly to blame here: vanity prompted her not to believe me and to insult me, although all this was perhaps unclear even to herself. In that case, of course, I was answering for des Grieux and was found guilty, though perhaps my guilt was not so great. It's true, all this was merely delirium; and it's also true that I knew she was delirious, and . . . paid no attention to that circumstance. Perhaps she can't forgive me for this now? Yes, but that's now; but what about then? You see, her delirium and illness were not so severe that she was completely unaware of what she was doing, when she came to me with des Grieux's letter. That means that she must have known what she was doing.

I made a slapdash effort to stuff all my banknotes and my pile of gold into the bed, pulled up the covers and left about ten minutes after Polina. I was certain that she had run back to her room, and I wanted to make my way to their quarters on the sly and ask the nanny about the young lady's health. Imagine my surprise when I learned from the nanny, whom I met on the stairs, that Polina had not yet returned home and that the nanny was coming to my room to look for her.

'Just now,' I said to her, 'she just now left my room, ten minutes ago, where could she have gone?'

The nanny looked at me reproachfully.

Meanwhile, a regular scandal had erupted, which was already making the rounds of the hotel. In the porters' room and the manager's office it was being whispered that this morning, at six o'clock, the *fraülein*[1] had run out of the hotel, in the rain, and had run off in the direction of the Hotel d'Angleterre. From what they said and the hints they gave, I noticed that they already knew that she had spent the whole night in my room. However, there was talk about all of the general's family: it was known that yesterday the general had lost his mind and had been weeping for all the hotel to hear. There was also talk that the grandmother who had come was his mother and that she had travelled from Russia itself in order to forbid her son to marry Mlle de Cominges, and that if he disobeyed she would disinherit him, and as he indeed had not obeyed, the Countess intentionally, right before his very eyes, gambled away all her money at the roulette table so that he would get nothing. '*Diese Russen!*'[2] the manager indignantly repeated, shaking his head. The others laughed. The manager was preparing the bill. People already knew about my winnings; Karl, my floor attendant, was the first to congratulate me. But I had other things on my mind. I rushed off to the Hotel d'Angleterre.

It was still early; Mr Astley was not receiving anyone; upon learning that it was I, he came out into the hall and stopped in front of me, silently fastening his lustreless look on me, and waited to hear what I had to say. I at once asked about Polina.

'She's ill,' Mr Astley answered, staring straight at me as before, not taking his eyes off me.

'Then she really is with you?'

'Oh, yes, she's with me.'

'So then you . . . you intend to keep her with you?'

'Oh, yes, I do.'

'Mr Astley, this will create a scandal; it's impossible. Besides, she's quite ill; perhaps you noticed?'

'Oh, yes, I noticed and I already said to you that she was ill. If she weren't ill, she wouldn't have spent the night in your room.'

'So you know that as well?'

'I do. She was coming here yesterday, and I would have taken her to a relative of mine, but since she was ill she made a mistake and went to you.'

'Just imagine! Well, I congratulate you, Mr Astley. By the way, you've given me an idea. Were you by any chance standing all night beneath my window? All night long Miss Polina kept having me open the window and look out to see whether you were standing there, and she laughed terribly.'

'Is that so? No, I wasn't standing beneath the window; but I was waiting in the hall and walking around.'

'But she needs to see a doctor, Mr Astley.'

'Oh, yes, I've already called a doctor, and if she dies, you'll answer to me for her death.'

I was astounded.

'For goodness' sake, Mr Astley, what do you mean?'

'And is it true that you won 200,000 thalers yesterday?'

'Only a hundred thousand florins.'

'Well then, you see! So then, off you go to Paris this morning.'

'Why?'

'All Russians who have money go to Paris,' Mr Astley explained in a voice and tone as if he were reading this from a book.

'What would I do now, in the summertime, in Paris? I love her, Mr Astley. You know that yourself.'

'Is that so? I'm convinced that you don't. Moreover, if you stay here, you'll be certain to gamble away everything, and you won't have anything to pay for your trip to Paris. Well, goodbye, I'm absolutely convinced that you'll leave today for Paris.'

'Fine, goodbye, only I'm not going to Paris. Just think, Mr Astley, what will be happening here. In a word, the general... and now this adventure with Miss Polina – you see, all this will make the rounds of the whole town.'

'Yes, the whole town; but I don't think the general is giving that any thought – he has other things on his mind. And what's more, Miss Polina is entitled to live where she pleases. As for that family, it can truly be said that the family no longer exists.'

I walked away and chuckled at this Englishman's strange certainty that I was going to Paris. 'However, he wants to kill me in a duel,' I thought, 'if Mlle Polina dies – yet more bother!' I swear that I felt sorry for Polina, but strangely enough, from the moment I touched the gaming table yesterday and started raking in packets of money – my love seemed to have retreated into the background. That's how I would put it now, but then I still hadn't clearly seen all this. Is it possible that I really am a gambler? Is it possible that I really... loved Polina so strangely? No, I love her to this day, as God is my witness! And then, when I had left Mr Astley and was going home, I was sincere in suffering and blaming myself. But... but then an utterly strange and silly thing happened to me.

I was hurrying to the general's, when suddenly a door not far from his suite opened and someone called out to me. It was Madame *veuve* Cominges and she was calling me at the request of Mlle Blanche.

They had a small suite, just two rooms. I could hear Mlle Blanche laughing and calling from the bedroom. She was just getting up.

'Ah, c'est lui! Viens donc, bêta. Is it true, *que tu as gagné une montagne d'or et d'argent? J'aimerais mieux l'or.*'[3]

'I did,' I answered, laughing.

'How much?'

'A hundred thousand florins.'

'*Bibi, comme tu es bête.* Yes, come in here, I can't hear anything. *Nous ferons bombance, n'est-ce pas?*'[4]

I went in to her. She was lolling under a pink satin blanket, from beneath which her dusky, strong, marvellous shoulders were on display – shoulders the likes of which one only sees in a dream – carelessly covered by a cambric camisole, trimmed with the whitest lace, which suited her dusky skin to a remarkable degree.

'*Mons fils, as-tu du coeur?*' she exclaimed upon seeing me, and burst out laughing. She always laughed very gaily and even sometimes sincerely.

'*Tout autre . . .*'[5] I began, paraphrasing Corneille.

'There, you see, *vois-tu*,' she suddenly began chattering, 'first of all, find my stockings, help me get them on, and in the second place, *si tu n'es pas trop bête, je te prends à Paris.*[6] You see, I'm going now.'

'Now?'

'In half an hour.'

Indeed, everything was packed. All her cases and things were ready. Coffee had been served long before.

'*Eh bien!* Do you want, *tu verras Paris. Dis donc qu'est ce que c'est qu'un outchitel? Tu étais bien bête, quand tu étais outchitel.*[7] Where are my stockings? Well, help me get them on!'

She held out her truly delightful little foot, dusky, tiny, not misshapen like most feet that look so charming in shoes. I laughed and began to pull on her silk stocking. Mlle Blanche meanwhile sat on the bed and chattered away.

'*Eh bien, que feras-tu, si je te prends avec?* First of all, *je veux cinquante mille francs.* You can give them to me in

Frankfurt. *Nous allons à Paris*; we will live together there *et je te ferai voir des étoiles en plein jour.*[8] You will see such women, the like of which you have never seen. Listen . . .'

'Wait a minute, if I give you 50,000 francs, then what will be left for me?'

'*Et cent cinquante mille francs*, you've forgotten, and besides I agree to live with you in your apartment for a month or two, *que sais-je!* We, of course, will go through those 150,000 francs in two months. You see, *je suis bonne enfant* and I tell you beforehand, *mais tu verras des étoiles.*'[9]

'What, all of it in two months?'

'What! Does that horrify you! *Ah, vil esclave!* But do you know that one month of life like that is better than your whole existence. One month – *et après le deluge! Mais tu ne peux comprendre, va!* Off you go, off you go! You're not worthy! Oh, *que fais-tu?*'[10]

At that moment I was putting the stocking on her other foot, but I couldn't help myself and I kissed it. She pulled it away and began to hit me in the face with the tip of her toes. In the end, she chased me out altogether.

'*Eh bien, mon outchitel, je t'attends, si tu veux*;[11] I'm leaving in a quarter of an hour!' she called out after me.

Upon returning home, my head was already spinning. Now then, I was not to blame that Mlle Polina had thrown an entire packet in my face and as of yesterday preferred Mr Astley over me. Some of the banknotes that had been scattered about still lay on the floor; I picked them up. At that minute the door opened and the manager himself (who hadn't even wanted to look at me before) appeared with an invitation: Wouldn't I like to move downstairs into the magnificent rooms just vacated by Count V?

I stood there for a moment, thinking.

'My bill! I'm leaving now, in ten minutes,' I cried. 'If it's to be Paris, then Paris it is!' I thought to myself. 'Evidently, it was meant to be!'

A quarter of an hour later the three of us were indeed sitting in a family carriage: Mlle Blanche *et* Madame *veuve* Cominges and myself. Mlle Blanche laughed loudly, almost to the point of hysterics, as she looked at me. *Veuve* Cominges seconded her; I can't say that I was very cheerful. My life had been broken in two, but since yesterday I had already grown accustomed to betting everything I had on a single card. Perhaps it was indeed true that I was unable to take the money in stride and had lost my head. *Peut-être, je ne demandais pas mieux.*[12] It seemed that for a time – but only for a time – the scenery was being changed. 'But in a month I'll be here again and then . . . and then we'll be rivals once again, Mr Astley!' No, as I now recall, I was terribly sad even then, though I was laughing as loudly as that little fool Blanche.

'But what's the matter with you? How silly you are! Oh, how silly you are,' Blanche exclaimed, interrupting her laughter and beginning seriously to take me to task. 'Well, yes, well, yes, yes, we'll go through all of your 200,000 francs, but in return, *mais tu seras heureux, comme un petit roi*; I'll tie your necktie for you myself and introduce you to Hortense. And when we've gone through all your money, you'll come back here and break the bank again. What did those Jews say to you? The main thing is courage, and you have it, and you'll bring money to me in Paris more than once. *Quant à moi, je veux cinquante mille francs de rente et alors . . .*'[13]

'And what about the general?' I asked her.

'The general, as you know, every day at this hour goes to get me a bouquet. This time I deliberately requested that he find me some very rare flowers. The poor thing will return, and the little bird will have flown away. He'll come flying after us, you'll see. Ha-ha-ha! I'll be very glad. He'll be of use to me in Paris; Mr Astley will pay for his stay here . . .'

And that was how I came to set out for Paris then.

Chapter 16

What can I say about Paris? Of course, it was all delirium and folly. I spent just over three weeks in Paris, and in that time my hundred thousand francs were completely finished. I'm speaking only of the hundred thousand; the remaining hundred thousand I'd given Mlle Blanche in cash – fifty thousand in Frankfurt and three days later in Paris I gave her a promissory note for another 50,000 francs, which, however, she redeemed for cash from me a week later, '*et les cent mille francs, qui nous restent, tu les mangeras avec moi,*[1] *mon outchitel*'. She always called me tutor. It's difficult to imagine anything on this earth more conniving, mean and stingy than the class of creatures like Mlle Blanche. But that's only where spending her own money was concerned. As for my hundred thousand francs – she frankly announced to me later that she needed them for the initial costs of setting herself up in Paris. 'So that now I have begun in grand style once and for all, and nobody will knock me down for a long time – at least that's how I've arranged things,' she added. However, I hardly saw that hundred thousand; she kept the money the whole time, while my note-case, the contents of which she would apprise herself every day, never held more than a hundred francs, and almost always less than that.

'But what do you need money for?' she would say at times with the most guileless demeanour, and I didn't argue with her. But on the other hand, she put the finishing touches to her apartment very, very nicely with that money, and when she later took me to her new home and showed me the rooms, she said: 'You see what can be done with care and taste on the most paltry sums.' The price of this paltriness, however, was exactly 50,000 francs. She acquired horses and a carriage with the remaining 50,000;

moreover, we gave two balls, that is, two evening parties, which were attended by Hortense and Lisette and Cléopâtre – women remarkable in many, many respects and not at all bad looking. I was made to play the very foolish part of host at those two parties, to greet and entertain some nouveau riche and utterly dimwitted merchants, assorted, impossibly ignorant and shameless army lieutenants and pathetic little authors and journalistic vermin, who made their appearance in fashionable tailcoats, pale yellow gloves and with a sense of self-esteem and an arrogance of such proportions inconceivable even in Petersburg – and that's saying a great deal. They even took it into their heads to laugh at me, but I got drunk on the champagne and lay sprawled out in the back room. I found all this to be loathsome in the highest degree. 'C'est un outchitel,' Blanche would say about me, 'il a gagné deux cent mille francs[2] and without me he wouldn't know how to spend them. And afterwards he'll enter the ranks of tutors again; does anybody know of a position? Something must be done for him.' I began turning to champagne quite often, because I was invariably very sad and extremely bored. I lived in the most bourgeois, the most mercantile milieu, where every sou was counted and rationed out. Blanche didn't like me at all for the first two weeks, I noticed. True, she dressed me like a dandy and daily tied my necktie for me herself, but in her heart she frankly despised me. I didn't pay this the slightest attention. Bored and despondent, I started going to the Château des Fleurs, where I regularly got drunk every night and learned the cancan (which they dance vilely there) and even acquired some notoriety for this later on. Finally, Blanche figured me out: she had somehow earlier got the impression that during the entire period of our cohabitation I would walk behind her with pencil and paper in hand and would add up how much she had spent, how much she had stolen, how much she was going to spend and how much more she would steal. And, of course, she was sure that we would have rows over every ten francs. To my every assault, which she had pictured to herself beforehand, she had prepared her justification well in advance; but seeing that no assaults were forthcoming from me, she at first would launch into the justifications anyway. Sometimes she would begin ever so heatedly, but when she saw that I remained silent – more often than not I was lolling about on the couch and staring intently at the ceiling – she would end up being surprised. At first she thought that I was simply a fool, '*un outchitel*', and would simply break off her explanations, probably thinking to herself: 'After all, he's a fool; there's no reason to keep on about it if he doesn't understand.' She would leave, but sometimes ten minutes later would come back again – this happened during the period of her most frenzied spending, when she was spending completely beyond our means: for example, she changed her horses and bought a pair for 16,000 francs.

'Well, so, *bibi*, you're not angry?' she came up to me.

'No-o-o! I'm sick to death of you!' I said, waving her away with my hand, but she found this so curious that she immediately sat down beside me.

'You see, if I decided to pay so much it was only because they were such a bargain. They can be resold for 20,000 francs.'

'I believe you, I believe you; the horses are handsome; and now you have a splendid turnout; they'll come in handy; well and that's enough of that.'

'So you're not angry?'

'Why should I be? You're acting sensibly by providing yourself with some essential things. All this will come in handy later on. I see that you really need to put yourself on a footing like this; otherwise, you won't make your million. Our hundred thousand francs is only the beginning, a drop in the ocean.'

For Blanche, who had expected from me anything but reasoning like this (instead of shouts and incriminations!), this came like a bolt from the blue.

'So you... so that's what you're like! *Mais tu as de l'esprit pour comprendre! Sais-tu, mon garçon,*[3] even though you're a tutor – but you should have been born a prince! So you don't regret that the money is going so quickly?'

'Well, so what – the quicker the better!'

'*Mais ... sais-tu ... mais dis donc*, are you rich? *Mais sais-tu*, you see, you despise money too much. *Qu'est ce que tu feras après, dis donc?*'[4]

'*Après* I'll go to Homburg[5] and win another hundred thousand francs.'

'*Oui, oui, c'est ça, c'est magnifique!* And I know that you will win without fail and bring it here. *Dis donc*, and you'll make me really love you! *Eh bien*, for being like this I will love you the whole time and won't be unfaithful to you even once. You see, even though I didn't love you all this time, *parce que je croyais, que tu n'est qu'un outchitel (quelque chose comme un laquais, n'est-ce pas?)*, but nevertheless I have been faithful to you, *parce que je suis bonne fille.*'[6]

'Come on, you're lying! What about Albert, that swarthy little officer, do you think that I didn't see you last time?'

'*Oh, oh, mais tu es...*'

'Come on, you're lying, you're lying; and what do you think, that I'm angry? And to hell with it; *il faut que jeunesse se passe.*[7] You can't send him packing if he was here before me and you love him. Just don't give him any money, do you hear?'

'So you're not angry about that either? *Mais tu es un vrai philosophe, sais-tu? Un vrai philosophe!*' she exclaimed ecstatically. '*Eh bien, je t'aimerai, je t'aimerai – tu verras, tu sera content!*'[8]

And indeed, from that time on she really did seem to

become somewhat attached to me, even friendly, and that was how our last ten days passed. I didn't see any of the promised 'stars'; but in certain respects she really did keep her word. What is more, she introduced me to Hortense, who was quite a remarkable woman in her own way, and whom our circle had dubbed *Thérèse-philosophe*[9] . . .

However, there's no need to enlarge on that; it might make a story on its own, with its own colouring, which I don't want to insert into this tale. The fact of the matter is that I wished with all my might that it would all end as quickly as possible. But our hundred thousand francs sufficed, as I said earlier, for almost a month, which genuinely surprised me: at the very least, Blanche spent 80,000 of that money buying things for herself, and we lived on no more than 20,000 francs and – nevertheless it sufficed. Blanche, who towards the end was almost candid with me (at least she wasn't lying to me about some things), owned up that at least the debts that she had been forced to incur wouldn't fall on me. 'I didn't have you sign any of the bills or notes,' she said to me, 'because I felt sorry for you; another woman would certainly have done so and got you sent to prison. You see, you see how much I love you and how good I am! This damned wedding alone is going to cost me a lot!'

We really did have a wedding. It took place at the very end of our month together, and it may be assumed that the very last dregs of my hundred thousand francs went to pay for it; that was the end of the business, that is, that was how our month together ended, after which I formally retired.

This was what happened: the general arrived a week after we settled in Paris. He came straight to Blanche and from the very first visit all but lived with us. He had, it's true, a little apartment of his own somewhere. Blanche greeted him joyfully, with shrieks and laughter, and even rushed to embrace him; it transpired that she wouldn't let go of him and he had to follow her around everywhere: on the boulevard, riding in the carriage, to the theatre and to visit acquaintances. The general was still fit for such things; he was rather imposing and decent looking – almost tall, with dyed side whiskers and moustaches (he had served in the Cuirassiers),[10] with a distinguished face, although it was somewhat flabby. His manners were impeccable, a tailcoat sat well on him. In Paris he started wearing his decorations. With such a man not only was it possible to take a stroll on the boulevard, but if one may put it like this, it's even to be *recommended*. The good and clueless general was terribly pleased by all this; he hadn't counted on it at all when he came to see us on his arrival in Paris. He made his appearance practically shaking with fear; he thought that Blanche would start shouting and order that he be sent packing; and that's why when things worked out as they did, he went into raptures and spent the whole of that month in a state of inane rapture; and that was how I left him. It was here that I learned the details of what happened to him after our sudden departure from Roulettenburg – that very same morning he had some sort of fit. He fell unconscious, and then for a whole week was almost like a raving madman. He was under the care of doctors, but he suddenly stopped all that, got on the train and turned up in Paris. It goes without saying, Blanche's reception proved to be the very best medicine for him; but symptoms of his illness lingered long afterwards, despite his joyful and rapturous state of mind. He was utterly incapable of reasoning or even of carrying on any sort of mildly serious conversation; in such instances, he would merely keep repeating 'Hm!' to every word that was said and nodding his head – that was how he would get out of it. He often laughed, but it was a nervous, unhealthy laugh, as if he were about to go off into uncontrolled peals; sometimes he would sit for hours on end as dark as night, knitting his bushy eyebrows. There was a lot that he did not even remember; he had become dreadfully absent-minded and had adopted the habit of talking to himself. Blanche was the only one who could breathe some life into him; and the fits of dark and gloom, when he would hide himself in the corner, merely signified that he had not seen Blanche for a long time, or that Blanche had gone somewhere and not taken him with her, or, that as she was leaving, she hadn't cosseted him. At the same time, he wouldn't say what he wanted, and didn't know himself that he was dark and sad. After sitting for an hour or two (I observed this twice, when Blanche had gone out for the whole day, probably to see Albert), he suddenly began to look about, started fussing, stole a glance over his shoulder and tried to recall something, as if he were searching for somebody; but not seeing anybody and not recalling what he wanted to ask, he would fall back into oblivion until Blanche herself would suddenly appear, gay, frisky, all dressed up, with her ringing laugh; she would run up to him and begin to pester and even to kiss him, which was something, however, she rarely granted. Once the general was so delighted that he even burst into tears – I was even surprised.

From the very moment of his arrival, Blanche had immediately begun to plead his case before me. She even waxed eloquent; she reminded me that she had been unfaithful to the general because of me, that she had almost been his fiancée, that she had given him her word; that because of her he had abandoned his family and that, finally, I had been in his employ and I ought to appreciate this, and that – I ought to be ashamed . . . I kept my silence, while she chattered on terribly. Finally, I burst out laughing, and with that the matter came to an end; that is, first she thought that I was a fool, but towards the end she settled on the notion that I was a very good and sensible person. In a word, towards the end I had the good fortune to earn without reservation the good favour of this worthy young lady. (Blanche, however, really was a very kind girl – but in her own way, it goes without saying; I didn't appreciate her at first.) 'You are an intelligent and kind man,' she would say towards the end, 'and . . . and . . . it's just a pity that you're such a fool! You'll never, never make your fortune!'

'*Un vrai russe, un calmouk!*'[11] She sent me several times to take the general out for a walk, exactly as if she were sending a lackey to walk her greyhound. I, however, took him to the theatre, the Bal Mabille[12] and restaurants. Blanche would give me money for this, even though the general had his own and liked taking out his note-case in front of people a great deal. Once I almost had to use force to keep him from spending 700 francs on a brooch that tempted him in the Palais Royal and which he wanted to make a present of to Blanche in the worst way. Well, what was a seven-hundred-franc brooch to her? And the general didn't have more than a thousand francs altogether. I never did find out where he got it from. I suppose from Mr Astley, seeing as he had paid their hotel bill. As far as the general's disposition towards me during this whole period is concerned, I don't believe that he even suspected my relationship with Blanche. Although he had heard somewhat vaguely that I had won a fortune, he probably supposed that I was some kind of private secretary to Blanche or perhaps even her servant. In any event, he invariably spoke with me just as condescendingly as before, was just as overbearing, and sometimes even ventured to blow up at me. Once he made me and Blanche laugh an awful lot as we were having our morning coffee. He wasn't a person quick to take offence; and here he'd suddenly taken offence at me, for what? – I still don't understand. But, of course, he didn't understand himself. In a word, he launched into a speech without beginning or end, *à batons-rompus*,[13] shouting that I was just a little boy, he would teach me... he would make me understand... and so on and so forth. But nobody could understand a thing he said. Blanche broke out into peals of laughter; finally, he was placated somehow or other and taken out for a walk. On many occasions, however, I noticed that he would become sad, that he felt sorry for someone and about something, that he missed someone, even despite the presence of Blanche. A couple of times during moments like these he started talking to me, but could never make himself understood; he would recall his military service, his late wife, his family, his estate. He'd hit on a certain word and be delighted with it, and repeat it a hundred times a day, even though it did not in the least express either his feelings or his thoughts. I tried to talk with him about his children; but he evaded the questions with a bit of his former prattling – 'Yes, yes! The children, you're right, the children!' – and quickly changed the subject. Only once did he become deeply moved – we were on our way to the theatre: 'Those poor children!' he said suddenly, 'yes, sir, yes, those poor, poor children!' And several times later that same evening he repeated the words: 'poor children!' When I once brought up the subject of Polina, he became enraged. 'She's an ungrateful woman,' he exclaimed, 'she's wicked and ungrateful! She has brought disgrace on the family! If there were laws here, I would make her knuckle under! Yes, sir, yes!' As far as des Grieux was concerned, he couldn't even bear to hear his name. 'He ruined me,' he would say, 'he robbed me blind, he was my undoing! He's been my nightmare for two whole years now! I have dreamed of him for whole months on end! He's – he's a... Oh, never speak of him to me.'

I saw that things were going well for them, but as usual

I kept my silence. Blanche was the first to declare herself: this was exactly a week before we parted ways.

'*Il a de la chance*,' she chattered away to me. '*Babouchka* really is ill now and will certainly die. Mr Astley sent a telegram; you must admit that still and all he's her heir. And even if he weren't, he won't hinder me in any way. First of all, he has his own pension, and second, he'll live in the spare room and be perfectly happy. I will be "Madame la Générale". I will get into a good circle,' (Blanche dreamed about that constantly), 'and later I'll be a Russian landowner, *j'aurai un château, des moujiks, et puis j'aurai toujours mon million*.'[14]

'Well, and what if he starts getting jealous, demands... God knows what – do you understand?'

'Oh, no, *non, non, non*! He wouldn't dare! I've taken measures, don't worry. I have already had him sign several promissory notes of Albert's. The littlest thing – and he'll be punished at once; but he wouldn't dare!'

'Well, marry him...'

The wedding took place without any particular fanfare, a quiet family affair. Albert and a few other close friends were invited. Hortense, Cléopâtre and the others were very definitely kept away. The fiancé was extremely interested in his position. Blanche tied his necktie herself, and pomaded his hair; and he looked *très comme il faut* in his tails and white waistcoat.

'*Il est pourtant très comme il faut*,'[15] Blanche announced to me, as she was leaving the general's room, as if the idea that the general should be *très comme il faut* surprised even her. I entered into the details so little, taking part in all this only in the capacity of idle spectator, that I have forgotten a lot of what transpired. I remember only that Blanche turned out not to be de Cominges at all, just as her mother was not *veuve* Cominges, but du Placet. Why they both had been de Cominges up to this point – I do not know. But the general was very pleased by this as well, and he liked du Placet even more than de Cominges. On the morning of the wedding, after he was dressed, he kept pacing back and forth in the hall and repeating to himself, with an unusually serious and weighty air: 'Mlle Blanche du Placet! Blanche du Placet! Du Placet! Miss Blanche du Placet! ...' And a certain complacency shone on his face. In the church, at the mayor's and at home over the *zakuski*,[16] he was not only joyful and pleased, but even proud. Something had happened to both of them. Blanche, too, had started to have a special dignity about her.

'I now need to behave completely differently,' she said to me extremely seriously. '*Mais vois-tu*, I hadn't thought of one horrible thing: just think, I still haven't learned my new surname: Zagoryansky, Zagoziansky, madame le générale de Sago-Sago, *ces diables des noms russes, enfin madame la générale à quatorze consonnes! Comme c'est agréable, n'est-ce pas?*'[17]

Finally, we parted, and Blanche, that silly Blanche, even shed a few tears as she said goodbye to me. '*Tu étais bon enfant*,' she said, whimpering. '*Je te croyais bête es tu en avais l'air*, but it suits you.' And, after shaking my hand for the last time, she suddenly exclaimed: '*Attends!*', and rushed to her boudoir and a minute later brought me two thousand-franc notes. I would never have believed it possible! 'This will come in handy, you might be a very learned *outchitel*, but you're a terribly foolish man. I won't give you more than 2,000 under any circumstances, because you'll only squander it gambling. Well, goodbye! *Nous seron toujours bons amis*, and if you win again, come see me without fail, *et tu seras heureux!*'[18]

I still had about 500 francs left myself; besides, I had a magnificent watch worth a thousand francs, diamond studs and so forth, which I could stretch out for a rather long time without worrying. I deliberately settled down in this little town to catch my breath and, above all, to wait for Mr Astley. I had found out for certain that he would travel through here and stay for a day on business. I'll find out about everything . . . and then – then straight to Homburg. I won't go to Roulettenburg, except maybe next year. Indeed, they say that it's a bad omen to try your luck twice in a row at the same table, and the real gambling is in Homburg.

Chapter 17

It's already been a year and eight months since I've taken a look at these notes, and only now, in anguish and sorrow, did I take it into my head to read through them to amuse myself. So I stopped them then when I was about to go to Homburg. My God! With what a light heart, comparatively speaking, did I write those last lines! That is, not so much a light heart, but with what confidence and what unshakeable hopes! Did I have any doubts whatsoever about myself? And now more than a year and a half has gone by and, in my opinion, I'm far worse off than a beggar! What am I saying – beggar! To hell with beggary! I've simply ruined myself. However, there's almost nothing to compare it with, and it's no use giving myself a lecture on morals. Nothing could be more ridiculous than a morality lecture at a time like this! Oh, self-satisfied people: with what proud self-satisfaction are these chatterboxes ready to deliver their sententious lectures! If they knew to what extent I myself understand the complete loathsomeness of my present situation, then of course they wouldn't be able to bring themselves to lecture me. Well, what, what can they tell me that I don't know? And is that really the point? The point here is that everything changes with one turn of the wheel, and these same moralists will be the first (I'm sure of it) to come and congratulate me with their friendly jokes. And they won't all turn away from me like they do now. But to hell with them all! What am I now? *Zéro*. What can I be tomorrow? Tomorrow I may rise from the dead and begin a new life! I may find the man in me, before he's done for!

I really did go to Homburg then, but ... afterwards I was in Roulettenburg again, and in Spa, I was even in Baden, where I went as valet to Councillor Hintze, a scoundrel and my former master here. Yes, I was even a lackey for five whole months! That happened right after prison. (You see, I was in prison in Roulettenburg for a debt of mine here. An unknown person bought me out of prison – who was it? Mr Astley? Polina? I don't know, but the debt was paid, 200 thalers in all, and I was set free.) Where was I to go? And so I started working for this Hintze. He's a young and frivolous man, likes to laze about, and I know how to speak and write in three languages. At first I worked as some sort of secretary, for thirty gulden a month; but I ended up working as a real lackey: he found that he didn't have the means to employ a secretary, and so he reduced my salary; I didn't have anywhere to go and so I stayed – and thus became a lackey through my own doing. I didn't have enough to eat or drink, but on the other hand I saved up 70 gulden in five months. One evening, in Baden, I announced to him that I wished to part with him; that same evening I set off for the roulette table. Oh, how my heart pounded! No, it was not the money that was dear to me! Then I merely wanted all these Hintzes, all these hotel managers, all these magnificent Baden ladies to talk about me the next day, tell my story, marvel at me, praise me and admire me for my new winnings. All this is childish dreams and cares, but ... who knows; maybe I would meet Polina, I would tell her everything and she would see that I was above all these ridiculous strokes of fate . . . Oh, it wasn't the money that was dear to me! I'm sure that I would have squandered it on some Blanche again and would have driven around Paris again for three weeks with a pair of my own horses that cost 16,000 francs. You see, I know for certain that I'm not stingy; I even think that I'm extravagant – but meanwhile, with what trembling, with what a sinking heart do I hear the croupier's cry: *trente et un, rouge, impaire et pass!* or: *quatre, noir, pair et manque!* With what avidity do I look at the gaming table on which lie scattered louis d'or, friedrichs d'or and thalers, at the little piles of gold as they fall from the croupier's shovel in heaps of burning fire, or at the two-foot-long pillars of silver that lie around the wheel. As I am still making my way to the gaming room, I almost go into convulsions two rooms away, when I hear the clink of the money as it is being poured out.

Oh, that evening when I took my seventy gulden to the gaming table was also remarkable. I began with ten gulden on *passe* again. I have a partiality for *passe*. I lost. I had sixty gulden in silver coins left; I gave it some thought – and decided on *zéro*. I started by staking five gulden at a time on *zéro*; *zéro* came up on the third stake; I almost died with happiness, when I got 175 gulden; I wasn't this happy when I'd won 100,000 gulden. I at once staked 100 gulden on *rouge* – and won; all 200 on *rouge* – and won; all 400 on *noir* – and won; all 800 on *manque* – and won; counting what I had before there were 1,700 gulden, and this was in less than five minutes! Yes, at such moments you forget all your previous failures! You see, I obtained this by risking more than life, I had dared to take a risk and – now again I was a man among men!

I took a room, locked myself in and until three o'clock sat there counting my money. That morning I was no longer a lackey when I woke up. I decided to leave that very day for Homburg: I hadn't been a lackey in service there, or in prison. A half-hour before the train I set off to place two stakes, no more, and I lost 1,500 florins. However, I moved to Homburg all the same and it's a month I've been here now . . .

Of course, I live in constant anxiety, I play for the smallest stakes and wait for something; I make calculations, I stand for days on end by the gaming table and *observe* the play, I even see them playing in my sleep, but all that notwithstanding I seem to have become numb, as it were, as if I'd become mired in some sort of mud. I conclude this on the basis of my impressions on meeting Mr Astley. We had not seen each other since that time, and met by chance; this is how it was. I was walking in the garden and had figured that I had almost no money left, but I did have fifty gulden, and besides, the day before yesterday I had paid my bill in full at the hotel where I occupied a closet of a room. And so I had only one more opportunity to go to the roulette tables – if I won something at least, I could continue playing; if I lost – I'd need to go back to being a lackey again if I didn't right away find some Russians who could use a tutor. Engrossed in these thoughts, I went out for my daily walk through the park and the forest, to the neighbouring principality. Sometimes I would walk like this for four hours at a time and return to Homburg exhausted and famished. I had just left the garden and was entering the park when I suddenly espied Mr Astley on the bench. He had noticed me first and called out to me. I sat down beside him. Noticing a certain reserve about him, I at once restrained my gladness; but I was terribly happy to see him.

'So then, you're here! I thought that I would run across you,' he said to me. 'Don't bother telling me your story: I know, I know everything; your whole life this past year and eight months is known to me.'

'Well, you certainly keep track of your friends!' I responded. 'It does you credit that you don't forget... Wait a minute, however, you've given me an idea: was it you who bought me out of prison in Roulettenburg, where I was being held for a debt of 200 gulden? An anonymous person paid my debt.'

'No, oh, no; I did not buy you out of prison in Roulettenburg, where you were being held for a debt of 200 gulden, but I knew that you were being held in prison for a debt of 200 gulden.'

'That means you nevertheless know who paid my debt?'

'Oh, no, I can't say that I do.'

'Strange; none of our Russians knows me, and the Russians here likely wouldn't pay my debt; that happens there, in Russia, when the Orthodox take care of their fellow Orthodox. And so I thought that some eccentric Englishman did it on a whim.'

Mr Astley listened to me with some surprise. I believe he thought that he would find me dejected and crushed.

'However, I'm very glad to see that you've retained in full all your independence of spirit and even cheerfulness,' he uttered with a rather unpleasant air.

'That is, you're racked with vexation on the inside that I'm not crushed and not humiliated,' I said, laughing.

He didn't understand right away, but once he did, he smiled.

'I like your remarks. I recognize in these words my former intelligent, old, enthusiastic and at the same time cynical friend; some Russians can encompass, at one and the same time, so many contradictions. Indeed, a person likes to see his best friend humiliated before him; a large part of friendship is based on humiliation; and all intelligent people know this old truth. But in the present instance, I assure you, I am sincerely happy that you are not dejected. Tell me, don't you intend to quit gambling?'

'Oh, the devil take it! I'd quit right now, if only . . .'

'If only you could win back what you've lost? I thought so; don't bother finishing what you were going to say – I know you said it unintentionally, and consequently, you spoke the truth. Tell me, apart from gambling, do you have any other occupation?'

'Nothing . . .'

He began to put me through an examination. I had scarcely glanced at the newspapers and positively not cracked open a single book.

'You've become apathetic,' he observed, 'not only have you renounced life, your interests both personal and social, your duty as a man and a citizen, your friends (and all the same you did have friends); not only have you renounced any goal whatsoever, apart from winning, you have even renounced your own memories. I remember you at an ardent and intense moment of your life; but I'm certain that you've forgotten all your best impressions of that time; your dreams, your most urgent desires now don't go further than *pair* and *impair*, *rouge*, *noir*, the twelve middle numbers and so forth and so on, I'm certain of it!'

'Enough, Mr Astley, please, please, don't remind me,' I cried out in vexation and almost with malice. 'You should know that I have forgotten absolutely nothing; but I merely have driven all this out of my head, even my memories – for the time being, until I radically improve my circumstances; then . . . then you will see, I will rise up from the dead!'

'You will still be here in ten years' time,' he said. 'I'll wager that I will remind you of this, if I am alive, right here on this very bench.'

'Well, that's enough,' I broke in with some impatience, 'and to prove to you that I'm not so forgetful of the past, allow me to ask: where is Miss Polina now? If it wasn't you who paid my debt, then it must certainly have been she. I have had no news of her since that time.'

'No, oh, no! I don't think that it was she who paid your debt. She's in Switzerland now, and you would be doing me a great favour if you stopped asking me about Miss Polina,' he said resolutely and even angrily.

'That means that she must have hurt you very badly as well!' I began to laugh involuntarily.

'Miss Polina is the best being of all beings who are most worthy of respect, but I repeat, you would be doing me a big favour if you stopped asking me about Miss Polina. You never knew her and I consider her name on your lips to be an insult to my moral sensibilities.'

'So that's how it is! However, you're wrong; and judge for yourself – what else is there for me to talk to you about besides that? You see, all our memories consist of nothing else. However, don't worry, I don't need to know your inner, secret affairs . . . I'm only interested in Miss Polina's external situation, as it were, only her present outward circumstances. That can be conveyed in a few words.'

'All right, on the condition that it ends with these few words. Miss Polina was ill for a long time; she's ill now too; she lived for a while with my mother and sister in northern England. Six months ago her grandmother – you remember that crazy woman – died and left her, personally, a fortune of 7,000 pounds. Miss Polina is now travelling with my married sister's family. Her little brother and sister were also provided for by the grandmother's will and are studying in London. The general, her stepfather, died of a stroke a month ago in Paris. Mlle Blanche treated him well, but she managed to have transferred to her own name all that he received from the grandmother . . . there, that seems to be everything.'

'And des Grieux? Isn't he travelling in Switzerland as well?'

'No, des Grieux is not travelling in Switzerland, and I do not know where des Grieux is; moreover, I warn you once and for all to avoid such remarks and ignoble associations, otherwise you will definitely have to answer to me.'

'What! Despite our former friendly relations?'

'Yes, despite our former friendly relations.'

'I beg your pardon a thousand times, Mr Astley. But allow me nonetheless: there's nothing insulting or ignoble about it; you see I do not blame Miss Polina for anything. Moreover, a Frenchman and a Russian young lady, generally speaking, is an association, Mr Astley, the likes of which neither you nor I could explain or fully understand.'

'If you will not mention the name of des Grieux together with that other name, then I would ask you to explain to me what you mean by the expression: "a Frenchman and a Russian young lady"? What is this "association"? Why is it precisely a Frenchman and why without fail a Russian young lady?'

'You see, you are interested. But it's a lengthy subject, Mr Astley. You need to know a lot beforehand. However, it's an important question – no matter how ridiculous it looks at first glance. The Frenchman, Mr Astley, is a finished, beautiful form. You, as a Briton, may disagree with this; I, as a Russian, also disagree, well, maybe, from envy; but our young ladies are of a different opinion. You might find Racine[1] unnatural, distorted and perfumed; you probably wouldn't even bother to read him. I also find him unnatural, distorted and perfumed, and even ridiculous from a certain point of view; but he is delightful, Mr Astley, and the main thing, he is a great poet, whether we like it or not. The national form of a Frenchman, that is, a Parisian, began to develop its elegant form when we were still bears. The Revolution succeeded the nobility. Now the most vulgar little Frenchy can have manners, methods, expressions and even thoughts quite elegant in form, without taking part in this form through his own initiative, or his soul or his heart; all this comes to him by way of inheritance. Of course, they may be shallower than the shallowest and more base than the basest. Well, Mr Astley, I tell you now that there is not a being in the world more trusting and open than a good, bright and not too affected Russian young lady. Des Grieux, by appearing in some role, by appearing masked, can conquer her heart with unusual ease; he has an elegant form, Mr Astley, and the young lady takes this form to be his real soul, the natural form of his heart and soul, and not garments that came to him by way of inheritance. To your great displeasure, I must declare to you that Englishmen, by and large, are awkward and inelegant, and Russians can discern beauty rather deftly and have a weakness for it. But to discern a beautiful soul and original personality, one needs incomparably more independence and freedom than our women have, especially the young ladies – and, in any event, more experience. Now Miss Polina – forgive me, you can't take back what's been said – needs a very, very long time to make up her mind to prefer you to that scoundrel des Grieux. She will appreciate you, become your friend, open up her heart to you; but nevertheless the loathsome scoundrel, the nasty and petty moneylender des Grieux will reign in her heart. This will even persist, so to speak, out of stubbornness and pride alone, because this same des Grieux appeared to her once with the halo of an elegant marquis, a disillusioned liberal who brought ruin upon himself (supposedly?) by helping her family and the frivolous general. All these shams were revealed afterwards. But it doesn't matter that they were revealed: all the same, give her the former des Grieux now – that's what she wants! And the more she hates the present des Grieux, the more she yearns for the former one, even though the former existed only in her imagination. You're a sugar refiner, aren't you Mr Astley?'

'Yes, I'm a partner in the well-known sugar refinery Lowell and Co.'

'Well, then, you see, Mr Astley. On the one hand you have a sugar refiner, and on the other Apollo Belvedere;[2] they have nothing in common. And I'm not even a sugar refiner; I'm simply a petty gambler at the roulette table, and I was even a lackey, which is probably already known to Miss Polina, because she seems to have good detectives.'

'You're embittered, and that's why you're talking all this nonsense,' Mr Astley said coolly, after giving it some thought. 'Besides, your words lack originality.'

'I agree! But that's precisely what's so terrible, my noble friend, that all these accusations of mine, no matter how out-of-date, however banal, however vaudevillian – they are true nevertheless! You and I have nevertheless achieved nothing!'

'That's vile nonsense... because, because... See here now!' Mr Astley uttered in a trembling voice, his eyes flashing. 'See here now, you ignoble and unworthy, petty and unfortunate man, I have come to Homburg expressly at her bidding in order to see you, to have a long heart-to-heart talk with you, and to convey to her everything – your feelings, thoughts, hopes and ... memories!'

'Really! Really?' I cried and the tears flowed from my eyes in torrents. I couldn't hold them back and I believe this was the first time it happened in my life.

'Yes, you unfortunate man, she loved you, and I can reveal that to you, because you are a ruined man! What's more, even if I were to tell you that she loves you to this day, you would remain here all the same! Yes, you have brought ruin upon yourself. You had certain abilities, a lively nature, and you weren't a bad fellow; you might even have proved useful to your fatherland, which is in such need of men, but you will remain here and your life is over.

THE GAMBLER

I do not blame you. As I see it, all Russians are like that or inclined to be so. If it's not roulette, then it's something else like it. Exceptions are rare. You are not the first not to understand what work is (I'm not speaking about your peasants). Roulette for the most part is a Russian game. So far you have been honest and would rather become a lackey than steal . . . but I dread to think what it will be like in the future. Enough, goodbye! You, of course, need money? Here are ten louis d'or from me, I won't give you any more, because you'll gamble it away all the same. Take it and goodbye! Now take it!'

'No, Mr Astley, after all that has been just said . . .'

'T-a-k-e it!' he cried. 'I'm convinced that you are still a noble person and I give this to you as one true friend to another. If I could be certain that you would quit gambling, leave Homburg and go to your fatherland – I would be prepared to give you a thousand pounds at once so that you might begin a new career. But I'm not giving you a thousand pounds, but only ten louis d'or, precisely because at the present time it's absolutely one and the same to you – you'll gamble it away all the same. Take it and goodbye.'

'I'll take it if you'll permit me to embrace you at parting.'

'Oh, with pleasure.'

We embraced sincerely, and Mr Astley walked away.

No, he's wrong! If I was harsh and foolish about Polina and des Grieux, then he was sharp and rash about Russians. I won't say anything about myself. However . . . however, for the time being all this is beside the point. All this is words, words and words, when it's action that is called for! Now the main thing is Switzerland! Tomorrow first thing – oh, if only it were possible to set out tomorrow! To be reborn, to rise up from the dead. I need to show them . . . To let Polina know that I can still be a man. All I need to do is . . . now, however, it's late – but tomorrow . . .

Oh, I have a presentiment and it can't be otherwise! I now have fifteen louis d'or, and I began with fifteen gulden! If one begins carefully... And really, really, am I such a baby! Do I really not understand that I am a ruined man. But – why shouldn't I rise up from the dead? Yes! All it would take is just once in my life to be careful and patient and – and that's all there is to it! All it would take is to stand firm just once, and I can change my whole destiny in a single hour! The main thing is standing firm. Just remember what happened to me in similar circumstances seven months ago in Roulettenburg, before my final loss. Oh, that was a remarkable instance of resolve: I had lost everything, everything... I'm leaving the casino, and I see that I still have a single gulden knocking about in my waistcoat pocket. 'Ah, so I'll be able to buy myself some dinner!' I thought, but after taking about a hundred steps, I changed my mind and went back. I staked that gulden on *manque* (this time it was *manque*), and there really is something peculiar in the feeling, when you're alone, in a foreign country, far from your native land and friends, and you don't know if you're going to eat that day, you stake your last gulden, the very, very last one! I won and twenty minutes later I walked out of the casino with 170 gulden in my pocket. That is a fact, sir! That's what your last gulden can mean sometimes! And what if I had lost heart, if I hadn't dared to bring myself to do it?...

Tomorrow, tomorrow it will all be over!

1866

A Nasty Business

A Story

This nasty business took place just at the time when the renaissance of our beloved fatherland[1] was beginning with such irrepressible force and with such touchingly naive fervour, when all its valiant sons were seeking new destinies and hopes. Then, one winter, on a clear and frosty night, even though it was already past eleven, three extremely respectable gentlemen were sitting in a comfortable and even elegantly appointed room, in a handsome two-storey house on the Petersburg Side,[2] and they were engaged in a solid and superior conversation on quite an interesting subject. All three of these gentlemen held the rank of general.[3] They were sitting around a little table, each in a fine, soft armchair, quietly and comfortably sipping champagne as they talked. The bottle stood on the table in a silver bucket filled with ice. The fact of the matter was that the host, Privy Councillor Stepan Nikiforovich Nikiforov, an old bachelor of about sixty-five, was celebrating moving into his recently purchased house and, incidentally, his birthday, which fell at the same time and which he had never celebrated before. However, the celebration was nothing special; as we have seen, there were only two guests, both of them former colleagues and former subordinates of Mr Nikiforov, to wit: Actual State Councillor[4] Semyon Ivanovich Shipulenko and the other, also an actual state councillor, Ivan Ilyich Pralinsky. They had arrived at about nine o'clock, had tea, then switched to wine, and they knew that at exactly half past eleven they would need to start for home. The host had loved regularity all his life. A couple of words about him: he had begun his career as a petty civil servant without means, quietly performed his drudgery for some forty-five years, knew very well what rank he would have when he finished his service, could not bear it when people tried to reach for the stars, even though he already had two,[5] and particularly disliked voicing his own personal opinion on any subject whatsoever. He was honest as well, that is, he had never had to do anything particularly dishonest; he was a bachelor because he was an egoist; he was far from stupid but couldn't bear displaying his intelligence; he particularly disliked slovenliness and enthusiasm – believing it to be moral slovenliness – and towards the end of his life he had completely sunk into some sort of sweet, lazy comfort and systematic solitude. Although he did sometimes visit people of the better sort, ever since he was a young man he couldn't bear having guests at his place, and lately if he didn't lay out a game of grand-patience,[6] he would content himself with the society of his mantel clock and for whole evenings on end would placidly listen to it tick under its glass shade on the fireplace, while dozing in his armchair. He was clean-shaven and quite respectable in appearance, looked younger than his years, was well preserved, promised to live for a long time yet and adhered to the strictest gentlemanliness. He had a rather comfortable position: he sat on some commission and signed some things. In a word, he was considered a most outstanding man. He had only one passion or, rather, one burning desire: to have his own house, and precisely one built like a manor house and not an apartment block. This desire at last was fulfilled: he had found and bought a house on the Petersburg Side; true, it was rather far away,[7] but the house had a garden and, moreover, was elegant. The new owner judged that it was just as well that it was a bit further out: he didn't like receiving guests, and for visiting somebody or going to the office he had a handsome, chocolate-coloured two-seat carriage, Mikhey the coachman and a pair of small, but strong and handsome horses. All this had been acquired by forty years of fastidious economy, so that his heart rejoiced at it all. That is why after acquiring the house and moving into it, Stepan Nikiforovich felt such contentment in his tranquil heart that he even invited guests on his birthday, which before he had scrupulously kept secret from his closest acquaintances. He even had special designs on one of those he had invited. He himself occupied the top floor of the house, while the lower floor, which was built and laid out identically, required a tenant. Stepan Nikiforovich was counting on Semyon Ivanovich Shipulenko and that evening had even brought up the subject twice. But Semyon Ivanovich had kept silent on that matter. He was also a man who had made his way with difficulty and over a long period, with black hair and side whiskers and with the complexion of one who has constant bilious attacks. He was married, was a morose stay-at-home, kept his household in a state of fear, performed his duties with self-confidence; he, too, knew very well how far he would go, and what's even better – that he would go no further; he held a good position and held it firmly. Even though he regarded the incipient new order not without bile, he wasn't particularly alarmed: he was very sure of himself and listened to Ivan Ilyich Pralinsky's lofty words on the new ideas not without derisive malice. However, all of them were a bit tipsy, so much so that even Stepan Nikiforovich himself condescended to engage in a small debate with Mr Pralinsky about the new order. But a few words about His Excellency Mr Pralinsky, all the more so as it is he who is the main character of the forthcoming story.

Actual State Councillor Ivan Ilyich Pralinsky had been called His Excellency for all of four months, in a word, he was a young general. He was still young in years as well, about forty-three and certainly no more than that, and he looked and liked looking even younger than he was. He was a handsome man, tall, flaunted his clothes and the refined respectability of his choice in clothes, wore a significant order on his neck with great skill, and from childhood had known how to acquire some high-society ways and, being a bachelor, dreamed of a wealthy and even high-society wife. He dreamed about a great deal besides, though he was far from stupid. At times he talked big and even liked to assume parliamentary poses. He came from a good family, was the son of a general and never had to dirty his hands with physical work; in his tender childhood he wore velvet and cambric, was educated in an aristocratic institution; and although he didn't carry much knowledge away with him, he had enjoyed success in his career and was made a general. His superiors considered him to be a capable man and even pinned their hopes on him. Stepan Nikiforovich, under whose command he had begun and then continued his service almost until he was made a general, never considered him a very businesslike man and pinned no hopes on him whatsoever. But he liked the fact that he was from a good family, had a fortune – that is, a large apartment house with a manager – was related to some of the best people and, on top of that, possessed a certain bearing. Stepan Nikiforovich silently criticized him for excess imagination and flippancy. Ivan Ilyich himself sometimes felt that he was too proud and even testy. Strangely enough, at times he had morbid attacks of conscientiousness and even some slight regret for something. With bitterness and a secret nagging in his heart, he sometimes admitted to himself that he had not flown as high as he had thought he would. At moments like these he would even sink into some sort of despondency, particularly when his haemorrhoids played up, and call his life *une existence manquée*, stop believing even in his parliamentary abilities – silently it goes without saying – and call himself a *parleur*, a *phraseur*,[8] and although all this, of course, was much to his credit, it in no way prevented him from raising his head again half an hour later and even more obstinately and more arrogantly taking heart, and assuring himself that he would still manage to prove himself and that he would not only be a high official but even a statesman whom Russia would long remember. At times he even imagined monuments. From this one can see that Ivan Ilyich aimed high, although he hid his vague dreams and hopes deep within himself, even with a certain amount of fear. In a word, he was a good man and even had the soul of a poet. In recent years, painful moments of disappointment had begun to visit him more frequently. He had become somehow particularly irritable, suspicious and quick to view any objection as an insult. But the revitalization of Russia had suddenly given him high hopes. Making general had been the finishing touch. He took heart; he raised his head. He suddenly began to speak eloquently and a great deal, to talk on the newest subjects, which he extremely quickly and unexpectedly mastered until they became a passion. He sought out opportunities to speak, travelled all over the city and in many places succeeded in being accorded the reputation of a desperate liberal, which gratified him a great deal. On this evening, having drunk some four glasses, he was particularly expansive. He wanted to persuade Stepan Nikiforovich, whom he had not seen for a long time and whom he had hitherto always respected and even obeyed, to change his mind about everything. For some reason he considered him a retrograde and attacked him with uncommon ardour. Stepan Nikiforovich raised almost no objections, merely listened slyly, even though the subject interested him. Ivan Ilyich got excited and in the heat of the imaginary argument sipped from his glass more frequently than he should have. Then Stepan Nikiforovich would take the bottle and at once fill his glass, which for some unknown reason, suddenly began to offend Ivan Ilyich, all the more so because Semyon Ivanych Shipulenko, whom he particularly despised and moreover even feared for his cynicism and malice, sat there right beside him keeping his silence most insidiously, and smiling more often than he should have. 'It seems they take me for a little boy,' flashed in Ivan Ilyich's head.

'No, sir, it's time, it's already high time,' he continued with fervour. 'It's long overdue, sir, and in my opinion humaneness is the first thing, humaneness towards one's subordinates, remembering that they, too, are people. Humaneness will save everything and set everything on the right path . . .'

'He-he-he-he!' could be heard from Semyon Ivanovich's direction.

'But why is it that you're giving us such a tongue-lashing?' Stepan Nikiforovich finally objected, smiling amiably. 'I confess, Ivan Ilyich, that I still don't grasp what it is that you wish to explain. You advocate humaneness. Does that mean love of your fellow man?'

'Yes, if you will, even love for your fellow man. I . . .'

'Excuse me, sir. As far as I'm able to judge, there's more to it than that. Love of one's fellow man has always been called for. The reforms aren't confined to that. Questions have been raised about the peasantry, the courts, agriculture, tax-farming,[9] morality and . . . and . . . and there is no end to them, these questions, and all of them taken together, all of them at once might give rise to large-scale, so to speak, instability. That's what we're afraid of, it's not just a matter of humaneness . . .'

'Yes, sir, the matter is a bit deeper, sir,' Semyon Ivanovich observed.

'I quite understand, sir, and allow me to observe, Semyon Ivanovich, that I by no means consent to lag behind you in the deepness of my understanding of things,' Ivan Ilyich observed sarcastically and much too harshly, 'but, then, I will nevertheless take the liberty of observing to you as well, Stepan Nikiforovich, that you have failed to understand me at all . . .'

'No, I haven't.'

'Meanwhile, I precisely hold to and advance the idea that humaneness, and precisely humaneness to one's subordinates, from official to scribe, from scribe to household servant, from servant to peasant – humaneness, I say, might serve, so to speak, as the cornerstone of the impending reforms and in general for the revitalization of things. Why? Because. Take the syllogism: I am humane, consequently, they love me. They love me, therefore, they trust me. They trust me, therefore, they believe me; they believe me, therefore, they love me . . . that is, no, I mean to say that if they believe, then they will believe in reform, they will understand, so to speak, the very essence of the matter, so to speak, they will embrace one another morally and decide the entire matter amicably, thoroughly. What are you laughing at, Semyon Ivanovich? Isn't it clear?'

Stepan Nikiforovich silently raised his eyebrows; he was surprised.

'It seems that I've had a bit too much to drink,' Semyon Ivanych observed venomously, 'and therefore I'm having difficulty grasping it. My mind's somewhat clouded.'

Ivan Ilyich winced.

'We won't bear it,' Stepan Nikiforovich uttered suddenly, after a slight hesitation.

'What do you mean "we won't bear it"?' Ivan Ilyich asked, surprised at Stepan Nikiforovich's sudden and scrappy remark.

'Just that, we won't bear it,' Stepan Nikiforovich clearly had no wish to elaborate any further.

'You're not thinking about the new wine in new wineskins,[10] are you?' Ivan Ilyich objected not without irony. 'No, no, sir; I can answer for myself.'

At that moment the clock struck half past eleven.

'It's time for us to be going,' Semyon Ivanych said, as he made to get up from his seat. But Ivan Ilyich anticipated him, stood up from the table at once and took his sable hat from the mantel-piece. He looked aggrieved.

'So then, Semyon Ivanych, you'll give it some thought?' Stepan Nikiforovich said, as he was seeing his guests out.

'About the apartment, sir? Yes, I'll think about it, sir.'

'Let me know as soon as you can, when you have made up your mind.'

'Still talking about business,' Mr Pralinsky observed amiably with a certain ingratiating air as he played with his hat. He thought that they had forgotten about him.

Stepan Nikiforovich raised his eyebrows and kept silent, as a sign that he was not detaining his guests. Semyon Ivanych hurriedly took his leave.

'Oh . . . well . . . as you wish . . . if you don't understand common courtesy,' Mr Pralinsky decided to himself, and he somehow with a particularly independent manner held out his hand to Stepan Nikiforovich.

In the entryway Ivan Ilyich wrapped himself up in his light, expensive fur coat, for some reason trying not to notice Semyon Ivanych's worn-out raccoon coat, and they both started to make their way down the stairs.

'Our old man seemed offended,' Ivan Ilyich said to the silent Semyon Ivanych.

'No, why should he?' the other answered quietly and coldly.

'Lackey!' Ivan Ilyich thought to himself.

They came out on to the porch, and up drove Semyon Ivanych's sledge with its unprepossessing grey horse.

'What the devil! Where has Trifon gone with my carriage!' Ivan Ilyich cried, when he didn't see his trap.

There was no carriage to be seen, neither this way nor that. Stepan Nikiforovich's man knew nothing about it.

A NASTY BUSINESS

They turned to Varlam, Semyon Ivanych's coachman, and received the answer that he had been there the whole time and that the carriage had been there as well, but now it was nowhere to be seen.

'A nasty business!' Mr Shipulenko uttered, 'would you like me to give you a lift?'

'The common folk are scoundrels!' Mr Pralinsky cried out in fury. 'He asked me, the rascal, if he could go to a wedding, here on the Petersburg Side, some godmother or other was getting married, the devil take her. I strictly forbade him to absent himself. And now I'll bet that's where he's gone!'

'He actually did go there, sir,' Varlam observed, 'and he promised to be back in a minute, that is, right on time.'

'Well, then! I just knew it! Wait till I get hold of him!'

'You'd be better off having him whipped a few times at the police station, then he'll carry out his orders,' Semyon Ivanych said, as he covered himself with a rug.

'Please, don't trouble yourself, Semyon Ivanych!'

'So you don't want a lift?'

'Have a pleasant journey, *merci*.'[11]

Semyon Ivanych drove off, while Ivan Ilyich walked along the little wooden footway, intensely irritated.

'No, wait till I get hold of you, you rascal! I'm deliberately going on foot so that you'll understand, so that you'll be frightened! He'll come back and find out that the master left on foot . . . the swine!'

Ivan Ilyich had never cursed like that before, but he was so very infuriated, and to top it off his head was pounding. He was not a drinking man, and so he quickly felt the effects of those five or six glasses. But the night was delightful. It was frosty, but unusually quiet and still. The sky was clear, starry. The full moon flooded the earth with a suffused silver brilliance. It was so nice that Ivan Ilyich, after walking some fifty paces, had almost forgotten about his misfortune. He was beginning to feel somehow particularly contended. Besides, when people are a bit tipsy they're very impressionable. He even began to like the homely little wooden houses on the empty street.

'You know, it's marvellous that I left on foot,' he thought to himself. 'It's a lesson for Trifon and a pleasure for me. Really, I should walk more often. What's the big deal? I'll find a cab right away on Bolshoy Prospekt.[12] It's a marvellous night. Look at the little houses here. Must be the small fry that live here, officials . . . merchants, maybe . . . that Stepan Nikiforovich! And what retrogrades they all are, those old simpletons! Precisely simpletons, *c'est le mot*. But he's an intelligent man, he's got that *bon sens*,[13] a sober, practical understanding of things. But then, these old men, old men! They don't have that . . . what's it called now! Well, they don't have something . . . We won't bear it! What did he mean by that? He even became lost in his thoughts when he said it. However, he didn't understand me at all. But how could he not? It's more difficult not to understand than to understand. The main thing is that I'm convinced, convinced with all my heart. Humaneness . . . love of one's fellow man. To return man to himself . . . to revive his self-respect and then . . . Get down to business with this ready material. Seems clear enough! Yes, sir! Allow me, Your Excellency, now take this syllogism: we meet, for example, a clerk, a poor, downtrodden clerk. "Well . . . who are you?" Answer: "A clerk." Fine, a clerk; further: "What kind of clerk are you?" Answer: "I'm such and such," he says, "kind of clerk." "Are you employed?" "I am!" "Do you want to be happy?" "I do." "What do you need to be happy?" Such and such. "Why?" Because . . . And you see the man understands me right from the start: my man is a man who has been caught, so to speak, in the net and I can do anything with him that I wish, that is, for his own good. That Semyon Ivanych is a nasty man! And what a nasty mug he has... Whip him at the police station – he said that on purpose. No, it's all lies – whip him yourself, I'm not going to whip anyone; I'll wear down Trifon with words, I'll wear him down with reproaches – and then he'll feel it. As for birch rods, hm... it's a question that has yet to be settled, hm... But maybe I should drop in on Emerans? Ugh! The devil take it! These damned footways!' he cried out, after suddenly taking a wrong step. 'And this is the capital! Enlightenment! You could break your leg! Hm. I hate that Semyon Ivanych; a most disgusting mug. It was he who was sniggering when I said: they will embrace one another morally. Well, let them embrace, what business is it of yours? But I'm not going to embrace you; I'd rather embrace a peasant... If I meet a peasant, I'll have a talk with him. However, I was drunk and maybe I didn't express myself properly. And maybe even now I'm not expressing myself properly... Hm. I'm never going to drink. You talk a lot of nonsense in the evening, and the next day you repent. Now then, you see I'm not staggering, I'm walking... But all the same they're all crooks!'

So Ivan Ilyich reasoned, in fragments and incoherently, as he continued to walk down the sidewalk. The fresh air was having an effect on him and arousing him, so to speak. Five minutes more and he would have calmed down and wanted to go to bed. But suddenly, just a stone's throw away from Bolshoy Prospekt, he heard music. He looked around. On the other side of the street in a ramshackle wooden house, which was only one-storeyed but long, a sumptuous feast was being given, the violins hummed, the double bass squeaked and the flute shrilly broke out into a very merry quadrille[14] tune. An audience was standing under the windows, mainly women in quilted coats and with kerchiefs on their heads; they were straining with all their might to catch a glimpse of something through the cracks in the shutters. Clearly, the merrymakers were enjoying themselves. The din from the dancers' stomping reached the other side of the street. Ivan Ilyich noticed that there was a policeman nearby and walked over to him.

'Whose house is that, my good fellow?' he asked, as he threw open his expensive fur coat a bit, just enough so that the policeman could notice the important decoration on his neck.

'It belongs to the clerk Pseldonimov, the legistrator,'[15] the policeman answered, drawing himself up to his full height, after making out the decoration in a flash.

'Pseldonimov? Bah! Pseldonimov! . . . What's he doing? Getting married?'

'Getting married, Your Honour, to the titular councillor's daughter. Titular Councillor Mlekopitayev . . . He used to serve in the local authority. The house comes with the bride, sir.'

'So now it belongs to Pseldonimov, it's no longer Mlekopitayev's house?'

'Pseldonimov's, Your Honour. It was Mlekopitayev's and now it's Pseldonimov's.'

'Hmm. I'm asking you, my good man, because I'm his superior. I am the general in the very place where Pseldonimov works.'

'Just so, Your Excellency.' The policeman drew himself up even more, while Ivan Ilyich fell deep in thought, as it were. He stood and pondered . . .

Yes, Pseldonimov really was in his department, in his own office; he recalled that. He was a petty clerk, with a salary of about ten roubles a month. Since Mr Pralinsky had only quite recently assumed charge of his office, he might not remember all of his subordinates in great detail, but he remembered Pseldonimov, precisely on account of his surname.[16] It had caught his attention the very first time, so that right away his curiosity had been piqued to have a closer look at the owner of such a surname. He recalled now that the man who was still quite young, with a long hooked nose, a shaggy towhead, gaunt and malnourished, wearing an impossible uniform and unmentionables that were even impossibly indecent. He recalled that the idea had occurred to him then to give the poor fellow ten roubles towards the holiday so that he might put himself right. But since the face of this poor fellow was so glum and there was quite an unpleasant, even repellent, look about him, the kind thought somehow vanished of its own accord, so that Pseldonimov remained without a bonus. Less than a week ago this same Pseldonimov amazed him all the more with his request to marry. Ivan Ilyich recalled that for some reason he hadn't had time to deal with this matter more thoroughly, so that the matter about the wedding was decided lightly, hastily. But nevertheless he remembered with exactitude that Pseldonimov's bride came with a wooden house and four hundred roubles in cash; this circumstance had surprised him then; he recalled that he had even lightly made a joke about the conjunction of the names Pseldonimov and Mlekopitayev. He remembered it all clearly.

He was remembering and became more and more lost in his thoughts. We know that entire discourses sometimes take place in our heads in an instant, in the form of some sensations, without translation into human language, much less literary language. But we shall attempt to translate all our hero's sensations and present to the reader at the very least the essence of these sensations, so to speak, what was most indispensable and plausible in them. Because, you see, many of our sensations, when translated into ordinary language, seem highly unlikely. That's why they are never brought out into the world, but everybody has them. It goes without saying that Ivan Ilyich's sensations and thoughts were a bit disjointed. But then you know the reason for that.

'All right!' flashed through his head, 'here we all talk and talk, but when it comes to action, then damned all happens. Take, for example, this same Pseldonimov: he's just come from his wedding, excited and hopeful, anticipating the taste of ... It's one of the most blessed days of his life ... Now he's busy with his guests, throwing a feast – modest, poor, but cheerful, joyful, sincere ... What if he were to learn that at this very moment I, I, his superior, his chief superior, were standing right here outside his house and listening to his music! But really what would he think? No, what would he think if I suddenly up and walked in now? Hmm ... It goes without saying that at first he would be frightened, become speechless from embarrassment. I might put him out ... I might upset everything ... Yes, that's what would happen if any other general were to walk in, but not me ... But that's just it, any other general, but not me ...

'Yes, Stepan Nikiforovich! You didn't understand me earlier, but here's a ready example for you now.

'Yes, sir. We keep clamouring about humaneness, but we're incapable of heroism, of performing a great feat.

'What sort of heroism? This sort. Just think: given the present relations between all members of society, for me, for me to walk in after midnight on the wedding of a subordinate of mine, a registrator, who earns ten roubles a month, well that's an embarrassment, that's a transposition of ideas, the last day of Pompeii,[17] chaos! Nobody will understand it. Stepan Nikiforovich will die without understanding it. After all, it was he who said: we won't bear it. Yes, but that's you, you old people, you people with your paralysis and inertia,[18] but I will *bear it*! I will turn the last day of Pompeii into the sweetest day of my subordinate's life, and a wild act into a normal, patriarchal, lofty and moral one. How? Like this. Kindly be so good as to lend an ear ...

'Well... now let's assume that I walk in: they're astounded, stop the dancing, look about wildly, back away. All right, sir, but here's where I show what I'm made of: I walk right up to the frightened Pseldonimov and with the gentlest smile, I say in the simplest words possible: "And so then," I say, "I was visiting His Excellency Stepan Nikiforovich. I suppose you know he lives here, in this neighbourhood..." Well, and then lightly, in a somewhat comic vein, I'll tell them about my adventure with Trifon. From Trifon I'll move on to how I set out on foot... "Well, I hear the music, I satisfy my curiosity by asking a policeman and I learn, brother, that you're getting married. And so I think to myself, why don't I drop in on my subordinate and see how my clerks enjoy themselves and... get married. After all, I don't suppose you'll throw me out!" Throw me out! What fine words for a subordinate. What the devil do I mean – throw me out! I think he'll lose his mind, rush as fast as his legs will carry him to sit me down in an armchair, tremble with delight and at first he won't even grasp what's happening!...

'Well, what could be simpler, more graceful than conducting oneself like that! Why did I come? That's another question! That now is the moral side of the matter, so to speak. Now that's the very essence!

'Hm... Now what was I thinking about? Yes!

'Well, of course, they'll seat me with the most important guest, some titular councillor or a relative, a retired staff-captain with a red nose... Gogol[19] described these originals marvellously. Well, I'll be introduced to the young bride, it goes without saying, I'll praise her, put the guests at their ease. I'll ask them not to be shy, to enjoy themselves, to go on with their dancing, I'll be witty, I'll laugh, in a word – I'll be amiable and kind. I'm always amiable and kind, when I'm pleased with myself... Hm... It's just that I still seem to be a bit... that is, I'm not drunk, but just...

'... It goes without saying that I, as a gentleman, am on

an equal footing with them and by no means require any particular signs of... But morally, morally it's a different thing altogether: they'll understand and appreciate that... My conduct will resurrect all the nobility in them... Well, I'll sit for a half an hour. Even an hour. I'll leave, it goes without saying, before the supper itself, or they'll start bustling about, baking, roasting, they'll bow down ever so low, but I'll only drink a glass, wish them well and decline supper. I'll say: business. And as soon as I utter this "business", everyone's face will become respectfully solemn all at once. In this way I'll delicately remind them that they and I are different, gentlemen. Earth and sky. It's not that I want to bring it up, but one needs to... it's necessary even in the moral sense, no matter what you say. However, I'll smile right away, I'll even laugh a bit, perhaps, and everyone will cheer up in a flash... I'll joke a bit more with the bride; hm... You know, I'll even hint that I'll come again in exactly nine months on the dot to stand godfather, he-he! She'll certainly give birth by then. After all, they breed like rabbits. Well, and everybody will burst out laughing, the bride will blush; I'll kiss her on the forehead with feeling, I'll even give her my blessing and... and tomorrow my deed will be known in the office. Tomorrow once again I am stern, tomorrow once again I am exacting, even implacable, but everybody will know what sort of person I am. They will know my soul, they will know my essence: "As a boss he's stern, but as a person – he's an angel!" And then I've won; I've caught them with one small little deed, which would not even occur to you; they're already mine; I am the father, they're the children... Well then, Your Excellency, Stepan Nikiforovich, you just try doing something like that...

'... And do you know, do you understand that Pseldonimov will tell his children how the General himself feasted and even drank at his wedding! And, you know, these children will tell their children, and they will tell their grandchildren, as a most sacred story about how a high official, a statesman (and I'll be all that by then) favoured them . . . and so on and so forth. And you see, I'll morally raise up the humiliated, I'll restore him to himself . . . You see, he has a salary of ten roubles a month! And you see, if I repeat this or something else like it, five times, or ten times, then I'll acquire popularity everywhere . . . I will be imprinted on everybody's heart, and the devil only knows what might come of it later, this popularity! . . .'

This or something like it was how Ivan Ilyich reasoned (gentlemen, what doesn't a person say to himself sometimes, moreover when he's in a somewhat unconventional condition). All these debates flashed through his head in about half a minute, and of course he might have limited himself to these dreams and after shaming Stepan Nikiforovich in his thoughts, he might have quietly set out for home and gone to bed. And it would have been splendid if he had done just that! But the whole misfortune stemmed from the fact that the moment was an unconventional one.

As if on purpose, suddenly, at that very moment, the smug faces of Stepan Nikiforovich and Semyon Ivanovich appeared in his excited imagination.

'We won't bear it!' Stepan Nikiforovich repeated, laughing condescendingly.

'He-he-he!' Semyon Ivanovich echoed him with his nastiest smile.

'Well, let's just see how we won't bear it!' Ivan Ilyich said decisively, and his face even became flushed. He stepped down from the footway and with firm steps made straight for the house across the street that belonged to his subordinate, the registrar Pseldonimov.

His star carried him along. He boldly walked in the open gate and disdainfully brushed aside with his foot the gruff, shaggy little dog, which more for appearance's sake than any other concern had rushed at his feet with a wheezy bark. He walked along the wooden plankway to the covered porch, which looked out on to the yard like a sentry box, and walked up the three ramshackle wooden steps to the tiny entrance-way. Even though somewhere in the corner the end of a tallow candle or something in the way of a lampion[20] was burning, but this did not prevent Ivan Ilyich just as he was, wearing galoshes, from putting his left foot into the galantine, which had been set out to cool. Ivan Ilyich bent down and, after having a look round to satisfy his curiosity, he saw that there were two other dishes with some sort of jelly, and another two moulds, evidently of blancmange.[21] The trampled galantine put him in an embarrassing position, and for just a moment the idea flashed through his head: Shouldn't I slip away at once? But he considered this to be too base. After reasoning that no one had seen it and that they would certainly not think it was he, he quickly wiped off his galosh in order to hide the traces, groped for the door upholstered in felt, opened it and found himself in the tiniest entrance-hall. One half of it was literally crammed full of overcoats, greatcoats, cloaks, bonnets, scarves and galoshes. The other half had been taken over by the musicians: two violins, flute and double bass; all four men, it goes without saying, brought in right off the street. They sat behind a little unpainted wooden table, with a single tallow candle, and were sawing away with all their might at the final figure of a quadrille. From the opened door one could just make out in the drawing room the dancers in the dust, smoke and fumes. It was somehow deliriously gay. One could hear laughter, shouts and women's screams. The men stomped like a squadron of horses. Over all this hullabaloo resounded the commands of the man calling the dances, probably an extremely free-and-easy and even unbuttoned person: 'Gentlemen, step forward, *chaîne de dames, balancez!*'[22] and so on, and so forth. Ivan Ilyich in some agitation threw off his fur coat and galoshes and with his hat in his hands entered the room. However, he was no longer capable of reasoning.

For the first minute nobody noticed him: everybody was dancing the last steps of the number that was coming to an end. Ivan Ilyich stood as though he were stunned and couldn't make out anything in this bedlam. Women's dresses, gentlemen with cigarettes clenched in their teeth flashed past... Some lady's light-blue scarf, which brushed against his nose, flashed by. After her in mad rapture a medical student tore past, his hair swept by the whirl of the dance, and shoved him hard as he went by. An officer of some detachment who seemed as tall as a signpost flashed by. Somebody in an unnaturally shrill voice shouted out: 'Eh-h-h, Pseldonimushka!' There was something sticky under Ivan Ilyich's feet: evidently the floor had been polished with wax. In the room, which was quite large, by the way, there were some thirty guests.

But a minute later the quadrille came to an end, and almost at once took place exactly what Ivan Ilyich had pictured to himself when he was still daydreaming on the footway. Some sort of rumbling, some sort of odd whispering made the rounds of the guests and dancers, who had not yet had a chance to catch their breath and wipe the sweat from their faces. All eyes, all faces quickly began to turn in the direction of the guest who had just entered. Then everybody at once began little by little to fall back and retreat. Those who hadn't noticed were tugged by their clothes and brought to their senses. They looked around and at once beat a retreat with the others. Ivan Ilyich was still standing in the doorway, not taking a single step forward, and the open space between him and the guests, strewn with innumerable sweet wrappers, tickets and cigarette butts, kept growing and growing. Suddenly into this space timidly stepped a young man, wearing a uniform, with wispy flaxen hair and a hooked nose. He moved forward, stooping, and looked at the unexpected guest with the exact same expression as a dog looks at his master, who has called it to give it a kick.

'Hello, Pseldonimov, don't you recognize me?' Ivan Ilyich said, at once sensing that he had put it awkwardly; he also sensed at that moment that perhaps he was committing a most terrible act of foolishness.

'Y-y-y-our-r-r Ex-cel-len-cy!' Pseldonimov mumbled.

'Well, that's right. Brother, I've dropped in on you utterly by chance, as you yourself can probably imagine . . .'

But Pseldonimov apparently couldn't imagine anything. He stood, with his eyes wide open, in terrified bewilderment.

'Well, I don't suppose that you're going to throw me out . . . Happy or not, you must make the guest feel at home! . . .' Ivan Ilyich continued, feeling that he was becoming unbearably embarrassed, and wishing to smile, but unable to do so; the humorous story about Stepan Nikiforovich and Trifon was becoming more and more impossible. But Pseldonimov, as if on purpose, didn't come out of his stupor and continued to look on with an utterly foolish expression. Ivan Ilyich winced; he felt that one more minute like this and unbelievable chaos would break out.

'I hope I'm not disturbing anything . . . I'll go!' he just barely got out, and a nerve in the right corner of his mouth began to twitch . . .

But Pseldonimov was already coming to his senses . . .

'Your Excellency, excuse me, sir . . . The honour . . .' he mumbled, bowing hurriedly, 'be so kind as to sit down, sir . . .' And after coming to his senses even more, he pointed with both hands to the sofa, which they had moved for the dancing . . .

A NASTY BUSINESS

His mind at rest, Ivan Ilyich sank down on to the sofa; somebody at once rushed to move over a table. He took a fleeting look around and noticed that he was the only one sitting, while all the others were standing, even the ladies. A bad omen. But it wasn't time yet to remind and encourage. The guests were still backing away, and Pseldonimov, still understanding nothing and far from smiling, still stood alone in front of them, bent over. In short, it was nasty: at this moment our hero endured such anguish that indeed the invasion of his subordinate in the manner of Harun-al-Rashid,[23] for the sake of principle, might be considered an heroic deed. But suddenly another little figure turned up alongside Pseldonimov and began to bow. To his inexpressible satisfaction and even happiness, Ivan Ilyich at once recognized his chief desk officer, Akim Petrovich Zubikov, with whom, of course, he was not acquainted, but whom he knew to be an efficient and quiet official. He immediately stood up and offered his hand – his entire hand and not just two fingers – to Akim Petrovich. The latter embraced it with both his palms with the most profound respect. The General was triumphant; all had been saved.

And indeed, now Pseldonimov was, so to speak, not the second, but the third person. Ivan Ilyich could address his story directly to the desk officer, whom out of necessity he could welcome as an acquaintance, and a close one at that; Pseldonimov meanwhile could just keep silent and quake with reverence. Consequently, the proprieties were being observed. But a story was essential; Ivan Ilyich sensed that; he saw that all the guests were expecting something, that even all the household were crowding both doorways and were practically climbing on top of one another in order to see and hear him. But it was nasty how the desk officer, owing to his stupidity, still wouldn't sit down.

'Come now!' Ivan Ilyich said, awkwardly indicating the place next to him on the sofa.

'For goodness' sake, sir ... I'll be fine here, sir ...' and Akim Petrovich quickly sat down on the chair, which had been placed under him almost on the fly by Pseldonimov who stubbornly remained standing.

'Can you imagine what I've been through,' Ivan Ilyich began, addressing himself exclusively to Akim Petrovich in a somewhat trembling voice that had already become unduly familiar. He was even drawling and separating his words, stressing each syllable, and he began pronouncing the letter 'a' somewhat like 'eh';[24] in a word, he sensed and was aware that he was behaving affectedly, but he could no longer control himself; some external force was having its way. At that moment he was excruciatingly aware of a great many things.

'Can you imagine, I've just come from Stepan Nikiforovich's, maybe you've heard of him, the privy councillor. Well ... he's on that commission ...'

Akim Petrovich respectfully leaned forward with his whole body as if to say: 'How could I not have heard, sir.'

'He's your neighbour now,' Ivan Ilyich continued, addressing Pseldonimov for a moment for the sake of propriety and to put him at ease, but he quickly turned away, upon seeing at once from Pseldonimov's eyes that it made absolutely no difference to him.

'The old man, as you know, has been mad about buying a house his whole life ... Well, and he's bought one. And it's a nice little house. Yes ... And then it was his birthday today, and he had never celebrated it before, you see, he had even kept it a secret from us, didn't let on about it on account of his stinginess, he-he! But now he's so happy with his new house that he invited me and Semyon Ivanovich. You know – Shipulenko.'

Akim Petrovich leaned forward again. He leaned forward with zeal! Ivan Ilyich took some comfort. It had already occurred to him that the desk officer might suspect that at that moment he was an essential point of support for His Excellency. That would have been nastiest of all.

'Well, the three of us sat there for a bit, champagne was served, we talked about business . . . Well, about this and that . . . about *is-sues* . . . We even *ar-gued* a bit . . . He-he!'

Akim Petrovich respectfully raised his eyebrows.

'Only that's not the point. I was finally saying goodbye to him, he's a punctilious old man, goes to bed early, you know, he's getting old. I go out . . . and my Trifon's not there! I become alarmed, and I ask: "Where did Trifon go with my carriage?" It comes to light that he was hoping that I'd stay late and had gone off to the wedding of some godmother or cousin . . . God only knows. Right here somewhere on the Petersburg Side. And happened to take the carriage with him.' The General again for propriety's sake cast a glance at Pseldonimov. The latter immediately bent over double, but not at all as one needs to do for a general. 'No sympathy, no heart,' flashed through his head.

'Well, I never!' Akim Petrovich said, profoundly astonished. A slight rumble of surprise spread through the whole crowd.

'Can you imagine my situation . . .' (Ivan Ilyich cast a glance at all of them.) 'There was nothing to be done, I set off on foot. I thought, I'll make my way to Bolshoy Prospekt, and then I'll find some cabby . . . He-he!'

'Hee-hee-hee!' Akim Petrovich respectfully rejoined. Again a rumble, but now in a cheerful register, spread through the crowd. At that moment the glass chimney of a wall lamp shattered with a loud crack. Somebody zealously rushed over to take care of it. Pseldonimov roused himself and grimly looked at the lamp, but the general didn't even notice and everything calmed down.

'I'm walking . . . and it's such a beautiful night, so still. Suddenly I hear music, stomping feet, dancing. A policeman satisfies my curiosity – Pseldonimov is getting married. And you, my good man, you're throwing a party for the whole of the Petersburg Side? Ha-ha,' he suddenly addressed Pseldonimov once again.

'Hee-hee-hee! Yes, sir,' Akim Petrovich rejoined; the guests again stirred a bit, but the stupidest thing of all was that Pseldonimov even though he made another bow, now he didn't even smile, as though he were made of wood. 'What a fool!' Ivan Ilyich thought, 'even an ass would smile now, and everything would have gone along swimmingly.' Impatience raged in his heart. 'I think, let's drop in on my subordinate. After all, he won't throw me out . . . whether you are happy about it or not, you must make a guest welcome. Please forgive me, my good man. If I've disturbed you, I'll go . . . You see, I only wanted to drop in and have a look . . .'

But little by little a general movement was beginning. Akim Petrovich looked on with a sweet expression, as if to say, 'How could you be a disturbance, Your Excellency?' All of the guests began to stir and started to show the first signs of being at ease. Almost all of the ladies were sitting now. A good and positive sign. The bolder of them were fanning themselves with their kerchiefs. One of them, wearing a shabby velvet dress, was saying something in a deliberately loud voice. The officer, whom she had addressed, wanted to answer her even more loudly, but since the two of them were the only ones being loud, he shrank from doing so. The men, most of whom were clerks with two or three students, exchanged glances as if urging one another to become more at ease; they coughed and even began to take a few steps in different directions. However, nobody was particularly timid: they were all merely shy and almost all of them silently regarded with hostility the personage who had burst in upon them and disturbed their merrymaking. The officer, ashamed of his faint-heartedness, began to approach the table little by little.

'Now listen, my good fellow, allow me to ask, what is your name and patronymic,' Ivan Ilyich asked Pseldonimov.

'Porfiry Petrov,[25] Your Excellency,' the latter answered, wide-eyed, as if he were on review.

'So, introduce me, to your young bride, Porfiry Petrovich ... Take me ... I ...'

And he manifested a desire to get up. But Pseldonimov had rushed off as fast as his legs would carry him to the drawing room. The young bride, however, had been standing right there in the doorway, but she hid herself as soon as she heard that they were talking about her. A minute later Pseldonimov led her out by the hand. Everyone stepped aside to make way for them. Ivan Ilyich solemnly rose to his feet and turned to her with the most amiable smile.

'Very, very pleased to make your acquaintance,' he said with the worldliest of half-bows, 'particularly on such a day ...'

He gave a most calculating smile. The ladies became pleasantly excited.

'*Charmé*,'[26] the lady in the velvet dress uttered almost aloud.

The bride stood next to Pseldonimov. She was a skinny little thing, all of seventeen years old, pale, with a very small face and a sharp little nose. Her small eyes, quick and furtive, were not bashful in the least; on the contrary, their staring gaze even had a hint of some sort of menace about them. Evidently, Pseldonimov had not married her for her beauty. She was dressed in a white muslin dress over a pink chemise. Her neck was skinny, her body was like a chicken's with the bones all sticking out. To the general's greeting she managed to say absolutely nothing.

'My, what a pretty thing she is,' he continued in a low voice, as if he were addressing Pseldonimov alone, but deliberately so that the bride could hear as well. But Pseldonimov replied absolutely nothing to this, and didn't even lurch forward this time. It even seemed to Ivan Ilyich that there was something cold in his eyes, suppressed, wily, peculiar, malignant. And yet come what may Ivan Ilyich must strive for sensitivity. After all that's why he had come.

'But what a pair!' he thought. 'However...'

And once again he addressed the young bride who had taken a seat next to him on the sofa, but to his two or three questions he had not received more than 'yes' and 'no', and even those, to tell the truth, came grudgingly.

'If only she'd turn bashful,' he continued to himself. 'Then I could start joking. Otherwise, my position is hopeless, isn't it?' And Akim Petrovich kept silent as well, as if on purpose, and even though it was out of stupidity, it was still unforgivable.

'Ladies and gentlemen! I'm afraid I've interrupted your party,' he addressed everybody in general. He sensed that his palms were even sweating.

'No, sir... Don't worry, Your Excellency, we'll start again right away, but for now... we'll take it easy,' the officer replied. The bride looked at him with pleasure: the officer was still young and was wearing some sort of regimental uniform. Pseldonimov was standing right there, hunched forward, and seemed to be brandishing his hooked nose even more than earlier. He listened and watched, like a lackey who stands holding a fur coat, waiting for his masters to finish their farewells. Ivan Ilyich made that comparison himself; he had become flustered, he felt he was being awkward, terribly awkward, that the ground was slipping out from under his feet, that he had gone somewhere and couldn't get out, as if he were in the dark.

Suddenly everybody stepped aside and a short, stout woman appeared, already up in years, simply dressed, although she had dolled herself up, with a large shawl around her shoulders that was pinned at the throat, and wearing a bonnet, which clearly she was not in the habit of doing. She was holding a small, round tray on which there stood a bottle of champagne that was untouched but already uncorked and two glasses, no more and no less. The bottle evidently was intended for only two guests.

The elderly woman made straight for the general.

'Please forgive me, Your Excellency,' she said, bowing, 'but since you did not disdain us, and have done us the honour of coming to my son's wedding, then would you please be so kind as to drink to the young couple's health. Don't disdain us, do us the honour.'

Ivan Ilyich latched on to her as his salvation. She was not an old woman at all, about forty-five or forty-six, no more. But she had such a kind, ruddy, such an open, round, Russian face, she was smiling so good-naturedly, she bowed so simply that Ivan Ilyich almost took comfort and began to hope.

'So *you* are the *mother* of your *son*?' he said, getting up from the sofa.

'The mother, Your Excellency,' Pseldonimov muttered, stretching his long neck and once again brandishing his nose.

'Ah! Very glad, *very* glad to make your acquaintance.'

'Then you won't refuse, Your Excellency.'

'With the greatest pleasure.'

The tray was set down, Pseldonimov ran up and poured the wine. Ivan Ilyich, still standing, took a glass.

'I am particularly, particularly happy on this occasion that I can . . .' he began, 'that I can . . . bear witness . . . In a word, as your superior, I wish you, madam' (he turned to the young bride) 'and you, Porfiry, my friend – I wish you complete, prosperous and lasting happiness.'

And it was even with some feeling that he drank his

glass, the seventh that evening. Pseldonimov was looking serious and even morose. The General was beginning to feel an excruciating hatred for him.

'And that towering fellow' (he cast a glance at the officer) 'just hangs about. At least he could shout "Hurrah!" And then someone else would, and then someone else . . .'

'And you too, Akim Petrovich, have a drink and congratulate them,' the old woman added, turning to the desk officer. 'You're his superior, he's your subordinate. Look after my little son, I ask you as a mother. And don't forget us in the future, my dear Akim Petrovich, you're a good man.'

'How nice these old Russian women are!' Ivan Ilyich thought. 'She's livened them all up. I've always liked the ways of the common folk . . .'

At that moment another tray was brought to the table. It was carried by a girl wearing a rustling calico-print dress, which was so new it had yet to be laundered, and a crinoline. She could barely get her arms around the tray it was so large. On it were countless little plates with apples, sweets, meringues, marmalade, walnuts and so on and so forth. The tray until now had been in the drawing room for the enjoyment of all the guests. But now it was carried over to the general alone.

'Please don't turn up your nose at our victuals, Your Excellency. You're welcome to whatever we have,' the old woman repeated, bowing.

'How kind . . .' Ivan Ilyich said, and with evident pleasure he took a walnut and cracked it between his fingers. He had already made up his mind to be popular to the end.

Meanwhile, the young bride suddenly began to giggle.

'What is it, madam?' Ivan Ilyich asked with a smile, happy to see signs of life.

'It's Ivan Kostenkinych, sir, he's making me laugh,' she replied, casting her eyes downwards.

A NASTY BUSINESS

The General indeed did discern a fair-haired youth, not at all bad looking, who was hiding on a chair on the other side of the sofa and who was whispering something to Madame Pseldonimov. The youth got to his feet. He, to all appearances, was very bashful and very young.

'I was talking about the "dream-book" Your Excellency,' he mumbled, as if he were apologizing.

'And which dream-book is that?' Ivan Ilyich asked indulgently.

'There's a new dream-book, sir, a literary one, sir. I was telling them, sir, that if you see Mr Panayev[27] in your dreams that means you'll spill coffee on your shirt front, sir.'

'What innocence,' Ivan Ilyich thought, even with malice. The young man, though he became very flushed from saying this, was incredibly happy to have spoken about Mr Panayev.

'Well, yes, yes, I've heard . . .' His Excellency rejoined.

'No, here's something even better,' another voice said right beside Ivan Ilyich. 'A new lexicon is being published and they say that Mr Krayevsky will write the articles on Alferaki . . . and *eks*posé literature . . .'[28]

This was said by a young man, not the bashful one, but a rather unceremonious one. He was wearing gloves and a white waistcoat and was holding his hat in his hands. He had not been dancing, had an arrogant look about him, because he was one of the contributors to the satirical journal the *Brand*,[29] was used to setting the tone and had ended up at the wedding by accident, invited as an honoured guest of Pseldonimov, with whom he was on familiar terms and with whom just last year he had lived together in poverty in a 'corner' they rented from a certain German woman. He did, however, drink vodka and he had already repeatedly absented himself to a cosy back room, to which all knew the way. The general took an awful dislike to him.

205

'And that's funny, sir, because,' suddenly broke in cheerfully the fair-haired youth who had been telling the story about the shirt front and whom the contributor in the white waistcoat looked upon with hatred as a result. 'It's funny, Your Excellency, because the author supposes that Mr Krayevsky doesn't know how to spell and thinks that "exposé literature" should be written "*eks*posé literature"...'

But the poor youth was scarcely able to finish. He could see by the general's eyes that he had understood long before, because the general himself was also embarrassed, as it were, evidently because he had understood it. The young man became incredibly ashamed. He managed to retire to the background somewhere and for the rest of the evening he was very sad. In lieu of him the unceremonious contributor to the *Brand* came even closer, and it seemed as though he intended to sit somewhere nearby. Such lack of ceremony seemed somewhat ticklish to Ivan Ilyich.

'Yes! Tell me, please, Porfiry,' he began, just so as to say something, 'why – I keep meaning to ask you about this personally, why is your surname Pseldonimov and not Pseudonymov? After all, you're probably Pseudonymov, right?'

'I can't say with any certainty, Your Excellency,' Pseldonimov answered.

'It probably got mixed up on his father's papers when he entered the service, sir, and so he remains Pseldonimov even now,' Akim Petrovich rejoined. 'That happens, sir.'

'Cer-tain-ly,' the general picked up with great feeling, 'cer-tain-ly, because, just judge for yourself: Pseudonymov, you see, comes from the literary word "pseudonym". Well, but Pseldonimov doesn't mean anything.'

'It's just stupidity, sir,' Akim Petrovich added.

'But what exactly is just stupidity?'

'The Russian folk, sir; it's just stupidity that they sometimes change the letters, sir, and sometimes they pronounce

A NASTY BUSINESS

things their own way as well, sir. For example, they say *imvalid* when you ought to say invalid.'

'Well, yes . . . *imvalid*, he-he-he . . .'

'They also say *mumber*, Your Excellency,' the tall officer blurted out, who had felt an itch for a long time now to distinguish himself somehow.

'But what does mumber mean?'

'Mumber instead of number, Your Excellency.'

'Ah, yes, mumber . . . instead of number . . . Well, yes, yes . . . he-he-he! . . .' Ivan Ilyich was obliged to titter for the officer as well.

The officer straightened his tie.

'And here's something else they say: *aboot*,' the contributor to the *Brand* interjected. But His Excellency tried not to hear that. He wasn't going to titter for everybody.

'*Aboot* instead of *about*,' pestered the 'contributor', visibly irritated.

Ivan Ilyich looked at him sternly.

'Now why are you pestering him?' Pseldonimov whispered to the contributor.

'But what do you mean, I'm making conversation. Talking's not allowed, is that it?' the latter began to argue in a whisper, but then he fell silent and walked out of the room, barely concealing his rage.

He stole straight to the tempting little back room, where early in the evening for the dancing gentlemen there had been set out on a little table, covered with a Yaroslavl[30] tablecloth, two kinds of vodka, herring, slices of pressed caviar and a bottle of very strong domestic sherry. With fury in his heart, he was about to pour himself some vodka, when suddenly the medical student with the tousled hair, the premier dancer and exponent of the cancan at Pseldonimov's party, ran in. He rushed to the decanter with greedy haste.

'They're going to start now!' he said, quickly helping

himself. 'Come and watch: I'll do a solo with my legs in the air, and after supper I'll risk doing the "fish".[31] That's just the thing for a wedding. A friendly hint to Pseldonimov, so to speak. That Kleopatra Semyonovna is a splendid woman, you can risk anything you like with her.'

'He's a retrograde,' the contributor answered darkly, as he drank off his glass.

'Who's a retrograde?'

'That one, the person over there by the bonbons. He's a retrograde, I tell you!'

'Well, come on now!' the student mumbled and rushed out of the room upon hearing the ritornello[32] of the quadrille.

The contributor, left on his own, poured himself another glass for fortitude and independence, drank it off, had a bite; never before had Actual State Councillor Ivan Ilyich acquired a more fierce enemy and more implacable avenger than the scorned contributor to the *Brand*, particularly after two glasses of vodka. Alas! Ivan Ilyich didn't suspect anything of the kind. Nor did he suspect yet another most important circumstance, which would have an effect on all further mutual relations between the guests and His Excellency. The fact of the matter is that even though he had for his part given a decent and even detailed explanation of how he came to be present at the wedding of his subordinate, this explanation really and truly didn't satisfy anybody, and the guests continued to feel embarrassed. But suddenly everything changed, like magic; everyone calmed down and was ready to enjoy themselves, laugh, scream and dance, just as if there were no unexpected guest in the room. The reason for this was the rumour, whispering and news that suddenly began to circulate, no one knew how, that the guest, it seems . . . was under the influence. And although at first glance this appeared to be the most awful slander, little by little it seemed to be justified, so that suddenly everything became clear. Besides, they suddenly became unusually relaxed. And then at that very same moment the quadrille began, the last one before supper, the one the medical student had been in such a hurry for.

And just as Ivan Ilyich was about to address the new bride once again, this time trying to engage her with some pun, the tall officer suddenly came running up to her and with a sweeping gesture got down on one knee. She at once jumped up from the sofa and flew away with him to get into line for the quadrille. The officer didn't even excuse himself, while she didn't even look at the general as she was leaving, even as if she were happy that she had escaped.

'However, she's really within her rights,' Ivan Ilyich thought, 'and besides they don't know the niceties.'

'Hm . . . you shouldn't stand on ceremony, Porfiry, my good man,' he turned to Pseldonimov. 'Perhaps you have something . . . in the way of things to see to . . . or something there . . . please, don't be shy.' 'Is he standing guard over me, or what?' he added to himself.

Pseldonimov with his long neck and eyes intently fixed on him was becoming unbearable. In a word, this was all wrong, quite wrong, but Ivan Ilyich was still far from wanting to admit it.

The quadrille began.

'May I, Your Excellency?' Akim Petrovich asked, respectfully holding the bottle in his hands and getting ready to pour a glass for His Excellency.

'I . . . I don't really know if . . .'

But Akim Petrovich with a reverential, beaming face was already pouring the champagne. Having filled the glass, he also poured himself one as well, almost surreptitiously, almost furtively, cowering and pulling faces, but with this difference – he gave himself an entire finger less, which seemed somehow more respectful. He was like a woman in labour, sitting next to his immediate superior. Indeed, what was he going to talk about? And yet he was obliged to entertain His Excellency, since he had the pleasure of his company. The champagne was a way out, and His Excellency found it pleasing that he had been poured a glass – not on account of the champagne, which was warm and the most ordinary rubbish, but he found it morally pleasing.

'The old man wants a drink himself,' Ivan Ilyich thought, 'but he doesn't dare have one without me. I shouldn't hold him back... And it's ridiculous for the bottle to just stand there between us.'

He took a sip, and at any rate it did seem better than just sitting there.

'I'm here, you see,' he began with pauses and emphases, 'You see, I'm here, so to speak, by chance and of course perhaps some might find... that it was, so to speak... *im-prop-er* for me to be present at such a... gathering.'

Akim Petrovich kept his silence and listened with timid curiosity.

'But I hope that you will understand why I'm here... You see, I didn't as a matter of fact come here to drink wine. He-he!'

Akim Petrovich was about to follow His Excellency's example and have a titter, but he somehow stopped short and again said absolutely nothing comforting in reply.

'I'm here... in order, so to speak, to encourage... to show, so to speak, the moral, so to speak, purpose,' Ivan Ilyich continued, annoyed at Akim Petrovich's obtuseness, but suddenly he fell silent as well. He saw that poor Akim Petrovich had even lowered his eyes, as if he were guilty of something. Feeling a certain embarrassment, the general hurried to take another sip from his glass, while Akim Petrovich, as if his entire salvation depended upon it, grabbed the bottle and topped it up again.

A NASTY BUSINESS

'You certainly don't have much in the way of resources,' Ivan Ilyich thought, looking sternly at poor Akim Petrovich. The latter, sensing the general's stern gaze on him, decided to keep completely silent and not raise his eyes. And they sat facing each other like that for about two minutes, two painful minutes for Akim Petrovich.

A couple of words about Akim Petrovich. He was as submissive as a hen, one of the old school, nurtured on servility, and for all that a good man and even a noble one. His people were Petersburg Russians, that is, both his father and his father's father were born, grew up and served in Petersburg without ever leaving Petersburg even once. This is a quite special type of Russian people. They don't have even the slightest understanding of Russia, which doesn't bother them in the least. Their entire interest is confined to Petersburg, and chiefly their place of work. All their cares are centred on preference[33] for kopeck stakes, the shops and their monthly salary. They don't know a single Russian custom, nor a single Russian song, except 'Luchinushka',[34] and they only know that one because the organ-grinders play it. However, there are two significant and reliable signs by which you can immediately distinguish a real Russian from a Petersburg Russian. The first sign is that all Petersburg Russians, without exception, never say *Petersburg News*, but *Academic News*.[35] The second, equally significant sign is that a Petersburg Russian never uses the word 'breakfast', but always says *Frühstück*,[36] with particular emphasis on the sound *frü*. By these two fundamental and distinctive signs you can always distinguish them; in a word, this is a humble type that has become fully developed over the last thirty-five years. However, Akim Petrovich was no fool. If the general had asked him about something suitable, he would have answered and kept up the conversation, but otherwise, you see, it was improper for a subordinate to answer such questions, even though Akim Petrovich was dying from curiosity to find out something in more detail about His Excellency's real intentions...

But meanwhile Ivan Ilyich was sinking deeper and deeper into thought and into a sort of whorl of ideas; with a preoccupied air, he was sipping from his glass imperceptibly, but constantly. Akim Petrovich repeatedly and most diligently would fill up his glass. Both were silent. Ivan Ilyich began to watch the dancing and soon it had somewhat engaged his attention. Suddenly, a certain circumstance even surprised him...

The dancing indeed was merry. They danced in the simplicity of their hearts to be merry and even go wild. There were very few nimble dancers; but those who were not stamped about so loudly that one might have taken them for nimble ones. The first to distinguish himself was the officer: he particularly liked the figures in which he danced alone, as in a solo. Here he would bend himself in an amazing manner, to wit: he would be as straight as a post and then suddenly bend to one side so that you would think that he would fall down, but with the next step he would suddenly bend in the opposite direction, at the same sharp angle to the floor. The expression on his face was most serious and he danced with the full conviction that everybody was amazed by him. Another gentleman, having imbibed quite a bit before the quadrille had begun, had fallen asleep beside his partner during the second figure, so that his partner was forced to dance alone. A young registrator, who had danced with his partner in the blue scarf, had played the same trick in all the figures of each quadrille, namely, he would fall behind his partner somewhat, snatch the end of her scarf, and when they passed one another as they changed positions, he would manage to brush this end of the scarf with a couple dozen kisses. And his partner would sail on in front of him as if she hadn't noticed anything. The medical student indeed performed his solo with his legs in the air, inciting frenzied delight, stomping of feet and shrieks of pleasure. In a word, there was an extraordinary lack of constraint. Ivan Ilyich, who was feeling the effects of the wine, had started to smile, but little by little a sort of bitter doubt started to creep into his heart: of course, he very much liked relaxed manners and lack of constraint; he had desired them, he had even sincerely invited them, these relaxed manners, when they were all backing away from him; but now these relaxed manners were already exceeding all bounds. One lady, for example, wearing a shabby blue velvet dress, bought fourth-hand, in the sixth figure had pinned up her dress in such a way that it looked like she was wearing bloomers. This was that same Kleopatra Semyonovna, with whom it was possible to risk everything, in the words of her partner, the medical student. And what can be said about the medical student? He was simply Fokine.[37] How had this happened? First, they backed away, and then all of a sudden they had become completely emancipated! It would seem to be nothing, but this transition was somehow strange: it portended something. It was as if they had all quite forgotten that there was such a one as Ivan Ilyich on this earth. It goes without saying that he was the first to laugh and even ventured to applaud. Akim Petrovich respectfully tittered with him in unison, although with visible pleasure and not suspecting that His Excellency was already beginning to nourish new doubts in his heart.

'You dance splendidly, young man,' Ivan Ilyich was obliged to say to the student, who walked past – the quadrille had just ended.

The student turned sharply towards him, pulled some sort of face, and bringing his face indecently close to His Excellency's, he crowed like a rooster for all he was worth. This was really too much now. Ivan Ilyich rose from the table. Despite this, a volley of unrestrained laughter followed, because the rooster's crow was amazingly natural, and his pulling the face so unexpected. Ivan Ilyich was still standing in bewilderment, when suddenly Pseldonimov himself appeared and, bowing, asked him to come to supper. His mother followed him.

'Your Excellency, sir,' she said, bowing, 'please do us the honour, don't disdain our poverty...'

'I... I truly don't know...' Ivan Ilyich began, 'you see, I didn't come for that... I... was already getting ready to go...'

Indeed, he was holding his hat in his hands. Besides, just then, at that very moment, he had promised himself that he would definitely leave, right away, no matter what, and wouldn't stay for anything and... and he stayed. A minute later he was leading the procession to the table. Pseldonimov and his mother walked in front of him, clearing the way for him. He was seated in the place of honour and once again an untouched bottle of champagne appeared before him. There were *zakuski*:[38] herring and vodka. He reached out his hand, poured himself an enormous glass of vodka and drank it. He had never drunk vodka before. He felt like he was sledding down a hill, flying, flying, flying, that he needed to hold on to something, to grab on to something, but that was impossible.

Indeed, his position was becoming more and more peculiar. More than that – it was some sort of mockery of fate. God only knows what had happened to him in something on the order of an hour. When he came in, he had held out his hands, so to speak, to embrace all of mankind and all of his subordinates; and now, not even an hour later, he sensed and knew with all his aching heart that he hated Pseldonimov, that he cursed him, his wife and his wedding. More than that: he could see by his face and by his eyes that Pseldonimov hated him, that his look practically said: 'I wish you'd get lost, damn you! Foisting yourself on me!...' All this he had read a long time ago in his look.

Of course, Ivan Ilyich even now, as he was sitting down at the table, would sooner have had his hand cut off than sincerely acknowledge, not only aloud, but even to himself, that all this was really the case. That moment had not yet quite come; now there was still some sort of moral balance. But his heart, his heart... it ached! It begged for freedom, for air, for rest. You see, Ivan Ilyich was much too good a person.

He knew, you see, he knew very well that he should have left a long time ago, or not merely leave but save himself. That all this had suddenly gone awry, that it had not turned out at all like he had imagined just now on the footway.

'Why did I come after all? Did I really come to eat and drink here?' he asked himself, as he was having a bite of herring. He even experienced denial. At moments irony occasioned by his exploit stirred in his soul. He was even beginning not to be able to understand himself why, as a matter of fact, he had come.

But how could he leave? To leave like that, without seeing it to the end, was impossible. 'What will people say? They'll say that I hang about indecent places. As a matter of fact, it will turn out just like that if I don't see it through to the end. What will they be saying tomorrow (because the word will get around everywhere); for example, what will Stepan Nikiforovich or Semyon Ivanych say; or what about at the offices, at the Shembels or the Shubins? No, I must leave so that they all understand why I came, I must bring out into the open the moral purpose...' But meanwhile, this pathetic moment just would not come. 'They don't even respect me,' he continued. 'Why are they laughing? They're so casual, it's as if they didn't have feelings! Yes, I have long suspected that the entire younger generation has no feelings! I must stay no matter what happens! ... Just now they were dancing, and now they'll gather round the table ... I'll talk about issues, about the reforms, about Russia's greatness ... I'll win them over yet! Yes! Perhaps nothing is completely lost yet ... Perhaps that's how it always is in reality. But just what should I start with, to engage them? What method should I devise? I'm at my wits' end, my wits' end ... And what do they need, what do they want? ... I see that they're smiling to one another over there ... I hope it's not about me, good heavens! But what is it I want ... why am I here, why don't I leave, what am I trying to achieve? ...' He was thinking this, and some sort of shame, some deep, unbearable shame was tearing at his heart more and more.

But everything kept going on in the same way, one thing leading to another.

Exactly two minutes after he sat down at the table, a certain terrifying idea took hold of his whole being. He suddenly felt that he was horribly drunk – that is, not like he had been earlier, but completely drunk. The reason for this was the glass of vodka, drunk after the champagne and which had an immediate effect. He felt, he sensed with his whole being that he was becoming completely weak. Of course, his courage had grown stronger, but his conscience did not abandon him, rather it cried out to him: 'This is bad, this is very bad, and even quite indecent!' Of course, his unsteady drunken thoughts could not settle on one point: suddenly there appeared within himself, even palpably, two sides, as it were. In one there was courage, the desire for victory, the overthrow of obstacles and a desperate certainty that he would achieve his goal. The other side let itself be known through an agonizing ache in his soul and some sort of gnawing pain in his heart.

A NASTY BUSINESS

'What will people say? How will it end? What will tomorrow bring, tomorrow, tomorrow!...'

Earlier he had somehow dimly sensed that he had enemies among the guests. 'That's probably because I was drunk before, too,' he thought with agonizing doubt. Imagine his horror now, when he really became convinced by unmistakable signs that he really did have enemies at the table and that there could no longer be any doubt about that.

'And for what! For what!' he thought.

Seated at this table were all of the thirty or so guests, some of whom were already completely plastered. The others behaved with a certain offhand, malignant independence – they shouted, all talked loudly, proposing premature toasts, trading volleys of bread bullets with the ladies. One fellow, an unprepossessing person in a soiled frock coat, fell off his chair as soon as he sat down at the table and remained there until supper was over. Another wanted without fail to climb on to the table and propose a toast, and it was only the officer, grabbing him by his coat-tails, who restrained his premature rapture. The supper was quite a mishmash, even though they had hired a cook, the serf of some general: there were galantine, tongue with potatoes, cutlets with green peas, and finally, there was a goose, and blancmange to end it all. To drink there was beer, vodka and sherry. Only the general had a bottle of champagne standing before him, which prompted him to pour some for himself and Akim Petrovich; the latter would not have dared allow himself such liberties at the supper table. The rest of the guests were supposed to drink their toasts with wine from the Caucasus or whatever there happened to be. The table itself was comprised of several tables that had been pushed together, among which there was even a card table. It was covered with several tablecloths, among which there was a coloured one from

Yaroslavl. The guests were seated with ladies and gentlemen alternating. Pseldonimov's mother did not wish to sit at the table; she was too busy fussing and giving orders. But then there appeared a malignant female figure, who had not shown herself earlier, in some sort of reddish silk dress, wearing a bandage on account of a toothache and a very tall bonnet. It turned out that this was the bride's mother, who had finally agreed to come out of the back room for supper. Until now she had not come out on account of her irreconcilable hostility for Pseldonimov's mother; but we shall make mention of this later. This lady was looking at the general spitefully, even mockingly, and clearly did not wish to be introduced to him. Ivan Ilyich thought this figure to be extremely suspect. But apart from her there were some other people who were suspect as well and inspired involuntary misgivings and unease. They even seemed to be in some sort of plot together, and one precisely against Ivan Ilyich. At least it seemed so to him, and during the course of the whole supper he became more and more convinced of it. To wit: one gentleman, with a beard, some sort of free artist, was malignant; he even looked at Ivan Ilyich several times and then, after turning to his neighbour, whispered something to him. Another, one of the students, who it was true was already quite drunk, but all the same, judging by certain signs, was suspect. Nor did the medical student bode well. Even the officer himself was not altogether trustworthy. But the contributor to the *Brand* shone with special and visible hatred: he was sprawled out so in his chair, had such a proud and arrogant look, and chortled with such self-assurance! And although the other guests paid no particular attention to the contributor (who had written only four little poems for the *Brand*, thus becoming a liberal), and it was even clear that they didn't like him, when suddenly a little bread bullet fell near Ivan Ilyich, obviously intended for him, he was prepared to stake his life that the culprit was none other than the contributor to the *Brand*.

All this, of course, had the most deplorable effect on him.

Particularly unpleasant was yet another observation: Ivan Ilyich was absolutely convinced that he was beginning to articulate his words unclearly and with difficulty, that he wanted to say a lot, but that his tongue wasn't moving. Then, that he suddenly began to forget himself, as it were, and the main thing, that he would begin snorting and laughing out of the blue, when there was nothing at all to laugh at. This mood quickly passed after another glass of champagne, which even though Ivan Ilyich had poured it himself, he didn't wish to drink, and then suddenly drank it somehow, completely by accident. After this glass he suddenly almost wanted to burst into tears. He sensed that he was sinking into the most eccentric sentimentality; once again he began to love everybody, even Pseldonimov, even the contributor to the *Brand*. He suddenly wanted to embrace them all, to forget everything and be reconciled. And more than that: to tell them everything frankly, everything, everything, namely, what a good and splendid person he was, with what excellent abilities. How he will be of use to the fatherland, how he knew how to make the fair sex laugh, and, the main thing, what a progressive he was, how humanely he was prepared to condescend to everyone, to the most lowly, and, finally, in conclusion, to tell them frankly of the motives that prompted him to come uninvited to Pseldonimov's, to drink two bottles of his champagne and to grace him with his presence.

'The truth, the sacred truth above all, and frankness! I'll bring them around with frankness. They'll believe me, I see it clearly; they even look hostile now, but when I reveal everything to them, I'll win them over incontrovertibly. They'll fill their glasses and with a cheer drink to my health. The officer, I'm sure, will break his glass on his spur. They might even shout "Hurrah!" I wouldn't resist even if they got it into their heads to toss me up into the air hussar fashion,[39] it would be quite a good thing even. I'd kiss the bride on the forehead; she's a sweet girl. Akim Petrovich is also a very good man. Pseldonimov, of course, will improve with time. He lacks that genteel lustre, so to speak ... And although, of course, the whole new generation is found wanting when it comes to this delicacy of the heart, but ... but I'll tell them about Russia's mission today among the other European powers. I'll mention the peasant question, and ... and they'll all love me, and I'll leave in glory! ...'

These dreams, of course, were very pleasant, but it was unpleasant that among all these rosy hopes Ivan Ilyich suddenly discovered in himself an unexpected ability: namely, to spit. At least saliva began to suddenly spring from his mouth quite against his will. He noticed this on Akim Petrovich, whose cheek he had showered and who sat not daring to wipe it off right away out of respect. Ivan Ilyich took a napkin and suddenly wiped it himself. But right away this seemed so absurd, so outside the bounds of what is sensible that he fell silent and began to wonder at himself. Akim Petrovich, though he had been drinking, nevertheless sat there as if he'd been scalded. Ivan Ilyich realized now that he had been talking for almost a quarter of an hour to him about some very interesting topic, but that Akim Petrovich, while listening to him, seemed not only embarrassed, but even frightened. Pseldonimov, sitting a chair away from him, had also craned his neck towards him and, with his head cocked to the side, was listening to him with a most unpleasant look. He really seemed to be keeping watch over him. As he glanced round at the guests, he saw that many were looking straight at him and chortling. But the strangest thing of all was that despite all that he wasn't in the least embarrassed; on the contrary, he took another sip from his glass and suddenly, for all to hear, began to speak.

'I've already said!' he began as loudly as he could, 'I've already said, ladies and gentlemen, to Akim Petrovich just now that Russia... yes, precisely Russia... in a word, you understand that I want to *say*... Russia is experiencing, in my considered opinion, hu-humaneness...'

'Hu-humaneness!' resounded from the other end of the table.

'Hu-hu!'

'Phooey, phooey!'

Ivan Ilyich faltered. Pseldonimov got up from his chair and began to look to see who had shouted. Akim Petrovich began furtively to shake his head as if he were reprimanding the guests. Ivan Ilyich observed this only too well, but suffered torments in silence.

'Humaneness!' he stubbornly continued. 'And just this evening... and just this very evening I was telling Stepan Niki-ki-for-o-vich... yes... that... that the renewal, so to speak, of things...'

'Your Excellency!' a voice loudly resounded from the other end of the table.

'What can I do for you?' Ivan Ilyich answered, as he tried to make out who had interrupted him with his shouting.

'Absolutely nothing, Your Excellency, I got carried away, continue! Con-tin-ue!' the voice called out again.

Ivan Ilyich winced.

'The renewal, so to speak, of these very things...'

'Your Excellency!' the voice shouted again.

'What can I do for you?'

'Hello!'

This time Ivan Ilyich couldn't bear it. He interrupted his speech and turned to the offender and transgressor of order. It was a student who was still very young, quite drunk and who had already aroused enormous suspicions in him. He had been yelling for some time and had even broken a glass and two plates, maintaining that this was what was done at weddings. At that moment, when Ivan Ilyich turned towards him, the officer sternly began to berate the shouting youth.

'What's wrong with you, why are you shouting? You should be thrown out, that's what!'

'It's not about you, Your Excellency, it's not about you! Continue!' the high-spirited schoolboy shouted, sprawled out on his chair. 'Continue, I'm listening, and am very, ver-ry, ver-ry pleased with you! Com-mend-able! Com-mend-able!'

'The boy's drunk!' Pseldonimov suggested in a whisper.

'I can see that he's drunk, but . . .'

'I was just telling an amusing story, Your Excellency!' the officer began, 'about a certain lieutenant in our company who spoke with his superiors in exactly the same way; so now he's imitating him. He kept repeating after his superior's every word: Com-mend-able, com-mend-able! It's been ten years now since he was discharged from the service on account of this.'

'Who is this lieutenant, then?'

'In our company, Your Excellency, he lost his mind with this "commendable". At first they admonished him mildly, then he was put under arrest . . . The superior appealed to his conscience like a father, but all he got was "Com-mend-able, com-mend-able!" And the strange thing about it is that the officer was a manly sort, six feet tall. They were going to bring him to trial, but then they realized he was mad.'

'Well then . . . he's a schoolboy. One doesn't have to be so severe over schoolboy pranks . . . I, for my part, am prepared to forgive . . .'

'There was a medical examination, Your Excellency.'

A NASTY BUSINESS

'What! They dissected him?'

'For goodness' sake, he was quite alive, you see, sir.'

A loud volley of laughter rang out from practically all the guests, who in the beginning had been behaving themselves with decorum. Ivan Ilyich became furious.

'Gentlemen, gentlemen!' he cried out, at first without even stammering, 'I'm perfectly able to apprehend that they don't dissect a man while he's alive. I had supposed that in his madness he was no longer alive . . . that is, that he had died . . . that is, I wish to say . . . that you don't love me . . . While I love all of you . . . Yes, and I love Por . . . Porfiry . . . I am humiliating myself by saying so . . .'

At that moment an enormous wad of saliva flew out of Ivan Ilyich's mouth and splattered the tablecloth in the most conspicuous place. Pseldonimov rushed to wipe it up with a napkin. This last misfortune had crushed him completely.

'Gentlemen, this is too much!' he cried out in despair.

'The man's drunk, Your Excellency,' Pseldonimov suggested once again.

'Porfiry! I see that you . . . all . . . yes! I was saying that I hope . . . Yes, I challenge all of you to tell me: how have I humiliated myself?'

Ivan Ilyich was practically in tears.

'Your Excellency, for goodness' sake!'

'Porfiry, I appeal to you . . . Tell me, for heaven's sake, if I came . . . yes . . . yes, to your wedding, I had a purpose. I wanted to morally raise . . . I wanted you to feel. I appeal to all of you: am I very humiliated in your eyes or not?'

Deathly silence. And that was precisely the problem, that there was deathly silence, and in answer to such a categorical question. 'Well, why don't they, why don't they at least give a shout at a moment like this?' flashed through His Excellency's head. But the guests merely exchanged glances. Akim Petrovich sat neither dead nor alive, while

Pseldonimov, dumb with fear, kept repeating to himself the horrible question that had occurred to him long before: 'And what will happen to me tomorrow for all this?'

Suddenly the contributor to the *Brand*, already very much in his cups but who until now had been sitting in morose silence, turned to face Ivan Ilyich and with eyes ablaze made his reply in the name of all those gathered there.

'Yes, sir!' he cried out in a thundering voice. 'Yes, sir, you have humiliated yourself, yes, sir, you are a retrograde... A retrograde!'

'Come to your senses, young man! Remember who you're speaking to!' Ivan Ilyich shouted furiously, once again jumping up from his seat.

'To you, and, in the second place, I'm not a young man... You have come to put on airs and seek popularity.'

'Pseldonimov, what is this!' Ivan Ilyich exclaimed.

But Pseldonimov had jumped up in such horror that he stood stock-still and had absolutely no idea what he should do. The guests sat there, petrified with fear, but the artist and the student were applauding, shouting, 'Bravo, bravo!'

The contributor continued to shout with irrepressible fury.

'Yes, you came to boast of your humaneness! You've interfered with everybody's merriment. You drank champagne without realizing that it's too expensive for a civil servant who makes ten roubles a month, and I suspect that you are one of those superiors who are fond of the young wives of his subordinates! Besides, I'm certain that you're in favour of tax-farming... Yes, yes, yes!'

'Pseldonimov, Pseldonimov!' Ivan Ilyich cried with his arms outstretched. He felt that the contributor's every word was like a new dagger in his heart.

A NASTY BUSINESS

'Right away, Your Excellency, please don't worry!' Pseldonimov energetically cried out, as he ran over to the contributor, grabbed him by the scruff of the neck and dragged him away from the table. One would not have expected such physical force from puny Pseldonimov. But the contributor was very drunk, and Pseldonimov was completely sober. Then he punched him in the back several times and threw him out the door.

'You're all scoundrels!' the contributor shouted. 'I'll publish caricatures of the whole lot of you tomorrow in the *Brand*!'

They all jumped up from their seats.

'Your Excellency! Your Excellency!' cried Pseldonimov, his mother and several of the guests, as they crowded round the general. 'Your Excellency, stay calm!'

'No, no!' the general cried, 'I'm crushed . . . I came . . . I wanted, so to speak, to bless. And here's what I get, this is what I get for everything!'

He sank down on to his chair, as if he were unconscious, placed both hands on the table and lowered his head on them, right into the plate with the blancmange. The general horror cannot be described. A minute later he got up, evidently wishing to leave, lurched, tripped on a leg of his chair, and fell flat on the floor and started snoring . . .

This sometimes happens to people who aren't drinkers when they get drunk by accident. They remain conscious until the bitter end, and then suddenly fall as if they had been cut down. Ivan Ilyich lay on the floor, having completely lost consciousness. Pseldonimov was pulling his hair and froze stock still in that position. The guests began to hurriedly disperse, each with his own interpretation of the events. It was already around three o'clock in the morning.

*

The main thing was that Pseldonimov's circumstances were really much worse than might have been imagined, the very unattractiveness of the present situation notwithstanding. And while Ivan Ilyich is lying on the floor, and Pseldonimov is standing over him, pulling his hair in despair, we will interrupt the narrative flow of our story and say a few explanatory words about Porfiry Petrovich Pseldonimov.

No more than a month prior to his wedding he was perishing utterly and irrevocably. He came from the provinces, where his father had at one time served in some capacity and had died while he was on trial. Five months before his wedding, Pseldonimov, who had been perishing in Petersburg for a whole year already, received his ten-rouble-a-month position; it was as if he had been resurrected, in both body and spirit, but he was again soon humbled by his circumstances. In the whole wide world, there remained only two Pseldonimovs, himself and his mother, who had left the provinces after her husband's death. Mother and son were perishing together in the freezing cold and living on food made from dubious materials. There were days when Pseldonimov would go to the Fontanka for water with a cup in hand so that he could slake his thirst. After receiving his position, he and his mother settled down somewhat in a corner somewhere. She began taking in laundry, while he scraped together his savings of four months to get himself somehow a pair of boots and the semblance of an overcoat. And the misfortunes he had to endure in the office: his superiors would approach him to ask whether it had been a long time since he had been to the bathhouse. A rumour circulated about him that there were nests of bedbugs beneath the collar of his uniform. But Pseldonimov was a man of firm character. In appearance he was submissive and quiet; he had very little education, he was almost never heard to take part in conversation. I don't know positively: whether he thought, whether he made plans and systems, whether he dreamed about anything. But to compensate for that he had developed some sort of instinctive, unshakeable, unconscious resolve to make his way out of his nasty situation. He had the stubbornness of an ant: if you destroy an anthill, they'll build it all over again at once, destroy it again – and they'll begin again, and so on tirelessly. This was a being, who was methodical and thrifty. It was written on his face that he would make his way, build his nest and perhaps even save up enough for an emergency. In the whole world only his mother loved him and she loved him to death. She was a firm woman, tireless, hard-working and yet kind. And they would have lived like that in their corner perhaps for another five or six years until their circumstances had changed if they hadn't crossed paths with retired Titular Councillor Mlekopitayev, formerly a paymaster who had served at one time in their province, and had recently come to Petersburg where he and his family had settled. He knew Pseldonimov and had been somehow obliged to his father for something. He had some money, of course, not very much, but still he had some; nobody knew how much he really had, not his wife, or his elder daughter, or his relatives. He had two daughters, and since he was a terrible bully, a drunkard, domestic tyrant and, moreover, a sickly man, he suddenly took it into his head to marry off one of his daughters to Pseldonimov: 'I know him,' he said, 'his father was a good man, and the son will be a good man.' Whatever Mlekopitayev wanted, he did; it was no sooner said than done. He was a very strange sort of bully. He spent most of his time sitting in an armchair, since he had lost the use of his legs with some illness, which didn't prevent him, however, from drinking vodka. For days on end he would drink and curse. He was a malicious man; he needed without fail to have somebody to torment non-stop. For this purpose he kept under his roof several distant relatives: his own sister, who was sick and a shrew; his wife's two sisters, who were malicious chatterboxes; and then there was his old aunt who had somehow managed to break a rib. He kept on another sponger, a Russified German woman, on account of her talent for telling him stories from the *One Thousand and One Nights*. All his pleasure consisted in needling these unfortunate hangers-on, to abuse them day and night for all he was worth, even though not one of them, including his wife, who was born with toothache, dared to so much as squeak in his presence. He would get them to fight among themselves, make up, and spread rumours and dissent among them, and then rejoice when he saw that they almost came to blows. He was quite delighted when his elder daughter, who had lived in poverty for ten years with her husband, some officer, and who had finally been widowed, came to live with him with her three sickly children. He couldn't stand her children, but since their appearance increased the material upon which he could conduct his daily experiments, the old man was quite pleased. This whole heap of malicious women and sickly children along with their tormentor were crowded together in a wooden house on the Petersburg Side, not getting enough to eat because the old man was stingy and doled out money kopecks at a time, though he didn't begrudge himself vodka; they didn't get enough sleep because the old man suffered from insomnia and demanded to be entertained. In a word, they all lived in poverty and cursed their fate. It was at this time that Mlekopitayev happened upon Pseldonimov. He was struck by his long nose and submissive air. His frail and plain younger daughter had just turned seventeen. Even though she at one time had attended some sort of German *Schule*,[40] she didn't get much out of it beyond her abc's. Then she grew up, scrofulous and emaciated under the crutch of her lame and drunken parent and amidst the squall of domestic gossip, spying and slander. She had never had any girlfriends, or any brains. She had been wanting to get married for a long time now. In company she was taciturn, but at home together with her mama and the hangers-on she was malicious and a shrill nag. She particularly liked to pinch and punch her sister's children, sneaking up on them for sugar and bread they had made off with, which was the cause of an endless and unquenchable quarrel with her older sister. The old man himself offered her to Pseldonimov. Poor though he was, the latter nevertheless asked for some time to think it over. He and his mother pondered on it for quite a while. But the house was to be registered in the bride's name, and even though it was wooden, and even though it was only one storey and a bit foul, it was still worth something. On top of that there was the 400 roubles – when could you ever save up that much yourself! 'After all, why am I taking a man into my house,' the drunken bully would shout. 'In the first place, because you're all women and I'm sick of having only women. I want Pseldonimov to dance to my tune as well, because I am his benefactor. In the second place, I'm taking him in because none of you wants it and you're all angry. So I'll do it to spite you. And I'll do what I've said! And you, Porfirka, beat her when she's your wife; she's had seven demons sitting inside her since birth. Drive them out, and I'll get the stick ready for you . . .'

Pseldonimov kept silent, but he had already made up his mind. He and his mother were received into the house before the wedding, washed up, dressed, shod, given money for the wedding. The old man was their protector, perhaps because the entire household had it in for them. He even liked old lady Pseldonimov, so he refrained from needling her. However, a week before the wedding he made Pseldonimov dance the *kazachok*.[41] 'Well, that's enough, I merely wanted to see that you didn't forget yourself with me,' he said when the dance had come to an end. He gave them only just enough money for the wedding and invited all his relatives and acquaintances. On Pseldonimov's side there was only the contributor to the *Brand* and Akim Petrovich, the guest of honour. Pseldonimov knew only too well that his bride loathed him and that she really wanted to marry the officer, and not him. But he bore it all, because that was the agreement with his mother. The entire wedding day and all evening the old man had been getting drunk and cursed using the nastiest words. On the occasion of the wedding, the entire family took shelter in the back rooms and were crowded together so that it stank. The front rooms were reserved for the party and supper. At last, when the old man fell asleep, completely drunk, at about eleven o'clock in the evening, the bride's mother, who had particularly been angry with Pseldonimov's mother that day, made up her mind to exchange her wrath for kindness and go out to the party and supper. The appearance of Ivan Ilyich upset everything. Mrs Mlekopitayev became embarrassed, got offended and began cursing them for not informing her that the general himself had been invited. They assured her that he had come on his own, uninvited – she was so stupid that she wouldn't believe them. The situation called for champagne. Pseldonimov's mother had only one rouble, Pseldonimov didn't have a single kopeck. They had to humble themselves before the malevolent old Mlekopitayev woman, beg for money first for one bottle, then another. They portrayed for her the future of his relationships in the office, his career; they appealed to her conscience. In the end she gave some of her own money, but she made Pseldonimov drink such a cup of gall and vinegar[42] that he had already repeatedly run into the little room, where the bridal bed was prepared, pulled his hair in silence and threw himself

A NASTY BUSINESS

head first on to the bed intended for heavenly delights, trembling all over with impotent rage. Yes! Ivan Ilyich did not know what those two bottles of Jackson had cost, which he had drunk that night. What then was Pseldonimov's horror, anguish and even despair, when the episode with Ivan Ilyich ended in such an unexpected way. He again foresaw trouble and maybe a whole night of screams and tears from the capricious new bride, and reproaches from the bride's dim-witted kin. His head was already aching without that, and the fumes and darkness had already clouded his eyes. And now Ivan Ilyich required help: he'd need to find, at three o'clock in the morning, a doctor or carriage to take him home, and it must be a carriage, because they couldn't send a person like him home in a droshky[43] in a state like that. But where was he to get money for a carriage? Mrs Mlekopitayev, infuriated that the general had not said two words to her and hadn't even looked at her during supper, announced that she didn't have a single kopeck. Perhaps she really didn't have a single kopeck. Where was he to get it? What was he to do? Yes, he had plenty of reasons for pulling his hair.

Meanwhile, for the time being they carried Ivan Ilyich to the small leather sofa that stood right there in the dining room. While they cleared the tables and put them back, Pseldonimov rushed about from corner to corner trying to borrow some money – he even tried to borrow from the servant girl – but nobody had any. He even risked bothering Akim Petrovich, who had stayed longer than the others. But he, though he was a kind man, upon hearing the word 'money' became so perplexed and so frightened, that he talked the most unexpected rubbish.

'Another time I would be delighted,' he mumbled, 'but now . . . really, excuse me . . .'

And, after picking up his hat, he ran out of the house as

quickly as he could. Only the kind-hearted youth, who had been telling the story about the dream-book, proved to be of any use, and inopportunely at that. He had also stayed longer than the rest, taking a sincere interest in Pseldonimov's misfortunes. In the end, Pseldonimov, his mother and the youth decided in general council not to send for a doctor, rather to send for a carriage and have the patient taken home, and for the time being, until the carriage arrived, to try some home remedies, such as daubing his temples and head with cold water, applying ice to the top of his head, and so forth. Pseldonimov's mother took this upon herself. The youth flew off in search of a carriage. Since at that hour there wasn't even a droshky on the Petersburg Side, he had to go some distance for the cabbies at the coaching inn and wake up the drivers. They began bargaining, saying that at this hour even five roubles was too little. They agreed, however, on three. But it was almost four o'clock when the youth arrived in the hired carriage at Pseldonimov's, where they had changed their minds long before. It turned out that Ivan Ilyich, who was still unconscious, had become so ill, was moaning and tossing about so that it had become absolutely impossible and even risky to move him or to have him taken home in this condition. 'What will happen next?' said the absolutely disheartened Pseldonimov. What was he to do? A new question arose. If they were to keep the sick man in their house, then where would they move him to and where could they put him? There were only two beds in the whole house: one was enormous, a double bed on which old man Mlekopitayev slept with his spouse, and the other one was a new purchase, imitation walnut, also a double bed, and intended for the newlyweds. All of the other inhabitants, or, rather, ladies who inhabited the house, slept on the floor, side by side, mostly on feather beds, already somewhat dilapidated and foul-smelling, that is, altogether

A NASTY BUSINESS

unseemly, and those were in limited supply; there weren't even enough to go around. Where could they put the sick man? A feather bed perhaps might be found – one could be dragged out from under somebody if worse comes to worst, but where and on what could they make up the bed? It turned out that the bed would need to be in the drawing room, since that room was the most removed from the bowels of the family and had its own exit. But what could it be made up on? Surely not chairs. Everybody knows that beds are made up on chairs only for schoolboys when they come home for a Saturday, but for such a person as Ivan Ilyich that would be disrespectful. What would he say tomorrow when he saw that he had been sleeping on chairs? Pseldonimov wouldn't even hear of it. Only one thing remained: to have him taken to the bridal bed. This bridal bed, as we said earlier, was set up in the small room, right off the dining room. On the bed there was a newly purchased, brand-new double mattress, clean sheets, four pink calico pillows in muslin pillowcases with frilled trim. The blanket was pink satin with a quilted pattern. Muslin curtains hung from a golden ring above. In a word, all was as it should be, and the guests, almost all of whom had visited the bedroom, praised the appointments. The bride, even though she couldn't stand Pseldonimov, during the course of the evening had popped in here furtively several times to see it. What was her indignation, her fury when she learned that they wanted to move to her bridal bed the sick man who had come down with what looked like cholerine![44] The mother of the bride took her part, cursing and promising to complain to her husband tomorrow; but Pseldonimov showed what he was worth and stood his ground: Ivan Ilyich was moved and a bed for the newlyweds was made on the chairs. The bride whined and was all set to pinch, but she didn't dare disobey: her papa had a crutch with which she was all too familiar, and she knew that her papa would be certain to demand a detailed accounting tomorrow. As consolation the pink blanket and pillows in their muslin cases were brought to the dining room. At this moment the youth arrived with the carriage; upon learning that the carriage was no longer required, he became terribly frightened. That meant paying for it himself, and he had never had so much as a ten-kopeck piece. Pseldonimov announced his complete bankruptcy. They tried persuading the cabbie, but he began making a row and even knocked on the shutters. I don't know the details of how it all ended. It seems that the youth set off in this carriage as a hostage to Peski, to Fourth Rozhdestvensky Street,[45] where he hoped to rouse a student who was spending the night with friends, and see if he had any money. It was well past four o'clock in the morning when the young people were left alone and the door to the drawing room was locked. Pseldonimov's mother stayed by the sufferer's bedside all night long. She retired on the floor, on a little rug, and covered herself with a fur coat, but she couldn't sleep, because she kept having to get up: Ivan Ilyich had a terribly upset stomach. Mrs Pseldonimov, a woman who was steadfast and magnanimous, undressed him herself, took off all his clothes and looked after him as if he were her own son, carrying out the necessary crockery from the bedroom through the hallway and back again all night long. And still the misfortunes of this night were far from over.

Not ten minutes had passed since the young couple had been locked up in the drawing room alone when suddenly a blood-curdling cry was heard, not a comforting cry, but of the most malignant sort. The cries were followed by a noise, a crash, as if some chairs had fallen, and in a flash a whole crowd of clamouring and frightened women in all manner of dishabille burst into the room, which was still dark. These women were: the mother of the bride, her older sister, who for the time being had abandoned her sick children, her three aunts, even the one with the broken rib had dragged herself along. Even the cook was there on the spot, and the German hanger-on, who told fairy tales and from under whom they had dragged by force her own feather bed for the newlyweds, the best one in the house and which comprised all she owned, even she dragged herself along with the others. All these estimable and perspicacious women had stolen out of the kitchen through the hallway on tiptoe a quarter of an hour ago and were eavesdropping in the anteroom, devoured by the most inexplicable curiosity. Now, somebody hastily lit a candle and everyone was presented with the most unexpected sight. The chairs, which had propped up the feather bed only at the edges and which couldn't support the double weight, had moved apart and the feather bed fell in between them on to the floor. The bride whimpered with fury; this time she was offended to the bottom of her heart. Pseldonimov, morally crushed, stood there like a criminal, whose villainy had been exposed. He didn't even try to justify himself. Exclamations and screams could be heard from all sides. Pseldonimov's mother came running at the noise, but this time the bride's mama had gained the upper hand. She began by showering Pseldonimov with strange and for the most part unjust reproaches on the theme: 'What sort of husband are you after this, my dear? What are you good for, my dear, after such shame?' – and so on and, finally, after taking her daughter by the hand, she led her away from her husband, to her own room, after personally taking responsibility for explaining to her stern father who would be demanding his accounting tomorrow. Everybody cleared off after her, oohing and aahing and shaking their heads. Only his mother remained with Pseldonimov and tried to console him. But he immediately drove her away.

He wasn't in the mood for consolation. He made his way to the sofa and sat down, lost in the gloomiest meditation, just as he was, barefoot and wearing only the most essential bits of underwear. His thoughts crossed and got muddled in his head. From time to time he would automatically, as it were, take a look around the room, where only recently the dancers had been going at it furiously and where cigarette smoke still hung in the air. Cigarette butts and sweet wrappers still littered the splattered and soiled floor. The ruins of the marriage bed and the overturned chairs bore witness to the transitory nature of the best and surest of earthly hopes and dreams. Thus he sat for almost an hour. Distressing questions kept occurring to him, for example: What awaited him at the office now? He was painfully aware that he needed to change his place of work no matter what, that remaining at his present position was impossible, precisely as a consequence of everything that had happened this evening. He also recalled Mlekopitayev, who tomorrow might make him dance the *kazachok* again, in order to test his meekness. He realized as well that even though Mlekopitayev had given him fifty roubles for the wedding day, which had been spent down to the last kopeck, he hadn't even suggested giving him the dowry of 400 roubles, nor had there been any mention of it. And the house itself had still not been formally registered. He recalled as well his wife, who had forsaken him at the most critical moment of his life, and the tall officer who had got down on one knee before his wife. He had managed to notice that; and he thought about the seven demons, who were sitting inside his wife, according to the testimony of her own parent, and about the stick prepared for their expulsion . . . Of course, he felt that he was strong enough to bear a good deal, but fate had dealt him such surprises that, in the end, he might doubt his own strength.

A NASTY BUSINESS

Thus Pseldonimov grieved. Meanwhile, the candle end was going out. Its flickering light, which fell directly on Pseldonimov's profile, reflected him in colossal proportions on the wall, with his long neck, hooked nose and the two tufts of hair that stood up on his forehead and on the back of his head. Finally, when he got a whiff of the morning freshness, he got up, chilled to the bone and spiritually benumbed, made his way to the feather bed that was lying between the two chairs, and without tidying it, without putting out the candle end and without even putting a pillow under his head, he crawled on all fours on to the bed and fell into that leaden, dead sleep, the likes of which is slept by those sentenced to be flogged to death on the square[46] the next day.

On the other hand, what could compare with the agonizing night that Ivan Ilyich spent on the unfortunate Pseldonimov's bridal bed! For some time the headache, vomiting and other most unpleasant attacks did not leave him for a minute. It was the torments of hell. Consciousness, although barely more than a flickering in his head, illumined such multitudes of horrors, such gloomy and disgusting pictures, that it would have been better had he not regained consciousness. However, everything was still confused in his head. He recognized, for example, Pseldonimov's mother – he heard her forgiving admonitions, such as: 'Be patient, my darling, be patient, my dear sir, you'll like it when you get used to it'; he recognized her but couldn't, however, logically account for her being near him. Disgusting apparitions appeared before him: most often Semyon Ivanych would appear, but as he peered more intently he noticed that it wasn't Semyon Ivanych at all, but Pseldonimov's nose. He also caught fleeting glimpses of the free artist, and the officer, and the old woman with the bandaged cheek. More than anything he was intrigued by the golden ring hanging above his head from which the curtains hung. He could discern it clearly by the dim light of the candle end that illuminated the room, and he kept trying to fathom it mentally: What purpose does this ring serve? Why is it here? What does it signify? He asked the old woman about it several times, but he obviously couldn't say what he wanted to say, and she evidently didn't understand him, no matter how hard he tried to explain. Finally, when it was almost morning, the attacks stopped and he fell asleep; he slept soundly, without any dreams. He slept for about an hour and when he woke up he had almost fully regained consciousness, his head ached unbearably and he had the nastiest taste in his mouth and on his tongue, which had turned into a piece of flannel. He sat up in the bed, looked around and started thinking. The pale light of the dawning day, which had stolen through the cracks in the shutters, trembled on the wall in narrow stripes. It was about seven o'clock in the morning. But when Ivan Ilyich suddenly realized and remembered everything that had happened to him since last evening; when he remembered all the adventures at the supper table, his stillborn heroic deed, his speech at the table; when he imagined all at once with horrible clarity everything that might now come of this, everything they would now say about him and what they would think; when he looked around and saw, finally, to what a sad and sorry state he had reduced the peaceful bridal bed of his subordinate – oh, then such terrible shame, such torments filled his heart that he cried out, covered his face with his hands and in despair threw himself down on the pillow. A minute later he jumped up from the bed, saw his clothes there on the chair, neatly folded and already cleaned, grabbed them and quickly, frantically, began pulling them on, all the while looking over his shoulder and horribly afraid of something. Right there on another chair lay his fur coat, his hat, and his yellow gloves were in his hat. He wanted to slip away quietly. But suddenly the door opened and old lady Pseldonimov walked in, carrying an earthenware basin and a jug. A towel hung from her shoulder. She put down the jug and without further ado announced that he most definitely must wash.

'Come now, my dear sir, wash yourself, you can't go without washing...'

And at that instant Ivan Ilyich realized that if there was one being in this whole world, with whom he could now be without shame or fear, it was precisely this old woman. He washed. And for a long time afterwards, at difficult moments in his life, he would remember, among other pangs of conscience, all the particulars of this awakening: the earthenware basin and the faience jug, filled with cold water in which little bits of ice still floated, and the soap in the pink wrapper, oval shaped and stamped with some letters, which cost fifteen kopecks and was obviously bought for the newlyweds, but which Ivan Ilyich now would be the first to use; and the old woman with the damask towel over her left shoulder. The cold water refreshed him; he dried himself and, without saying a word, without even thanking his sister of mercy, he grabbed his hat, threw over his shoulders the fur coat that was held out to him by Mrs Pseldonimov, and through the hallway, through the kitchen, in which the cat was meowing and where the cook, raising herself up on her bedding, followed him with her eyes with greedy curiosity, as he ran out into the courtyard, to the street and rushed to catch a passing cab. The morning was frosty; frozen yellow fog still hid from view the houses and all objects. Ivan Ilyich turned up his collar. He thought that everybody was looking at him, that they all knew him, that they would all find out...

For eight days he did not leave the house nor did he report to the office. He was ill, agonizingly ill, but more morally than physically. During these eight days he had lived through a whole hell, and it most likely was taken into account for him in the other world. There were moments when he would start thinking about becoming a monk. There really were. Then his imagination would ramble far and wide. He pictured quiet subterranean singing, an open coffin, living in an isolated cell, the forests and caves; but after coming to his senses, he would almost immediately acknowledge that this was all the most horrible nonsense and exaggeration and he would be ashamed of it. Then began the moral attacks concerning his *existence manquée*. Then shame once again would flare up in his heart, taking possession of it all at once and burning and aggravating everything. He would shudder, when he imagined various scenes. What would they say about him, what would they think when he walked into the office, what whispering would haunt him for a whole year, ten years, his whole life? The story about him would be handed down to posterity. He even sank at times into such faintheartedness that he was ready to go at once to Semyon Ivanych and ask for his forgiveness and friendship. He didn't even try to justify himself, he blamed himself completely: he could find no excuse and was ashamed even to look for one.

He also thought about immediately submitting his resignation and thus, simply, in solitude devote himself to the happiness of mankind. In any event, it was absolutely necessary to change all his acquaintances and in such a way as to eradicate all memory of him. Then he would think that this was nonsense as well and that increased sternness with his subordinates might still set the matter right. Then he began to have hope and cheer up. Finally, after eight whole days of doubts and torments, he felt that he could no longer bear the uncertainty, and *un beau matin*[47] he made up his mind to go to the office.

Before, when he was still staying home in anguish, he

had pictured to himself a thousand times how he would enter his office. With horror he had convinced himself that he would be certain to hear ambiguous whispering behind his back, see ambiguous faces, reap a harvest of the most malignant smiles. What was his amazement when in fact none of this took place. He was greeted respectfully; they bowed; everybody was serious; everybody was busy. His heart was filled with joy as he made his way to his own room.

He at once and very seriously got down to work, heard several reports and clarifications and proposed solutions. He felt that he had never before reasoned and come to a decision so intelligently, so efficiently as that morning. He saw that they were pleased with him, that they esteemed him, that they regarded him with respect. The most acute sense of suspicion would have been unable to detect anything. Things were going splendidly.

Finally, Akim Petrovich appeared with some papers. Upon his appearance something stabbed Ivan Ilyich right in the heart, as it were, but only for a moment. He attended to Akim Petrovich, expounded gravely, showed him how it should be done and explained it. He noticed only that he seemed to be avoiding looking at Akim Petrovich for too long, or rather that Akim Petrovich was afraid of looking at him. But now Akim Petrovich had finished and began to gather up his papers.

'And there's one more request,' he began as drily as possible, 'from the clerk Pseldonimov about his transfer to the department ... His Excellency Semyon Ivanovich Shipulenko has promised him a position. He requests your gracious assistance, Your Excellency.'

'Ah, so he's getting a transfer,' Ivan Ilyich said and he felt that an enormous weight had been lifted from his heart. He cast a glance at Akim Petrovich and at that moment their eyes met.

'All right, for my part... I will use,' Ivan Ilyich replied. 'I am prepared to help.'

Akim Petrovich clearly wanted to slip away as quickly as possible. But Ivan Ilyich suddenly, in a burst of nobility, made up his mind to have his say once and for all. Evidently he was once again visited by inspiration.

'Tell him,' he began, directing on Akim Petrovich a look that was clear and full of deep significance, 'tell Pseldonimov that I don't wish him ill; no, I don't!... That, on the contrary, I am prepared to even forget everything that took place, to forget everything, everything...'

But suddenly Ivan Ilyich stopped short, as he looked on in amazement at the strange behaviour of Akim Petrovich, who, for reasons unknown, instead of being a sensible man, suddenly turned out to be the most terrible fool. Instead of listening, and listening to the end, he suddenly turned an utterly foolish red, began somehow hurriedly and even indecently making some sort of little bows and at the same time backing away towards the door. His whole look expressed a desire to disappear, or rather to get back to his desk as quickly as possible. Left alone, Ivan Ilyich rose from his chair in confusion. He looked in the mirror and didn't recognize his own face.

'No, sternness, only sternness, nothing but sternness!'[48] he whispered almost unconsciously to himself, and suddenly his whole face turned bright red. He suddenly felt so ashamed, so miserable, more than he had been during the most unbearable moments of his eight-day illness. 'I couldn't bear it!' he said to himself and, overcome by weakness, sank into his chair.

1862

NOTES

6. *North Cape...Nizhny Novgorod*: The cape on the island of Mageroya in northern Norway, where the Norwegian Sea meets the Barents Sea, often called the northernmost point of Europe. Situated on the confluence of the Volga and Oka rivers, Nizhny Novgorod has a long history as a trading centre. In the nineteenth century the fair in the city attracted millions of visitors annually. Today it is the fourth largest city in the Russian Federation.

7. *I said this in French*: As demonstrated by the long passages in French in Tolstoy's *War and Peace*, in the early nineteenth century French was the language of the Russian aristocracy and polite society. However, by the time of the action of *The Gambler*, the use of Russian had become much more usual among all the educated classes. Note that both Alexey Ivanovich and Grandmother speak French poorly. Of course, in an international setting such as Roulettenburg, it would be the common language.

8. *Opinion nationale*: *National Opinion*, French daily newspaper, the organ of the liberal Bonapartists, which came out in Paris until 1879.

9. *Cela n'était pas si bête*: That wasn't so stupid.

10. *pan*: Sir, gentleman (Polish); *pani*, the feminine form, appears in Chapter 13.

11. *chasseur*: Literally, hunter; member of a French light-infantry regiment, known for their skill in rapid manoeuvres.

12. *Nadenka*: Earlier called Nadya, both are diminutive forms of Nadezhda, the girl's given name. See Appendix I, Names in Russian.

13. *"la baboulinka"*: French transcription of the Russian diminutive of *babushka* (grandmother).

14. *Schlangenberg*: Snake Mountain (German).

Chapter 2

1. *feuilletons*: From the French *feuillet*, sheet of paper, leaf, i.e. light fiction, sketches, reviews, chronicles that were printed as a supplement to the political news in French newspapers. In Russia, the feuilleton was generally a critical essay or a satirical article, and Dostoevsky's 'Petersburg Chronicle' is a good example.

2. *Rothschild*: The head of the well-known banking firm, Baron James de Rothschild (1792–1868) is alluded to in Dostoevsky's *The Adolescent* (1875), when Arkady Dolgoruky, the protagonist, reveals that his 'plan' consists of becoming a Rothschild.

3. *mauvais genre*: Bad form.

Notes

It gives me great pleasure to acknowledge my very large debt to the editors of the 'Academy' edition of Dostoevsky's *Complete Collected Works in Thirty Volumes* (*Polnoe sobranie sochinenii*), as many of my notes rely heavily on material that is published in the editors' commentary to the individual works. Quotations from Dostoevsky's works and other contemporary source materials (journals, newspapers, letters, etc.), unless otherwise noted, are from this edition.

All translations of foreign-language text are from French, unless otherwise specified. Quotations from the Bible refer to the Revised Standard Version.

All dates, unless otherwise indicated, are given according to the Julian calendar (Old Style), which remained in force in Russia until 1918. The Gregorian calendar, adopted in the West in the eighteenth century, was generally twelve days ahead.

The Gambler

Chapter 1

1. *Roulettenburg*: Based on the city of Wiesbaden, located on the Rhine River in Germany, famous in the nineteenth century for both its gambling and spas. Dostoevsky took the actual name from a Russian translation of a sketch by William Makepeace Thackeray ('The Kickleburys on the Rhine', 1850); the Russian version translated Thackeray's Rougetnoirebourg (Redand-blackcity) as Roulettenburg, which Dostoevsky had originally used as the title of his novel. He changed it to *The Gambler* at the publisher's request.
2. *thalers*: Silver coin that circulated throughout much of Europe. For information on the currencies referred to in the novel, see Appendix III, A Note about Money in *The Gambler*.
3. *comte et comtesse*: Count and countess.
4. *outchitel*: The Russian word for tutor or teacher, given in French transliteration.
5. *table d'hôte*: Meal at a fixed price served to guests in a hotel.

NOTES

4. *trente et quarante*: 'Thirty and forty', a French card game, also known as 'rouge et noir' (red and black).

Chapter 4

1. *Kirghiz*: Also Kyrgyz. Traditionally, nomadic people of Turkic origins in Central Asia.
2. *Tatar*: Also Tartar. Member of several Turkic-speaking peoples that for the most part are settled along the Volga River in central Russia and eastward to the Ural Mountains. Historically, the Mongol invaders of Russia in medieval times came to be known as Tatars.
3. *ten versts*: Russian unit of measure equal to 3,500 feet or 1.06 kilometres; so, here approximately 6½ miles.
4. *Vater*: Father (German).
5. *stork on the roof*: The folkloric role of the stork as a symbol of childbirth and the harbinger of good fortune likely originated in Germany and the Netherlands, where the stork often figures in nursery rhymes.
6. *save up money like Jews*: Dostoevsky's deep-seated xenophobia can be seen in the caricatures of Germans, Jews and Poles that appear in his fiction.
7. *Hoppe & Co.*: The Dutch banking firm Hope & Co. (only one 'p'), which was in operation for more than two centuries, had offices in Amsterdam and London.

Chapter 5

1. *copybook*: Collection of models for penmanship exercises. The short texts often comprised clichéd maxims and aphorisms.
2. *le coq gaulois*: The cockerel of Gaul, the national symbol of France.
3. *Wurmerhelm*: It has been suggested that Dostoevsky drew on the character Wurm (Worm, German), one of the most negative characters in Friedrich Schiller's play *Love and Intrigue* (1784). In any event, the name has obvious associations with 'worm'.

Chapter 6

1. *Madame la baronne . . . votre esclave*: Madame Baroness. I have the honour to be your slave.
2. *Hein*: Beat it (German, from *gehen*).
3. *nec plus ultra*: Nothing further beyond; to the utmost (Latin).

NOTES

4. *Jawohl . . . Sind Sie resend*: Indeed . . . Have you lost your mind? (German).
5. *junkers*: Country squires, titled landowners (German).

Chapter 7

1. *vos appointements*: Your salary.
2. *mon cher monsieur . . . n'est ce pas*: My dear sir, forgive me, I have forgotten your name, Monsieur Alexis? . . . isn't that right?
3. *Mais le general*: But the general.
4. *et madame sa mere*: And madame, her mother.
5. *le baron est . . . querelle d'Allemande*: The baron is so hot-tempered, the Prussian character, you know, he might start a groundless quarrel over nothing.
6. *que diable . . . comme vous*: The devil take it! A youngster like you.
7. *subalterne*: Subordinate; subaltern.
8. *Peut-être*: Perhaps.

Chapter 8

1. *miss*: In the narrator's rendition (in Russian) of Mr Astley's conversation, which we presume took place in French, Astley appropriately uses the Russian noun *miss* (in Cyrillic letters), rather than the more usual *baryshnia* or *devushka*, both of which can be translated as lady, miss or young girl.
2. *veuve*: Widow.
3. *Barberini*: Illustrious family name of the Roman nobility. In 1623, Cardinal Maffeo Barberini was elected Pope Urban VIII.
4. *un beau matin*: One fine morning.
5. *Spa*: Resort town in Belgium famed for its hot springs.
6. *garçon*: Waiter.

Chapter 9

1. *name and patronynic*: Russians are usually addressed by the first name and the second, which is the patronymic, formed from the name of the person's father.
2. *les seigneurs russes*: The Russian grandees.
3. *Praskovya*: Grandmother, the symbol of old Russia, as it were, calls Polina Alexandrovna, not by her adopted name abroad, Polina, but by her true Russian name.

NOTES

4. *une russe...duchesse de N*: A Russian, a countess, an important lady... Grand Duchess of N.
5. *à la barbe du pauvre general*: Under the poor general's nose.
6. *Oui, madame...surprise charmante*: Yes, madam... and believe me, I am so delighted... your health... it is a miracle... to see you here, a charming surprise.
7. *Bonjour*: Good day.
8. *pointe*: Peak.
9. *Cette vieille ... enfance*: This old woman has fallen into childhood.
10. *Mais...plaisir*: But, madam, it would be a pleasure.

Chapter 10

1. *Madame la générale princesse de Tarassevitcheva*: Madam, the General's wife, the Princess Tarasevicheva.
2. *Elle est... des bêtises*: She has fallen into childhood... left alone she'll do a lot of stupid things.
3. *Sortez, sortez*: Leave, leave!
4. *rouge et noir, pair et impair, manque et passe*: Red and black, even and odd, the low numbers 1–18 (*manque*) and the high numbers 19–36 (*passe*).
5. *trente-six*: Thirty-six.
6. *Faites le jeu... ne va plus*: Place your bets, gentlemen! Place your bets gentlemen! No more bets?
7. *Combien zéro? Douze? Douze*: How much is zero? Twelve? Twelve?
8. *Le jeu est fait*: No more bets!

Chapter 11

1. *Quelle victoire! ... Mais, madame, c'était du feu*: What a victory!... Why, Madam, that was brilliant!
2. *Madame la princesse... si généreux*: Madam Princess... a poor expatriate... Constant misfortune... the Russian princes are so generous.
3. *Que diable ... terrible vieille*: The devil take it, she's a terrible old woman!
4. *Was ist's der Teufel*: What the devil is it! (German).
5. *Mais, madame ... perdrez absolument*: 'But Madam... Your luck may change, only one unlucky move and you'll lose everything... above all, with your sort of game... it was terrible!' 'You'll certainly lose.'
6. *Eh! ce ... se trompe*: Eh! that's not it... My dear sir, our dear general is mistaken.

NOTES

7. *cette pauvre terrible vieille*: This poor, frightful old woman.
8. *O mon...bon*: Oh, my dear Monsieur Alexis, be so good.
9. *Quelle mégère*: What a shrew!

Chapter 12

1. *Nous boirons...l'herbe fraîche*: We will drink milk on the fresh grass.
2. *nature et la vérité*: Nature and truth. In his 'Winter Notes on Summer Impressions' (1863), Dostoevsky visits the grave of writer and philosopher, Jean-Jacques Rousseau (1712–78), whom he refers to as *'l'homme de la nature et de la vérité'* (man of nature and of truth), an allusion to Rousseau's *Confessions* (1781–8).
3. *Diantre...Elle vivra cent ans*: The devil take it! ...She'll live a hundred years!

Chapter 13

1. *Paul de Kock*: The racy, frothy and immensely popular novels of Parisian life by Charles-Paul de Kock (1793–1871) are the favoured reading of Stepan Verkhovensky in Dostoevsky's *Demons* (1871–2).
2. *łajdak*: Good-for-nothing, scoundrel (Polish).
3. *Balakirev*: Ivan Balakirev (1699–1763), servant in the imperial court of Peter the Great, was appointed court buffoon under Empress Anna Ivanovna (1693–1740). A book of anecdotes ascribed to Balakirev was published in 1839 and enjoyed widespread success.
4. *family carriage*: A private car on a train outfitted with tables, beds and samovar.

Chapter 14

1. *de la vieille dame ... gentilhomme et honnête homme*: The old lady ... a gentleman and honourable man.
2. *Les trois derniers coups, messieurs*: Last three turns, gentlemen!
3. *Vingt-deux...Trente et un*: Twenty-two! ...Thirty-one.
4. *Madame Blanchard ... balloon*: Marie Blanchard (b. 1778), widow of a pioneering hot-air balloonist, fell to her death during an exhibition over the Tivoli Gardens in Paris in 1819, when fireworks ignited the hydrogen in her balloon.
5. *Quatre*: Four!

NOTES

6. *a gagné déjà cent mille florins*: Has already won one hundred thousand florins.
7. *half a pood*: 18 lbs; 8.19 kilograms.

Chapter 15

1. *fraülein*: Young lady (German).
2. *Diese Russen*: These Russians!
3. *Ah, c'est lui ... mieux l'or*: Ah, it's him. Come here, you little fool! ... that you won a mountain of gold and silver? I would prefer the gold.
4. *Bibi, comme ... n'est-ce pas*: Darling, how stupid you are ... We'll have a feast, right? (Blanche uses the familiar form of 'you' throughout.)
5. *Mon fils, as-tu du coeur ... Tout autre*: My son, are you brave? ... As anyone else. Blanche and Alexey trade lines from Act I, scene 5 of *Le Cid* (1637), by the great French classical tragedian Pierre Corneille (1606–84).
6. *vois-tu ... à Paris*: You see ... if you're not too stupid, I'll take you to Paris.
7. *Eh bien ... tu étais outchitel*: Now then! ... you'll see Paris. Tell me, what's an *outchitel* [tutor]? You were very stupid when you were an *outchitel*.
8. *Eh bien ... en plein jour*: Well then, what will you do if I take you with me? ... I want 50,000 francs ... We're going to Paris ... and I will show you stars in broad daylight.
9. *Et cent cinquante mille ... des étoiles*: One hundred fifty thousand francs ... who knows! ... I am a good girl ... but you will see stars.
10. *vil esclave ... fais-tu*: Vile slave! ... and afterwards the flood! But you can't understand that, go! ... what are you doing? '*Après moi le deluge*' (after me the flood), to which Blanche alludes, has been attributed to Louis XV and his mistress Madame de Pompadour.
11. *je t'attends, si tu veux*: I'll wait for you, if you wish.
12. *Peut-être, je ne demandais pas mieux*: Perhaps, I wasn't asking for anything better.
13. *mais tu seras heureux ... et alors*: But you'll be as happy, as a little king ... As for me, I want an income of 50,000 francs and then.

Chapter 16

1. *et les cent mille ... avec moi*: And the 100,000 francs that we have left, you'll eat them up with me.

NOTES

2. *il a gagné deux cent mille francs*: He won 200,000 francs.
3. *Mais tu ... mon garçon*: But you have enough sense to understand! You know, my boy.
4. *Mais...sais-tu...dis donc*: Why...you know...tell me then... Why you know...What will you do afterwards, tell me?
5. *Homburg*: Dostoevsky frequented the roulette tables in Homburg during his stay at this fashionable German resort town in 1863.
6. *Oui, oui, c'est ça ... bonne fille*: Yes, yes, that's splendid! ... Because I thought that you were only an *outchitel* (something like a lackey, isn't that right?) ... because I'm a good girl.
7. *il faut que jeunesse se passe*: One must sow one's wild oats when one is young.
8. *Mais tu es...sera content*: But you are a true philosopher, do you know that? A true philosopher ... Well, I will love you, love you – you will see, you'll be pleased!
9. *Thérèse-philosophe*: The heroine of the book *Thérèse the Philosopher*, published anonymously in 1748; ascribed to the Marquis d'Argens. The Olympia Press, publishers of an English translation (2007), supplies this description: 'This first-person narrative by Thérèse is the charming tale of an innocent's initiation into sexual happiness. Self-discovery in a convent leads her to her confessor, Father Dirrag, and she is soon launched upon the path of reason that convinces her that passion and love of the Deity are equal gifts of God.'
10. *Cuirassiers*: Mounted cavalry soldiers, named for the breastplate armour they wore, the *cuirasse*.
11. *Un vrai russe, un calmouk*: A true Russian, a Kalmyk! The latter (also spelled Kalmuck) are a Mongol people who live in southwestern Russia, west of the Volga River, on the north-western shore of the Caspian Sea.
12. *Bal Mabille*: Notorious Parisian dance hall founded in 1831 by Mabille, a dance instructor. The dancers, who performed the scandalous cancan, were often available to gentlemen after hours. A number of photographs and drawings survive of the Bal Mabille dancers.
13. *à batons-rompus*: In fits and starts.
14. *Il a de la chance ... mon million*: He's lucky ... I will have a château, muzhiks, and then I'll always have my million. *Babouchka*: French form of the Russian *babushka* (grandmother).
15. *très comme il faut ... il faut*: Very proper ... He, nevertheless, is very proper.
16. *zakuski*: Hors-d'oeuvres (Russian).

NOTES

17. *Mais vois-tu... n'est-ce pas*: But you see... these devilish Russian names, in a word, Madam, the general's wife with fourteen consonants. Isn't that lovely? The general's surname is Zagoryansky, but for Blanche it might as well be Zagoziansky or the even more ludicrous and absolutely non-Russian sounding Sago-Sago.
18. *Tu étais bon enfant...et tu seras heureux*: You were a good boy... I thought you were stupid and you looked like you were... Wait!... We will always be friends... and you will be happy!

Chapter 17

1. *Racine*: The French classical dramatist, Jean Racine (1639–99), author of the verse tragedies *Iphigénie* (1674) and *Phèdre* (1677), was enthusiastically embraced and defended by the young Dostoevsky, despite the prevailing Romantic opinion held by many, including his brother, that Racine was somewhat outdated.
2. *Apollo Belvedere*: Marble copy of lost bronze original that was made in 350–325 BC. Rediscovered in the late fifteenth century, this statue of the Greek god Apollo has been considered for centuries the essence of classical perfection and the epitome of male beauty (now located in the Vatican Museum).

A Nasty Business

1. *the renaissance of our beloved fatherland*: Published in 1862, the story is set in the era of the 'Great Reforms' of the 1860s, instituted by Alexander II (1818–81, known as Alexander the Liberator) in order to modernize a backward Russia. The most important reforms included the emancipation of the serfs in 1861, followed three years later by judicial reforms and the implementation of the *zemstvo*, i.e. rural self-government.
2. *Petersburg Side*: Situated between Vasilyevsky Island and the Vyborg Side, this section of St Petersburg is located across the Neva River from the city centre.
3. *the rank of general*: The ranks in the Russian civil service held equivalent military titles. Thus Privy Councillor Nikiforov, a civil servant of the third class, is entitled to call himself general. See Appendix II, Table of Ranks.
4. *Actual State Councillor*: 'Actual' in this context implies a full, working member in active service.

NOTES

5. *stars, even though he already had two*: Stars were featured in a number of Russian Imperial orders and medals.
6. *grand-patience*: Solitaire or a card game for one person.
7. *rather far away*: That is, far from the city centre and 'official' Petersburg, where Nikiforov's office no doubt is located.
8. *une existence manquée ... parleur ... phraseur*: A failed life; talker, chatterbox; phrasemonger.
9. *tax-farming*: Purchasing the right from the government to collect certain taxes or the exclusive franchise to sell certain goods (salt, liquor, etc.)
10. *new wine in new wineskins*: 'And no one puts new wine into old wineskins; if he does, the wine will burst the skins ... but new wine is for fresh skins' (Mark 2:22).
11. *merci*: Thank you.
12. *Bolshoy Prospekt*: Major avenue (*bolshoy* means 'big') that crosses the Little Neva via the Tuchkov Bridge, runs the length of the Petersburg Side and spans the Karpovka River into Apothecary Island.
13. *c'est le mot ... bon sens*: That's the word; good sense.
14. *quadrille*: Originally of French origin, a dance performed by four couples in a square formation.
15. *Pseldonimov, the legistrator*: He, as we see later, is a registrator, that is, a collegiate registrar, the lowest of the fourteen ranks. 'Legistrator' appears to be an invention of the policeman.
16. *his surname*: Absurdly close to the Russian word for 'pseudonym' (*psevdonim*), which Ivan Ilyich brings up later. Even more absurd is that his bride is named Mlekopitayev, derived from the word for 'mammal'.
17. *last day of Pompeii*: Reference to the massive historical painting by Karl Bryullov (1799–1852), *The Last Day of Pompeii* (1830–33), which depicts the chaos and destruction of the city and its people caused by the volcanic eruption.
18. *inertia*: 'Inertia' (*kosnost'*) can also be rendered as 'sluggishness' or 'stagnation'. Dosteovesky uses it to denote the mechanical principle of inertia.
19. *Gogol*: Nikolay Gogol (1809–52), master of the Russian short story and author of the novel *Dead Souls* (1842), has composed the portraits of some of the oddest characters in Russian literature, for example, the lowly clerk Akaky Akakievich and his tailor Petrovich in 'The Overcoat' (1842).
20. *lampion*: Small oil lamp for the outdoors, usually with a coloured chimney; a carriage lamp.

NOTES

Encyclopedic Dictionary, Compiled by Russian Scholars and Litterateurs, much to the dismay of scholars and writers, since Krayevsky was neither. (His editorship ceased with volume 1 (1861).) Nikolay Alferaki (1815–63), a wealthy merchant in Taganrog, left behind a magnificent palace, which today houses the Taganrog Regional Museum. The ironic misspelling of *exposé* as *ekspozé* (*ablichitel'naya literatura*), favoured genre of the radical camp, is repeated in Dostoevsky's *Notes from Underground*.

29. *the Brand*: Easily decipherable as the *Spark*, one of the most popular publications of the 1860s, a weekly illustrated journal published in St Petersburg, known especially for its satire and caricatures.

30. *Yaroslavl*: The linen mills in Yaroslavl, situated 280 kilometres north-east of Moscow, on the confluence of the Volga and Kotorosl rivers, date from the time of Peter the Great.

31. *the "fish"*: This folk dance is described by Ivan Turgenev in his story 'Old Portraits' (1881): 'Ivan danced marvellously, especially the so-called "fish dance." When the chorus struck up a dance tune, the fellow would come into the middle of the ring, and then there would begin such a turning and skipping and stamping, and then he would fall flat on the ground, and imitate the movement of a fish brought out of the water on to dry land; such turning and wriggling, the heels positively clapped up to the head; and then he would get up and shriek—the earth seemed simply quivering under him' (*A Desperate Character and Other Stories*, tr. Constance Black Garnett (1899; reprinted New York: AMS Press, Inc. 1970)).

32. *ritornello*: Return (Italian). A recurrent musical theme.

33. *preference*: Game for 2–4 people played with a 32-card deck, popular in Russia and Eastern Europe.

34. *'Luchinushka'*: Russian folk song, performed by everybody from gypsy singers to the famous operatic bass Fyodor Chaliapin.

35. *Petersburg News . . . Academic News*: The daily newspaper's nickname *Academic News* comes from its publisher, the Academy of Sciences.

36. *Frühstück*: Breakfast (German). Reference to St Petersburg's significant German population – in 1869, the year of the first city-wide census, the German population accounted for 7 per cent of the population (Steven Duke, 'Multiethnic St. Petersburg', in *Preserving Petersburg: History, Memory, Nostalgia*, ed. H. Goscilo and S. M. Morris (Bloomington: Indiana University Press, 2008)). For literary examples of Germans in

NOTES

21. *galantine ... blancmange*: A galantine is a dish of boned meat or fish that is poached before it is set in a mould with its own jelly or in aspic. A blancmange is a sweet dessert made from milk or cream, often flavoured with almonds, and thickened with gelatine or cornstarch; it is usually set in a mould and served cold.

22. *chaîne de dames, balancez*: A figure in a quadrille: Ladies' chain, set to your partners!

23. *Harun-al-Rashid*: Caliph of Baghdad (763?–809), known for the opulence of his court and his participation in the Muslim holy war against Byzantium. According to legend, he made excursions at night around the city of Baghdad incognito, in order to become better acquainted with the life of his subjects. He is the subject of numerous songs and a cycle of tales from the *One Thousand and One Nights*, the collection of stories narrated by the clever Scheherazade, who captivates her murderous husband with her storytelling.

24. *pronouncing the letter 'a' somewhat like 'eh'*: This manner of pronouncing words indistinctly, with a poor articulation that results from speaking too quickly, carelessly or with one's mouth half-closed, in this instance, reducing the full 'a' sound to a short 'eh', signals the speaker's arrogant regard or disdain (even a disdain that is forced or assumed) for his interlocutor. Ivan Ilyich's affected speech, aimed at maintaining distance between master and servant, is wholly inappropriate for the situation and his position as advocate of 'humaneness'.

25. *Porfiry Petrov*: Instead of giving the expected 'Petrovich' as his patronymic, Pseldonimov, a recent arrival from the provinces, uses the old Russian form 'Petrov', the more plebian abbreviated patronymic.

26. *Charmé*: Charmed.

27. *Panayev*: A parody of a dream-book, written by N. F. Shcherbina in 1855–7, who says about Ivan Panayev (1812–62), the writer, critic and co-editor of the journal the *Contemporary*: 'Seeing Ivan Panayev in your dreams portends spilling coffee on a white waistcoat or buying a half-dozen Holland shirts at Lepter's.' Dream-books, or compilations of interpretations of dreams, enjoyed enormous popularity in Russia. For example, Pushkin's *Eugene Onegin*, whose heroine Tatyana is engrossed in a dream-book which she has purchased from a pedlar.

28. *A new lexicon ... eksposé literature*: The newspaper and journal editor Andrey Krayevsky (1810–89) was made editor of the

NOTES

Petersburg, see Pushkin's 'Queen of Spades' (1833) and Ivan Goncharov's *Oblomov* (1859).

37. *Fokine*: Famed and infamous dancer, 'hero of the can-can', known for his 'shameless entrechats', according to the literary critic A. M. Skabichevsky (*Literary Memoirs* (Moscow–Leningrad, 1929)).
38. *zakuski*: Hors-d'oeuvres (Russian).
39. *hussar fashion*: Hussar regiments in Russia, as in other European countries, were light-cavalry units. The hussar, in addition to his superior skill as a horseman, could be distinguished from men of other units by his elaborate and richly coloured uniform, which was matched by the wearer's fearless courage on the battlefield and reckless abandon in private life.
40. *Schule*: School (German).
41. *kazachok*: Ukrainian folk dance, in which the male partner kicks out his legs from a squatting position.
42. *cup of gall and vinegar*: The drink given to Christ before his crucifixion: 'They gave him vinegar to drink mingled with gall: and when he had tasted thereof, he would not drink' (Matthew 27:34 (King James Version)).
43. *droshky*: A light, uncovered four-wheeled carriage outfitted with a bench on which the passengers sit sideways or astride.
44. *cholerine*: Exact translation of the Russian *kholerina*, the diminutive of *kholera* (cholera), a word used as little today in Russian as in English. Cholerine signifies the condition of having mild symptoms associated with cholera, e.g. diarrhoea, but not the actual incidence of the disease.
45. *Peski, to Fourth Rozhdestvensky Street*: Quite a distance, indeed – across the Neva to a neighbourhood not far from the Moscow train station on Nevsky Prospekt.
46. *flogged to death on the square*: Public flogging, which often ended in death, was abolished in Russia in 1845.
47. *un beau matin*: One fine morning.
48. *sternness, only sternness, nothing but sternness*: In Gogol's 'The Overcoat', the Very Important Person holds the same 'stern' philosophy.

Appendix I
Names in Russian

All Russians have three names: the given name, the patronymic and the surname. Thus: Fyodor Mikhaylovich Dostoevsky; Anna Grigoryevna Dostoevskaya. The patronymic is the father's given name and the ending *-ovich* or *-evich* for males, *-ovna* or *-evna* for females. Patronymics can be abbreviated by omitting the *-ov/-ev*, as in 'A Nasty Business' with Semyon Ivan*ych*, rather than the expected Ivan*ovich*; such abbreviation usually connotes a degree of familiarity. Note that in *The Gambler*, Grandmother, as was customary, addresses her manservant by patronymic alone – Potapych.

Most given names have affectionate or diminutive forms, as in English. Thus, Nadezhda: Nadya, Nadenka; and Marfa: Marfusha, both characters in *The Gambler*.

Appendix II
Table of Ranks

Established by Peter the Great in 1722, the Table of Ranks classified all civil servants, military officers and court officials into fourteen classes (no. I is the highest rank). Only the civil and military classes appear in this volume. It was not uncommon for a civil servant to make use of the military equivalent of his rank. Thus the three generals in 'A Nasty Business' are, in fact, civil servants of the third and fourth classes (privy councillor and actual state councillor).

Until 1843, rank VIII conferred hereditary nobility to a civil servant, and rank X personal, or nonhereditary nobility; the lowest rank conferred nobility in the military. The Table of Ranks remained in force until 1918.

Rank	Civil Service	Army	Form of Address
I	Chancellor	Field Marshal	Your High Excellency
II	Actual Privy Councillor	General	//
III	Privy Councillor	Lieutenant General	Your Excellency
IV	Actual State Councillor	Major-General	//
V	State Councillor	*	Your High-Born
VI	Collegiate Councillor	Colonel	Your High Honour
VII	Court Councillor	Lieutenant Colonel	//
VIII	Collegiate Assessor	Major	//
IX	Titular Councillor	Staff-Captain	Your Honour
X	Collegiate Secretary	*	//
XI	Naval Secretary	*	//
XII	Secretary of Province	Second Lieutenant	//
XIII	Provincial Secretary	Ensign	//
XIV	Collegiate Registrar	*	//

*An asterisk indicates those ranks with no precise army equivalent.

Appendix III
A Note about Money in *The Gambler*

Money plays a prominent role from the very first page of the novel, when the general gives Alexey Ivanovich two thousand-franc notes to be changed. As befits the international scene in Roulettenburg, apart from the hotel and the casino, the only institution mentioned is the exchange bureau. Sums of money are referred to throughout *The Gambler*, in currencies and amounts that have meaning for the narrator, but not necessarily for the twenty-first-century reader.

Francs, Florins and Gulden

A uniform German currency, the deutschemark, was not established until after the creation of the German Empire in 1871. Wiesbaden, the model for Roulettenburg, was the capital of the duchy of Nassau from 1806 to 1866, when it became part of Prussia. The Latin Monetary Union was established in 1856 by Belgium, France, Italy and Switzerland to set standards and equivalents for their currencies: 4 gulden was the equivalent of 10 francs or 4 florins, all currencies which circulated widely throughout Europe and which are mentioned in *The Gambler*. (The exchange rates of the Latin Union were observed informally by many other states throughout Europe.) In the 1860s the French franc was the equivalent of US $0.20 (UK £1.00 was equal to 25 francs[1]); thus the 2,000 francs that Alexey Ivanovich changes in the opening of Chapter 1 corresponded to approximately $400, estimated to have the purchasing power of $5,500 in 2008 US dollars (£80, i.e.

APPENDIX III

£5,800) using the retail price index.[2] The 200,000 francs that Alexey Ivanovich and Blanche spend in Paris in under three weeks' time is indeed a fortune: $40,000 in 1865 had the equivalent purchasing power of over half a million US dollars in 2008 (£8,250 in 1865, with a purchasing power of almost £600,000 now).

Roubles and Thalers

Also in Chapter 1, the general gives Alexey Ivanovich an advance of 100 thalers against the 120 roubles he is owed (approximately $95 dollars; the rouble was valued at US $0.80). The thaler, a silver coin that circulated throughout Europe for almost four centuries, had been adopted by most of the German states in the 1860s with a value of 1 gulden equals 1.75 thalers. (In Chapter 6 Alexey has some fried eggs and wine for a thaler and a half.) The 100 thalers equals 60 gulden or 150 francs ($30; £6); in other words, far less than he was due.

Potapych reckons that Grandmother lost 'as much as 90,000 roubles in all that day', or $72,000, which in 2008 would have the purchasing power of close to a million dollars (£690,370) – a fortune, indeed! Finally, the 3,000 roubles (approximately $2,400) that Dostoevsky received from Stellovsky, the amount that keeps reappearing in Dostoevsky's works, is by no means a fortune, particularly when you consider he was supporting six people *and* paying off debts – its purchasing power would come to about $32,700 (£36,000) now.

Friedrichs D'or and Louis D'or

The friedrich d'or was a Prussian gold coin in circulation from the mid-eighteenth century through the mid-nineteenth. In Chapter 2, Alexey Ivanovich begins his

APPENDIX III

career at the roulette table with a stake of 5 friedrichs d'or, which he mentions is the equivalent of 500 gulden, putting the value of his first stake at 1,250 francs, i.e. $250 (£50), a purchasing power in 2008 of $3,400 (£3,600).

The louis d'or (gold Louis), a gold coin first minted under Louis XIII in 1640, depicted on one side the French king and the royal coat of arms on the reverse. Subsequent monarchs continued the practice, as did Napoleon. The value was set at 20 francs. In Chapter 2, when Alexey Ivanovich is describing his first visit to the roulette tables, he writes that a 'gentleman ... may stake 5 or 10 louis d'or, rarely more than that'; in other words all of 100 or 200 francs, i.e. $20 or $40 (£4 or £8); the lower figures come to a respectable $275 (£290) in terms of purchasing power in 2008.

Notes

1. For the sake of convenience I have rounded off amounts throughout; the British pound was actually valued at 25.22 francs.
2. I quote the figures for current (i.e. 2008) 'purchasing power' in US dollars and UK pounds, converted from their value in 1865, according to the conversion calculator on the website Measuring Worth: http://www.measuringworth.com. The website of the UK National Archive also has a currency converter for British pounds, which gives somewhat different but similar amounts: http://www.nationalarchives.gov.uk/currency/default.asp#mid.

POCKET PENGUINS

1. Emile Zola — The Beast Within
2. Willa Cather — O Pioneers!
3. Leo Tolstoy — The Cossacks *and* Hadji Murat
4. Alfred Russel Wallace — The Malay Archipelago
5. Rainer Maria Rilke — The Notebooks of Malte Laurids Brigge
6. Virginia Woolf — Mrs Dalloway
7. Karen Blixen — Out of Africa
8. Franz Kafka — Metamorphosis
9. Maxim Gorky — My Childhood
10. Emilia Pardo Bazán — The House of Ulloa
11. Guy de Maupassant — A Parisian Affair
12. Alessandro Manzoni — The Betrothed
13. Henry David Thoreau — Walden
14. Ivan Turgenev — Fathers and Sons
15. D. H. Lawrence — The Rainbow
16. H. P. Lovecraft — The Call of Cthulhu
17. Joseph Conrad — The Secret Agent
18. Jaroslav Hašek — The Good Soldier Švejk
19. Henri Alain-Fournier — The Lost Estate
20. Mikhail Bulgakov — The Master and Margarita
21. Fyodor Dostoevsky — The Gambler *and* A Nasty Business

22	Carson McCullers	The Heart is a Lonely Hunter
23	H. G. Wells	The Island of Doctor Moreau
24	Ernst Jünger	Storm of Steel
25	Daphne du Maurier	Don't Look Now
26	Suetonius	The Twelve Caesars
27	Antoine de Saint-Exupéry	Wind, Sand and Stars
28	Natsume Sōseki	Sanshirō
29	Arthur Schnitzler	Dream Story
30	Jean Rhys	Good Morning, Midnight
31	Evelyn Waugh	Put Out More Flags
32	Isaac Bashevis Singer	The Magician of Lublin
33	Honoré de Balzac	Eugénie Grandet
34	Jean-Paul Sartre	The Age of Reason
35	Ford Madox Ford	The Good Soldier
36	Eileen Chang	Lust, Caution
37	Vladimir Nabokov	Laughter in the Dark
38	John Reed	Ten Days That Shook the World
39	Nikolay Gogol	Dead Souls
40	Wu Ch'êng-ên	Monkey